# No Substitute for Momentum

Carolyn J. Rose

# No Substitute for Momentum

Carolyn J. Rose

2017

No Substitute for Momentum

Cover design by Dorion D. Rose, Broken Cork Photography

Interior design for print edition by Boulevard Photografica/Patty G. Henderson

Digital editions (epub and mobi) produced by Booknook.biz

Paperback ISBN: 978-0-9968645-8-9

Mobi edition ISBN: 978-0-9968645-9-6

Epub edition ISBN: 978-0-9995310-0-6

For Katlin, Gary, and all the laughter

# Chapter 1

"If Mrs. B wants to go shopping *again*, do I have to go with her?" Allison riffled the pink-inked pages of a notebook open on the dining room table. "My history final's tomorrow. I have to study this afternoon."

Dave and I exchanged stunned glances. I suspected he was also trying to figure out which sentence surprised him most—that his acquisitive and style-driven teenage daughter didn't want to go shopping, or that she wanted to study.

He blinked, released the sports section of the paper, and tugged at the lobes of his ears.

I tipped the Sunday comics to provide cover and wagged a finger, signaling that he shouldn't mock her. She'd been working at being a new-and-improved version of herself for only two months, and the process had been marked by setbacks and meltdowns. Focusing on matters other than her hair, nails, snacks, and boyfriend came hard to Allison. She was easily sidetracked. And our wealthy neighbor's boredom-driven shopping excursions were major distractions.

"Well?" Allison looked up from the notebook, tapped her nails on the table, and lapsed into the snarky teenage tone I heard so much of as a substitute teacher. "Anyone? Anyone? Dad? Barbara? Do I have to?"

"If Mrs. B wants you to help her burn up another credit card," I counseled, "be firm, but not mean or sarcastic. Explain that you're studying for the semester final. Tell her you want a good grade."

"Me? I have to tell her?" Allison adopted the fearful expression of a puppy facing a python. "I don't want her all mad at me. Why can't you or Dad tell her?"

The simple answer was that Dave and I had decided Allison should—mostly—fight her own battles. After all, she was 16, a proto-adult, and had recently demonstrated she had backbone to spare when she stood up to the woman who bumped off a fellow actor at the community theater. But along with fighting her own battles, we wanted her to learn to approach potential conflict with an eye toward avoiding, postponing, or negotiating. And we wanted her to find ways to win without painting her opponent as a total loser.

"Mrs. B won't be mad because you want to study," I responded.

"Besides," Dave added, "the last time we had one of our long talks you said you wanted me and Barbara to back off. That's one reason *you* need to tell Mrs. Ballantine. The other reason is we're not the ones she's asking to go shopping."

"Too bad." Allison flipped a few more pages. "Because you need shoes that don't stink and socks without holes and T-shirts that aren't all baggy and faded out."

Dave raised his eyebrows, then leaned back against the sofa cushions and kicked off his battered running shoes. He propped his feet on the coffee table and wiggled his toes. Three poked out of white athletic socks that sagged around his ankles, sprouting sprigs of broken elastic like scraggly whiskers.

Lola, his Golden Retriever, raised her head and sniffed the air, then sneezed, abandoned her spot by the door to the deck, and limped over to lick Dave's naked toes. Cheese Puff, my 10-

pound scruffy orange mutt, for once showed what I considered to be better taste. He curled his upper lip, and wedged himself between the arm and seat cushion of his favorite chair.

"Allison has a point about the socks," I said. "And the shoes."

"But not about this." Dave tugged at a once-black T-shirt, now a patchy gray. "It's a classic."

Allison held up her history book to show us a picture of the Founding Fathers. "So are the wigs and knee pants and stockings these guys wore."

"Point to Allison." I made a check in the air.

Dave ran his hand over the barely visible design on the front of the shirt, a copy of a poster advertising the Northwest tour of a Eugene group called Table Spread Tsunami. I'd once made the mistake of asking about the band and received a lengthy verbal report, beginning with the name. It had been chosen because the lead singer, a vegan, nixed names favored by other musicians in the group—Blood Pudding Psychos, Pigs' Feet Festival, and Honest Haggis. He'd also vetoed Margarine Tsunami because he felt that smacked too much of butter.

As for their music, Dave described it as a blend of classical grunge and mellow punk. The first and only tour had been billed as a watershed collision of sounds. But Table Spread Tsunami never caught on. The band was every bit as washed up as the T-shirt.

"This shirt is a collector's item," Dave insisted. "Like those wigs and pants. It's a piece of history."

"It's more like a piece of garbage," Allison shot back. "You definitely should go shopping with Mrs. B. If she calls, I'll tell her to take you to the outlet stores."

Now it was Dave's turn to paste on the imperiled-puppy expression. I patted his hand. "I'll save you from that fate. But only because I'm fond of *you*, not that T-shirt or many of its pals. Plus, you promised to take me to the movies later."

"But *I* have to save myself? And maybe make Mrs. B all mad? Even if you say she won't be?" Allison flipped a page in her notebook, tearing a corner. "I'm *studying*. Besides, there's no *point* in shopping now. All the winter stuff is picked over. And most of the spring and summer stuff isn't out yet."

I don't know much about sales and marketing, so I had no idea if that was an accurate assessment of the shopping landscape in Reckless River, Washington. I also didn't care enough to question her statement. But, even if I did care, I doubted I could muster the energy for further discussion.

The tail end of January wasn't my favorite time of year. I thought of it as the doldrums, and often pictured myself as a sailing ship becalmed, wallowing in the swells of a cold ocean, and waiting for a wind. The days were growing longer. But they were taking their sweet time. In the brief gaps between storms bringing torrential rain, the weather was dreary, dank, dismal, and depressing. Yesterday I'd spotted the tips of daffodils poking through the mud at the edge of the asphalt trail that ran along the bank of the Columbia River in front of our condo. It would be weeks, however, before the hardy plants produced bright blooms.

"That's something you could tell Mrs. B," I suggested. "She'd understand that you've shopped out the stores around here, wouldn't she?"

"I guess." Allison chewed at her pen—a sparkly model that lit up as she underlined her pink-inked notes with a thick trail of turquoise. "But she'd probably say we haven't hit all the stores in Portland yet. Just the ones at the big malls."

That left a lot of shopping venues. Portland was a big city filled with chain stores, boutiques, consignment shops, and more. But even if all the stores had been checked off her list,

4

Mrs. B still might sally forth. Her shopping mania was, I believed, the result of being without a project.

"When she was practicing her dance routine and *I* wanted to go shopping, *she* was too busy." Allison punched the pen against her notebook, leaving a string of bright blotches. "Well, now *I'm* the one who's too busy."

With a pout that would have put my lower lip in traction, she scooped up the notebook and stomped upstairs to her room.

"Point made." Dave did the hand-dusting thing, and began a series of range-of-motion exercises for the arm he'd broken when he and Lola tumbled down a mountainside during search and rescue training. "Guess that settles that."

"For Allison," I agreed. "But Mrs. B is definitely stuck. For a week after we got back from Las Vegas she was flying high. Then she hit a wall."

"She rebounded for the holidays," Dave observed as he shooed Lola away from his toes. "And the grand opening of the sandwich shop."

"And then she crashed again."

"If she had a job, she wouldn't have *time* to crash. Thanks to drug dealers and lowlife scum, I don't. Except on occasional weekends."

Usually, that was also the case for me. But lately I had time to crash on weekdays as well—too much time.

As a substitute, my schedule was at the mercy of teachers in need of someone to fill in. It was also affected by other subs seeking opportunities to spend quality time with America's youth. To land more jobs, I had to beat out the competition. To do that, I had to prove myself to teachers so they'd request me. I also had to keep a vigilant eye on absence postings and snatch jobs from the computerized system before other subs got to them.

This month, however, there had been darn few jobs to snatch. As the end of the first semester loomed and teachers scrambled to cram in material, few called in sick or took personal days. And during finals, days off were allowed only for illness or emergency situations. Three times in the past two weeks, after motivating myself by peeking at my bank balance, I'd had to accept jobs at—gasp!—middle school. I won't torture you with the harrowing and drama-laded details. Suffice it to say I was still shell-shocked.

(For the record, some subs prefer middle school. I admire them. But I don't aspire to be like them. For one thing, I don't have what it takes—nerves of titanium, the knack of maintaining a cone of serenity while chaos swirls around me, and the ability to rise the next day and do it again. Subbing in high school, while not exactly relaxing, doesn't leave me nearly as rattled.)

"Maybe you could have a chat with Mrs. B," Dave suggested. "And head off the next shopping safari."

"Why don't you do the chat thing? You're a trained police officer. Didn't you take classes in negotiating?"

"Yeah, but in my experience, negotiating isn't the prime go-to skill for dealing with meth freaks waving guns. Their brains are fried. Conversations don't track."

"But if you become a homicide investigator you might have to negotiate with a murderer about to kill again to try to cover up his crime." That sounded a little lame, but I pointed to the door to the deck with an air of authority. "You should go next door and polish your skills."

"Nice try." Dave reached for the remote and clicked on the TV. "But I hear a basketball game calling my name. Besides, you're the one who should talk with Mrs. B. You're like a daughter to her."

*Crap.*

He was right.

I hated that.

After a glance at the door, I unleashed a mammoth sigh.

Dave didn't shift his gaze from the screen.

I made a show of folding the comics and straightening the heap of papers on the coffee table. Then I sighed again, this time with less breath and a hint of a whimper.

Dave shifted his gaze to the refrigerator. A tiny frown line appeared between his eyes. His gaze shifted to the cabinet where we stored chips and crackers, then swung slowly my way.

I jumped to my feet. "Don't even think about it."

"Think about what?" he asked in a tone of offended innocence.

"Asking me to get up and get you a snack."

"Okay." He shot me a sly smile. "But since you're already up . . ."

"Forget it." I whistled for the dogs. "Let's go see Mrs. B."

I detected a note of triumph in Dave's chuckle, but didn't give him the satisfaction of turning to acknowledge his score with a Bronx cheer or an elevated finger.

I found Mrs. B in her usual comfy chair, a notepad on her lap, a pen in her hand, and the TV tuned to a shopping channel.

"Hello, dear. Just let me make a note of this and we can chat."

I glanced at the TV and saw that "this" was a white plastic bowl painted with what looked like tiny eggplants. At second glance, I decided those eggplants might be plums, or even large grapes. Moving closer to the set, I rubbed my eyes. Either the camera wasn't focused, or the bowl had been painted by an artist with a shaky hand and thin paint.

"I thought I'd use it for dinners on the deck this summer. For chips. Or fruit."

*Was she kidding me?*

Mrs. B possessed at least two matching sets of silver to go with two sets of dishes, as many as six different types of glasses, and enough bowls of various sizes and shapes to hold a supply of soup that could serve everyone in our condo complex. Beyond that, Mrs. B was the poster child for exquisite and subtle taste. And the bowl being displayed on TV, the bowl that might be painted with gigantic raisins or shriveled red cabbages, was far from subtle. It might be described as "exquisite" only by someone being paid to do so—like the woman displaying it and touting it as unique, versatile, and perfect for every occasion.

*As long as every occasion took place under cover of darkness.*

Mrs. B wrote the last of a string of numbers on her pad.

Clearly the time for drastic action had arrived.

I stepped to the TV and punched the power button. "You are NOT buying that bowl or any other type of kitchenware. Not today. Not this year. Further, you are not buying another article of clothing—not for yourself, not for Allison, not for me, and not for Cheese Puff or Lola."

Cheese Puff yipped as if to say he seconded that. In the past two weeks he'd returned from visits to Mrs. B's condo wearing a blue turtleneck sweater, a black leather jacket, green flannel pajamas, and a black-and-yellow costume that made him look like a giant bee.

Lola let out a single, sharp bark of agreement. She'd been subjected to a set of fluorescent pink rain booties, a tutu, and a floppy green sunhat decorated with enormous cloth daisies. None of the outfits lasted long. Cheese Puff managed to wiggle out of his, then freed Lola by tugging at or chewing through elastic. In his finest moment, while Lola stood still, he'd balanced on his hind legs and used his paws and teeth to unbuckle a collar studded with plastic fish.

Mrs. B's sapphire eyes widened and her lips parted, but I beat her to the conversational punch. "I love you. We all love you."

I sat on a hassock beside her chair and reached for her hand. "You're the kindest, most generous person I've ever known."

She folded her arms and frowned.

I persisted. "But lately you've been generous to a fault."

Her eyes narrowed. "Is this an intervention?"

# Chapter 2

I swallowed hard and, based on her threatening tone, steeled myself for a blast of wrath.

(For the record, I'm not exactly the steely type. I'm more like the sheet-of-aluminum-foil type. No, make that the thin-sheet-of-foil-in-a-stiff-breeze type.)

"Uh, um, yeah, uh, I suppose it is an intervention. I mean, I didn't come over with that in mind, but when I saw you were ready to order the world's tackiest bowl, I—"

"It's about time." Mrs. B smiled and grasped my hand. "Thank you. I was starting to wonder if anyone truly cared about me."

"We all care about you. We love you."

"And I'm grateful. Perhaps I should rephrase what I said." She stroked my hand then wove her fingers with mine. "What I meant was I'd begun to wonder whether anyone cared enough to tell me I had lost my way."

"Or whether anyone was *brave* enough to suggest you'd taken a wrong turn?"

Her fingers tightened around mine. "Am I a scary old bat?"

"Of course not." I feigned mock amazement. "You're not scary, you're not a bat, and you're not old."

That last part, of course, depended on how you defined "old." She had never divulged her age and, as far as I knew, no

10

one had been bold enough to ask. Her blue eyes, silvery hair, flawless skin, and slender body endowed her with timeless beauty. Working from the dates of her brief career as a Las Vegas showgirl, however, Dave and I estimated she had spent around seven decades on this planet.

As far as "scary" goes, like beauty, it was in the eye of the beholder. Mrs. B was smart and strong-willed. She'd had to be to escape a childhood of grinding poverty, make her way to Las Vegas, and rise to the top of the showgirl hierarchy without compromising herself or her reputation. And Mrs. B was wealthy. She'd married Marco Ballantine, a man with the funds to carry her off on an around-the-world adventure that lasted decades. He'd also had the savvy to make investments that kept on earning and churning out big bucks. There were those who found her combination of intelligence, will, and wealth threatening. I wasn't one of them. At least not most of the time.

Mrs. B leaned forward and planted a kiss on my cheek. "Thank you."

"You're welcome."

She set the notepad and pen on the occasional table beside her chair. "I know you don't feel a reward is necessary, but I think perhaps you might enjoy the contents of the red tin in the cabinet above the knife block."

Since I suspected the tin contained giant cashews, I didn't have to be told twice.

"There's a bag with a new brand of dog treats on the counter," Mrs. B said as I removed the plastic safety strip from the red tin. "I hope the terms of your intervention will allow me to indulge Cheese Puff and Lola with tidbits now and then."

"Definitely." I handed over the dog treats, then pried the lid off the tin and gazed lovingly at the contents. Dozens of nuts, each the size of my little finger. If fat cells could sing, mine would be rocking out "Best Day of My Life." "But you can

11

indulge the dogs only if you admit you define 'now and then' to mean every time you see them."

Mrs. B pondered the condition I'd set. "So, I'm required only to *admit* that? I'm not required to change my behavior? Or even attempt to change it?"

I nibbled the small end off a nut and considered. Who was I, a woman who couldn't pass up a tin of cashews or a package of cheesy snacks, to insist that she change? Altering habits and inclinations was tough. Even tougher if you weren't motivated. Or if those who benefited from your habits and inclinations—like Cheese Puff and Lola, who were scarfing down designer biscuits shaped like squirrels—wouldn't support efforts to change.

"Admitting works for me." I nibbled another quarter of the nut, fighting the urge to pop the whole thing in my mouth along with a few of its friends.

"Then I admit it." Mrs. B tossed another biscuit to Lola and broke the tail from one for Cheese Puff. "I admit I go overboard. But I love these two furry friends."

I popped the last of the nut in my mouth and checked the view through the glass door to the deck. The rain had ceased and the cloud cover had lightened. Instead of charcoal gray, it was now more of a silvery flint. For a stormy period at the end of January in the Pacific Northwest, this was as close to sunlight as we were liable to get. And the readout on the thermometer on the windowsill in the kitchen showed the temperature was a balmy 46. Practically a heat wave.

"Perhaps we could show our love by taking them for a walk," I suggested.

Mrs. B flipped each dog another treat. "All right. I'll go along if you admit you're afraid that if you leave me alone I'll pick up the phone and buy that bowl."

12

"I'll admit only that I'd enjoy taking a walk with you. We haven't done that for a long time." I replaced the tin in the cabinet, grabbed the biscuit bag, and sealed it. "And I'll admit the bowl is the stuff of nightmares. But I'm pretty sure if I left you alone, good taste would prevail, willpower would kick in, and you'd come to your senses before you gave out your credit card number."

Mrs. B smiled, tore the top sheet from the notepad, and crumpled it. "Let me put on a pair of walking shoes and get a waterproof coat and I'll meet you on the deck. Let's make it a long walk. You and I have a lot to talk about."

*Uh oh.*

When someone says there's a lot to talk about, it usually doesn't mean the talk will be about only good stuff. Or even mundane stuff. So I had a sinking feeling the upcoming conversation wouldn't involve an exchange of recipes or tips for removing chocolate stains. No, it would probably center on my future—or, more precisely, my future as Mrs. B envisioned it. And the diamond engagement ring on my left hand would undoubtedly figure in our conversation.

Just before Thanksgiving, Dave had presented me with the ring. Actually, he'd presented me with a white take-out box that had been lurking at the rear of the refrigerator for several weeks. Never suspecting it contained more than something growing mold, and attempting to make it clear tossing spoiled food shouldn't be my job alone, I hadn't opened the box until Dave dug it from his pocket as we flew to Las Vegas. The ring was a perfect fit and I'd agreed to marry him, but on condition we wouldn't do the aisle walk soon. Dave and I had a lot of baggage and I didn't want to haul it to the altar, or the courthouse, or a mountaintop, or beach, or wherever we decided to tie the knot. Dave was 100% with me, but there were others who seemed to feel a date should be set and wedding planning should get underway. As you've probably guessed, the ringleader of those "others" was Mrs. B.

So it was with moderate to high trepidation that I slipped the dogs into their harnesses, changed from fuzzy slippers to waterproof shoes, and snagged a rain jacket from the hall closet. "Going for a walk with Mrs. B," I told Dave.

He turned a thumb up but didn't shift his gaze from the tall athletes on the screen. I wondered if he'd heard me over the squeak of basketball shoes on hardwood, or whether he'd signaled agreement so I wouldn't say more and interfere with his viewing pleasure. You'd think a police officer, a man well aware of the many dangers in the world, would ask for details about where I was headed and when I expected to return. But perhaps, after more than a year together and several close encounters with wrong-doers, Dave figured that, one way or another, I'd emerge unscathed. Or at least not so scathed I wouldn't recover in a timely manner.

Mrs. B took Cheese Puff's leash and we trekked across the damp deck and down a short flight of wooden steps. Lola took them in a one-foot-at-a-time manner, favoring the right rear leg broken in her tumble with Dave last fall. With a stop for Cheese Puff to check his pee-mail, we navigated the narrow rose garden, and headed east on the riverfront trail. Thanks to near-record rainfall, the Columbia was creeping higher every day. I spotted a couple of small trees riding the current on their way to Astoria and a tug prodding a barge upstream.

We'd gone about five yards along the trail when Mrs. B launched into a complaint. "I had hoped to have that empty unit renovated so I could generate a little rental income."

Mrs. B needed "a little rental income" in the same way a millipede needed a few more legs. On the other hand, if she was set on renting the unit, she wasn't rushing ahead with the idea of tying it to mine and thereby providing space for the baby she hoped Dave and I would deliver before long. I teetered on the brink of a conversational gap for a few seconds before curiosity made me jump. "But?"

"But your friend Paulette tells me she's busy. Too busy to even take a look and make suggestions about paint and window coverings and carpet."

Paulette, who dabbled in a dozen projects, including interior design, wasn't putting Mrs. B off. She was busy. Fine with me. If Paulette came over to assess the one-bedroom unit I'd previously inhabited, she'd no doubt drop in to see me. And, having eyes an eagle would envy, she'd notice the living room and dining room furniture had shifted. Since she had placed each piece when I moved in, and since she'd given me firm instructions not to even think of nudging anything even a few inches, I could only assume she'd be less than happy. Far less than happy.

Now you may ask why, knowing it would lead to trouble, I'd moved the furniture.

The answer is that I hadn't.

Jim had.

Jim, who resembled Father Christmas in a plaid flannel shirt, was a member of the Cheese Puff Care and Comfort Committee, a group Mrs. B formed two years ago. The group's goal then was to see that my dog received treats and outings while I subbed and pursued a higher degree with an eye toward a teaching career. In November, I'd hired Jim to lend a hand with cleaning and organizing when my work schedule was hectic. Right from the start he'd gone above and beyond.

Unfortunately, that put him on a collision course with Paulette.

More unfortunately, it put me in danger because I'd be caught between them when the collision occurred.

15

"Paulette didn't make it to our usual water aerobics classes last week," I said. "She's working on a huge fundraiser for the county food banks and their meals programs."

"She's such a good soul." Mrs. B kicked a stone from the path. "Now I feel guilty about being miffed."

"A donation to the food banks might cure that."

"And of course I'll make one. But I was hoping to have a plan for that unit. I . . . I need a project."

"Couldn't you renovate the condo without Paulette?"

"Certainly I could do it alone." Her mournful tone made the word "alone" echo like we were in a stone cathedral. "But she's on top of all the latest trends and colors and products. I was looking forward to sharing ideas."

I got a vision of the two of them sharing—sharing in the same way most two-year-old kids do. Both women had definite, often inflexible, ideas. "What about getting some members of the Committee involved?"

She shot me a look of annoyed disbelief. "They're all busy. Except Sybil."

True. Other core members of the Committee had recently taken on time-consuming projects. Verna was overseeing the finances of the recently opened Reckless River Sandwich Shop. Jim, in addition to helping muck out my condo on school days, had started making parts runs and chauffeuring customers for Larry Tate at Start 'er Up Auto Repair. Others had a number of volunteer activities.

"Sybil's a lovely person," Mrs. B said, "but you know how she is."

Meaning first that Sybil was flighty, and second that she was in love with ruffles, fringe, frills, and flowered wallpaper. Her tiny condo looked like the aftermath of an explosion at a vintage flea market.

16

"If all you need is someone to bounce ideas off of, maybe I could—"

"No, dear. You have too much on your plate. And you need to get to work on your future."

While I pondered what she meant, she bent and snatched up an empty coffee container. "You'd think people who buy coffee from companies that tout themselves as having environmental consciences would have enough conscience of their own to toss their waste in a container."

"Or supply their own mugs so they don't make waste," I said, fueling her rant.

"Exactly. There are days I think I should sit out here with one of those guns that shoots balls of paint and aim it at every fool who drops a piece of litter."

"You'd get arrested so often they'd put a revolving door on the jail. And Angus Drummond would have to come out of retirement again."

She laughed and tossed the cup in a metal trash can chained to a post driven into the ground beside the low stone wall running along the south edge of the trail. "Dear Angus. He might be grateful. He's probably as bored as I am. A man can only play so much golf and indulge in so many two-martini lunches."

I knew plenty of men who might argue, one being Mrs. B's squeeze, Dario O'Brien. The assistant producer of the showgirl reality program *Still Got That Strut* continued to talk about retiring and leaving Las Vegas for Reckless River and a life with Mrs. B. But so far that was only talk. Dave insisted their dual-city relationship suited them, and maintained both were happier with long weekends than they would be if Dario was around all the time.

"They have huge personalities," he said. "Put them together in one tight place and it might work for a few months. But, unless they have other outlets, sooner or later the friction between them would lead to an explosion."

Plus, much as he loved the pace and warmth of summer in Reckless River, Dario wasn't wild about the gloomy, wet winters. An avid golfer, he hated searching for balls that came down hard and burrowed toward the center of the soggy earth.

"It would be fun to take aim at litter and litterbugs," I said, hoping to keep Mrs. B away from plans for my future.

"It would be great fun." Mrs. B mimed shooting a gun. "And it would be fun to renovate that condo. Or do a dozen other little projects. But our chat has convinced me taking steps to direct the course of your future must come first. For you *and* for me."

# Chapter 3

I felt cold. Then hot. Then cold again.

What was so perilous about the course I'd charted for my future that she needed to join me at the helm? Or, more likely, seize the helm?

"I know you don't want to look for a teaching job over in Portland or even in the next county."

True. I didn't want to face long commutes every morning and afternoon. And I especially didn't want to spend time idling on the freeway. Portland was just across the river, but bridges and bottlenecks created brutal gridlock. And not only during rush hours.

"I know you have your heart set on teaching at Captain Meriwether High School." She took my arm and pulled me closer. "So tell me what you're doing to make sure that happens."

"Well, I sub there as often as I can. I help with the Family Support Room and other projects." I took a breath. "I have my resume prepared and my references standing by. And I told the administrators I'm ready and willing—at least I told Tremaine Scott, the assistant principal. If I see Jerome Morrow, I'll tell him. But he's practically invisible."

In fact, on Friday he'd been so invisible that Ardette Johnson, a classroom aide, had been sent to search for him during fourth period. After scouring the building, she'd checked the parking lot—no simple task because roughly 400 spaces surrounded the high school and Morrow, an egalitarian kind of guy, eschewed a plum spot outside his office and stuck his pickup truck in random places. After an hour, Ardie had determined his ride wasn't on the premises or nearby streets. As she'd told me in an e-mail, "Maybe he ducked out after lunch. But no one remembers seeing him in the morning. So maybe he was never here. Maybe I got cold and wet for nothing."

"What else are you doing?" Mrs. B prompted.

"Um, I suck up to the head secretary."

"That's the woman they call Big Chill, correct?"

"Right." Wilhelmina Frost was the power behind the men in charge. Even in high heels and with her hair teased, she didn't top five feet. But she made up for what she lacked in size with attitude, experience, and knowledge about where the bodies were buried. Like others at the high school, I both respected and feared her. And, perhaps because I wasn't completely cowed by sarcastic remarks, and occasionally returned fire, she seemed to like me.

"Well, that's a good start, dear." Mrs. B raised her free hand and touched the single string of pearls at her throat. "But we can do more."

I shivered. When Mrs. B used the word "we" and commanded what she called "pearl power," there was no point in arguing or attempting to alter her plans. As Dave said, Mrs. B was a force of nature. All we could do was reckon with her.

So I didn't ask what she had in mind. I only hoped it wouldn't involve billboards or full-page newspaper ads or, worse yet, a TV commercial. The camera would add 15 pounds to the extra 10 distributed here and there on my frame. And who needed that?

We'd gone about half a mile when we met Verna and Sybil. As usual, they were dressed to the nines—providing you define that as wearing about nine more articles of clothing than necessary. Verna wore something that looked like a beekeeper's hat complete with a long veil, a green wool coat that came within an inch of the ground, a black scarf, black gloves, and high-heeled black boots with gold buckles. Sybil had donned a pink beret and anchored it with a paisley scarf that nearly hid her blond hair. A second scarf, checkered in black-and-white, swaddled her throat above the collar of a yellow plastic rain coat. She'd completed the ensemble with purple leggings and a pair of bright pink rubber boots.

Each woman carried a striped umbrella large enough to shelter a small herd of bison. Verna was using hers as a walking stick. She was also leaning on Sybil.

Mrs. B gasped and rushed toward them, towing Cheese Puff along. "Are you hurt, Verna? Did you fall?"

"No. I'm just tired."

"You're never tired," Mrs. B said.

"That's what I told her," Sybil agreed in a breathy voice. "She's never tired."

"Well I'm tired today," Verna snapped. "And you two parrots are making me more tired by the second."

"Sorry." Sybil backed away.

"Why don't we all walk home together," Mrs. B suggested. She moved into Sybil's place, bracing Verna, and hooked a thumb to direct me to the other side.

I took Verna's umbrella and offered my arm, but Lola squeezed me aside and wedged herself between us, nudging Verna's knee, whining, and gazing up at me and then at Verna. "I think she wants you to hold her collar."

Verna stroked Lola's silky ears. "She won't try to run or drag me down?" She cast a wary glance at Cheese Puff who had pulled his leash to its full length and was darting back and forth along the low stone wall, barking at a squirrel perched atop it. The squirrel, wearing a bring-it-on expression, showed no evidence of intention to make a speedy exit.

"Lola's much more other-directed than Cheese Puff. *And* she's obedient. But just in case, I'll hold the leash."

Mrs. B reeled in Cheese Puff, handed his leash to Sybil, and patted Verna's arm. "The little prince gets over-excited at times," she said, defending my entitled dog. "But he wouldn't do anything to hurt you. At least not on purpose."

I kept my mouth shut. Reminding her about the stress he'd put her through when he refused to practice their dance routine last fall would get me nowhere. She'd been steadily revising that snippet of history, and lately claimed she was never seriously worried he'd leave her in the lurch when it came time to compete. She was also compiling a list of excuses for his behavior including depression, dietary deficiency, hormonal imbalance, and an undiagnosed inner ear infection. Every one of those excuses, in my opinion, was bogus.

"Maybe it's because his head is smaller," Sybil said.

"What's because his head is smaller?" Verna asked in a testy voice.

"Why he's all about himself. Why he doesn't obey much."

Sybil pointed at Cheese Puff. He had played out the leash again the second she took control, and was trying to reach a gull pecking something at the edge of the trail. That something was yellowish-green and slimy. I hoped Sybil had sense enough to pull Cheese Puff away before he drove off the gull and got to it. I couldn't identify it, but I was experienced enough to know it had the look of something that would make a U-turn in his stomach and emerge again, probably on a chair, a bed, or the carpet.

Perhaps the small-head theory would also explain why he never barfed outside or on the linoleum. In fact, he never got sick in a place where cleaning up could be accomplished with a single paper towel instead half a roll and an array of spot-removing or odor-neutralizing products.

"It's true there isn't much room in his skull." Verna grasped Lola's collar and cast a sidelong glance at Mrs. B. "But I think it's more likely that his behavior is due to the fact that efforts to train and discipline him have been undermined by certain people we know."

"Including you." Mrs. B made a tutting sound. "It's true we've pampered him, but don't forget that Lola had the benefit of special training."

That special training taught her to sniff out drugs and obey the commands of her partner. But we'd discovered she also had strong protective instincts that extended to Dave's family and friends. And, since she broke her leg, she'd become even more mature, more of what you might call an "old soul."

Her relationship with Cheese Puff had changed, too. Where once she'd treated him like a boyfriend—a shrimpy boyfriend missing important boyfriend parts—she now treated him more as a pesky little brother.

Sybil reeled Cheese Puff in just as he lowered his head to sniff the noxious substance on the trail. "When is Lola going back to work?"

"Maybe in a week or so," I said, "depending on if the vet signs off."

"She's still limping," Mrs. B pointed out. "They should let her take early retirement."

I thought the same way, but Lola was barely middle-aged, and the Reckless River Police Department had a lot invested in her. The chief, and an HR director with all the flexibility of Mount Everest, wanted her back on the job. And they wanted Dave back on the drug beat full time. But Dave, who had been helping out with homicide investigations while his broken arm healed, had gotten a taste for putting together the puzzle pieces of murder cases. Since Reckless River was a fairly peaceful city and since crime was down, the chief saw no need to expand the homicide division. And, even if he did, Dave wouldn't be first in line for a position.

So, he was facing a problem similar to mine—to land the job he wanted, he might have to look elsewhere. And, for many reasons, both of us viewed that as a last resort. He was prepared to chase drug dealers in order to remain in Reckless River. And I was prepared to continue subbing for another year or so.

Could I make that clear to Mrs. B? Clear enough for her to cease meddling?

I smothered a laugh. That was about as likely to happen as Allison landing a full-ride scholarship to Stanford.

But perhaps, if Mrs. B found other projects, I'd get a break.

We eased our way toward the condo complex, Cheese Puff tugging Sybil from one side of the trail to the other, Mrs. B and I exchanging glances as we studied Verna. Even through the veil I could see that her skin was gray and her lips were clamped. Each slow step was a struggle and her breath came in strangled gasps.

"When we get back," Mrs. B said, "I'm taking you to the urgent care place downtown."

"I'm fine," Verna snapped. "I'm just tired."

"You've been working too hard at the sandwich shop," Sybil said.

"I have not. And besides, it's all accounting. It's crunching numbers, not heavy lifting."

"It's still stressful," Sybil insisted. "You worry about every penny that goes out. I don't understand why."

"Because accounts are supposed to balance," Verna panted. "Because we need to know if we're making mistakes, especially sloppy mistakes. We can't afford to lose money through carelessness and waste. The sandwich shop has to show a profit."

"Eventually," Mrs. B corrected. "And it will. But in the meantime, if the ends don't meet, I'm happy to make up the difference."

"But you already put in so much," Verna gasped.

"So what's a little more?" Mrs. B asked with a silvery laugh. "None of us could project exactly how large a slush fund would be required to get through the first few months. And we all knew business would be slow at the beginning, especially because it's winter. I specifically recall you referring to the first few months as a shakedown period."

Mrs. B patted the hand that gripped her arm. "Now if you come to me in June *and* July *and* August and tell me you need more money, a lot more money, then I'll be inclined to hide my checkbook."

"See." Sybil turned on one heel as Cheese Puff did an about-face in an attempt to pursue a stroller-riding tot nibbling on a large cookie. "That's just what I told you, Verna. And you know Lana Dylan wants to learn to do the books. But you like to have control. And you always know best. Just like you know best about going to the doctor. Anyone can see you're a lot more than tired."

"I'd be less tired if you stopped harping," Verna snapped.

"I'm not harping." Sybil spun again as Cheese Puff reversed direction to chase a burger wrapper caught by a twist of wind.

"You are." Verna turned to me, her voice more forceful, as if she was energized by conflict with her friend. "Isn't she, Barbara?"

*Urk.*

If you've been following my story, you know that one of the many things I try to avoid—along with fennel, liver, beets, and excessive exercise—is taking sides in a dispute between Verna and Sybil. Experience has taught me it's a lose-lose scenario. And, when the dust settled, I'd be the biggest loser because they'd put aside their differences and gang up on me.

So I wanted to dodge Sybil's question. But, like a cold engine, my brain refused to turn over, power up, and get me out of this jam.

"Well?" Verna asked.

"Well . . . um . . . Hey, we're almost home."

"We'll go to my place and rest for a few moments," Mrs. B told Verna. "And then I'll drive you to urgent care."

"You'll do nothing of the sort." Verna shook free of Mrs. B's arm, but kept a tight grip on Lola's collar. "I'm fine. Perfectly fine. Just tired."

"Of course you are," Mrs. B said in a soothing voice. "But what could it hurt to—?"

"Enough. I don't want to be poked and prodded, so stop pestering me." Still holding Lola's collar, Verna veered to the right and the paved path that wound around the upriver end of the condo and past a tiny walled garden and the pool. "I need a cup of tea. And I need some rest. I'll have a weekend's worth of sales to reconcile tomorrow."

Lola looked back at me, but stuck with Verna. As her retractable leash played out, I tagged along at a four-yard distance. From the corner of my eye I saw Sybil hand Cheese Puff's leash to Mrs. B and follow us. Verna reached her condo, fumbled in her pocket for her keys, and unlocked the door.

26

Without a word, she released Lola's collar, slipped inside, and closed the door with a thud. I heard not one, but two bolts slide into place.

Whining, Lola sat on the mat, nosing the door frame. I tugged on the leash. "Let's go home, girl."

Lola whined again, but got to her feet.

"How long has she been like this?" I asked Sybil.

"I don't know. The last time I saw her was Friday. No, Thursday. No, it must have been Wednesday." She smiled and clasped her hands. "I found a hundred dollars in the drawer where I keep my nightgowns, so I went on the bus that goes to the casino at the coast and I kept winning and losing and winning and losing and then I missed the bus and so when I finally got home I slept right around the clock."

Way more than I needed to know. Par for Sybil's course.

"Could you check on her later?"

"I'll give her time to take a nap and then call." She frowned at the closed door. "What if she doesn't answer?"

# Chapter 4

"If Verna doesn't answer, you check the parking lot to see if her car is here. If it is, knock on her door. If she doesn't open it, let yourself in."

Sybil's eyes widened. "How?"

"With your keys."

"I don't have keys."

I blinked. She and Verna were best friends and had been for years. I'd assumed they'd exchanged keys as many of us had. Both of them, being members of the Committee, had keys to my unit and were in and out regularly. In fact, with the notable exceptions of my sister and my ex-husband, it seemed everyone I knew had a key to my unit.

"I gave Verna a key to my place." Sybil gestured down the way toward her one-bedroom unit. "But Verna never gave me hers." She frowned and rubbed her chin. "I've never ever been inside."

*Huh?*

"But you go everywhere together. Walks. Shopping. Movies."

"We meet here." Sybil pointed to the sidewalk. "And walk around to the trail. Or to her car. Or wherever."

"What about all those nights you watch TV together? Those mystery shows you're always talking about?"

"She comes to my place. She gave me a big TV for my birthday a few years ago. And she pays my cable bill."

I stared at the glossy red paint on Verna's door, paint dampened beneath the handle where Lola's nose had pressed. I tried to remember if I'd ever been inside and concluded I hadn't. Verna had never hosted events like Mrs. B who seldom went a week without having friends in for dinner. And really, considering Mrs. B's lavish spreads, why would others bother?

That much I got. But what I couldn't wrap my brain around was the dynamics of Verna's friendship with Sybil. "So you've *never* been inside her place?"

"That's what I said. Never."

Her answer pushed me across the border between curiosity and nosiness. Verna didn't seem like an intensely private person. She'd shared a large house with several of us in Las Vegas this past November, and shared a bathroom there with Sybil. So why not let her best friend into her unit? Was she hiding something? Ashamed of something?

"Did you ever peek in the door when she came out?"

Sybil shook her head. "Why would I do that?"

I didn't attempt to answer. Sybil, it appeared, lacked curiosity. Or at least curiosity approaching my insatiable need to know. I not only would have tried to peer past Verna when she emerged, I might even have waited until she was away and then slipped across her deck and hunted for a gap in the blinds or shades where I could peep in the windows. In fact, I might creep over there later today.

"Okay. Well, call her. If she doesn't answer, check for her car, if it's here, knock on the door, if she doesn't answer, call me or Mrs. B. Got it?"

Sybil held up her left hand, fingers spread, and touched each one with the tip of her right index finger. "Call, check for her car, knock on the door, call you or Muriel."

29

"Right." I tugged on Lola's leash. "And keep me posted."

"But what if she answers when I call? What do I say?"

"Say you were calling to see if she was feeling better."

"She'll tell me to stop fussing. She doesn't like people to fuss. You saw how she was a few minutes ago."

Good point. "Then say you were calling to see if she was coming over to watch TV tonight."

"But she already said she was."

*Sheesh.*

I counted to 10 before I spoke. "Pretend you forgot."

"But I didn't. She always comes over on Sunday night."

"Pretend. Make believe."

"You mean lie?"

"Sure. Make something up."

"It's okay to do that?"

"Tonight it is."

"Okaaaayyy."

Telling myself I'd be the one to call Verna if I didn't hear from Sybil, I pulled Lola away from the door and headed home. Dave met me halfway, hand extended to seize Lola's leash. "Sorry. No movie. Gotta go to a drug house."

Lola flopped to the sidewalk, looked up at me, and whined.

I took the cue. "But she's still limping. She hasn't been cleared for duty yet."

"That's what I told the lieutenant."

"Her leg is weak." I didn't relinquish the leash. "I think she's still in pain."

"I told him that, too. But they've got a big fish in the net and they need more evidence." Dave bent and scratched Lola's ears. "It's a house. A small house. I'll lift you into the car, I'll drive right to the door, and I'll help you out. All you have to do is find where they hid the drugs so we don't have to tear the whole place apart."

30

I handed over the leash. Lola stood—but not until Dave tugged on her collar at least twice. Gazing back at me, she limped toward his beater of a car in the parking lot, sneezing as she went. Either the walk had worn her out and she'd developed new allergies, or she was chewing the scenery and going for the canine equivalent of an Academy Award.

"We'll be back for dinner," Dave called over his shoulder.

"What?" I cupped my hands around my ears. "Did you say you'd be back *with* dinner?"

"You mean you don't want to cook?"

"Does a frog want to live at the South Pole?"

He laughed, lifted Lola into the back seat, and took off. I cut through my unit, left my jacket in the hall closet, and nipped out the sliding glass door and along the deck to Mrs. B's. I found her spooning hot chocolate mix into a mug.

"Would you like a warm drink, dear? Or are you counting calories?"

I was almost always counting calories. But I almost never managed to bring the daily total in under a sum that would result in weight loss. "I'd love one. Hey, have you ever been inside Verna's unit?"

Mrs. B considered as she poured hot water, stirred, added a splash of brandy, and tossed on enough miniature marshmallows to satisfy a week's worth of cravings. "You know, I don't believe I ever have."

"I haven't either." I accepted the mug, sipped, and licked off my marshmallow mustache. "Neither has Sybil."

Noting her raised eyebrows, I went on to explain about assigning Sybil the task of checking on her friend and letting herself in if Verna didn't answer the door. "I thought for sure she'd have a key. Or maybe three. I heard two deadbolts click when Verna went inside. And there's the lock on the knob."

31

Mrs. B put the cocoa mix away and offered more marshmallows. I exercised what little willpower I possessed and declined. Cheese Puff stood on his hind legs and danced a circle around her, signaling that he'd be happy to gobble a few. When Mrs. B shook her head, he sulked off to the sofa.

"Three locks," Mrs. B mused. "We've never had a break-in here. We've never even had a prowler—if you don't count Dario or Jake or the boy we mistook for Bigfoot."

"Right. And another odd thing is Verna's so concerned about safety at the sandwich shop—about slips and falls and emergency procedures. I was sure she'd have arranged for Sybil to get into her condo in case of an emergency."

I didn't add that Sybil wasn't first on my list to turn to in an emergency. In fact, she was dead last. I knew she'd come running if I called, but her mind worked in mysterious ways. As for remaining calm and handling a crisis in a manner that wouldn't create another crisis . . .

Lest I spill my cocoa while chuckling at a vision of Sybil channeling Chicken Little, I sat at the dining room table. Unlike the table in my unit, this didn't have a wobbly leg and wasn't almost always littered with crumbs or smeared with syrup or jam. But neither was it one of those gleaming tables that had to be protected with a special cover and a tablecloth. Mrs. B had nice furniture, but she didn't go for things that had to be coddled.

"I would have bet Sybil had a set of keys," Mrs. B said. "Those two seem to live in each other's pockets."

"Right, but when they meet to go someplace, they link up outside." I sipped cocoa. "And, get this—Sybil has never tried to peek inside when Verna opens the door."

Mrs. B smiled and settled in a chair across from me. "Not everyone has as inquisitive a nature as you do, dear."

She didn't add "thank goodness," but I heard it in her tone. Slightly embarrassed, I held back from launching into a list of what Verna could be hiding behind locked doors.

Perhaps it was my silence that prompted Mrs. B to start her own list. "Verna has an orderly mind and her clothing is always spotless, so I doubt her place is dirty."

"Maybe the walls are filled with posters for political candidates she knows the rest of us despise."

Mrs. B shook her head. "As outspoken as she is, I think we'd be well aware if she supported some of the brain donors who manage to get on the ballot. Perhaps she never gave Sybil a key because she's one of those people who feel protective about privacy and personal space."

"I wondered about that, but she's never seemed concerned when we pack in here for a meeting or dinner. Or when we shared the house in Las Vegas."

"Well, whatever her reasons may be, we should honor them and respect her space." Mrs. B gazed out over the deck and toward Verna's unit as if she'd read my thoughts about sneaking along and peering in the windows. "Unless something happens. Then we get in to help her any way we can."

A few minutes later, I was wishing I had arranged a signal for someone to get in and help me. The reason for that was hammering at my front door and took the form of my sister. And a substantial form it was—with a personality to match. To say Indigo Zephyr was overbearing was like saying hippos might get a little testy if you took a sponge bath in their part of the river. When I could, I tried to avoid her. But I've had about as much success with that as I've had with avoiding pollen in the spring or repetitive holiday music in December.

And the truth was, when I tried to avoid her, I felt guilty. Iz had stepped in to raise me when my parents checked out emotionally after my brother's death, so I owed her the kind of debt that's hard to pay. Not that she hadn't extracted payment in various forms over the years. If I could cancel out the guilt and overcome obligation, I'd call us even. But I couldn't, so I opened the door a few inches.

"What took you so long?" Iz thundered.

The great conversationalists of the world had nothing on my sister when it came to kicking off a talkfest.

"I was next door."

"Imbibing something alcoholic no doubt." Iz shoved past me and tromped along the hallway toward the living room.

"No doubt," I echoed, thinking the splash of brandy in my cocoa wouldn't be enough to brace me for whatever was to come.

Cheese Puff emitted the bark signifying annoyance and scrambled for the stairs and the bedroom. So much for loyalty. If he followed his usual MO, he'd tunnel beneath the pillows and remain there until I called him for dinner.

Iz, meanwhile, made for the refrigerator and went into rummage mode, all the while mumbling criticisms of the contents of jars, bottles, and plastic containers. There was a time when I'd rise to the bait and defend my leftovers and shopping selections. But I'd been steadily growing a backbone, so I made myself comfortable on the sofa and waited for the demand of the day.

Lest you think I'm cold, hard, and generally insensitive to my sister's needs, be advised she's more of the same. When it comes to sensitivity, there are chunks of marble with more empathy, compassion, and warmth than my sister possesses. Iz was not the kind of person who waited for you to notice she required something. She never hinted, or even requested. She demanded. Usually in a strident tone.

But today, after loading a plate with tuna casserole and swilling most of a can of cola while the microwave did its thing, she ceased her criticisms far sooner than usual. "I'm at a dead end." She sat at the opposite end of the sofa and spoke between bites of casserole. "I'm stuck. I feel like my life is on hold."

Another victim of loss of momentum.

It was beginning to look like an epidemic. Allison, who had started singing lessons shortly after Thanksgiving, was stuck on the first set of scales. Her boyfriend Josh was obsessing over tiny details at the sandwich shop. High school teachers Aston Marsden and Brenda Waring were stuck in their on-again-off-again relationship. Bernina Burke hadn't proposed new nitpicky condo regulations in weeks, and Jim had stopped reorganizing my kitchen drawers and alphabetizing the canned goods in the pantry.

Even the weather seemed stuck. We'd had no major storms as in previous winters. We'd also had no week-long stretches of sunny days when the temperature, thanks to chill winds blowing down the Columbia Gorge, never topped the freezing mark. All we'd had was fog, low clouds, and more varieties of rain than I'd thought were possible.

I didn't miss the icy winds, but I did miss the sun. Despite increasing my intake of Vitamin D and beaming on a special light for half an hour every day, my energy seemed to be draining away. I wasn't just stuck in a rut; I'd sunk into a funk.

"I've never been uncertain before," Iz moaned. "At least not since I was a little kid. But now I don't know who I am or where I'm headed."

*Uh-oh.*

This was worse than a loss of momentum. This was even worse than a long-term funk. This was the dreaded identity crisis.

# Chapter 5

I repressed a shudder. Two months ago Dave and I went through an identity crisis with Allison. Granted, it lasted only a day or two and was cut short when her brief breakup with Josh came to an end, but it had been painful for all of us. This was bound to be worse. Iz, who had made a name for herself as a rabble-rousing public speaker and advocate for women intent on fulfilling their destinies, had a *huge* identity. This was a crisis with a capital C.

"What about your career as a private investigator?" I offered.

"Career?" Iz snorted. "One case doesn't make a career. Especially a money-losing case."

I nodded. Concerned her many arrests for protesting would stand in the way of getting a license, Iz had flown under the radar. That involved renting a disreputable baby-poop-brown van and spending a week following a plumber whose wife believed he was cheating. She'd gotten exactly no evidence of infidelity, and received exactly no money from her client. Since Iz, astute businesswoman that she was, failed to work up a contract or get the woman's signature on any form of agreement, small claims court wasn't a possibility.

Iz stuffed in another bite of casserole then set the half-full plate on the coffee table. Unusual behavior for a woman who sucked food like an industrial-strength vacuum cleaner and almost always went back for seconds. Behavior so unusual it worried me.

I shuddered again. The only thing scarier than my sister carrying a full load of arrogant self-confidence was my sister revealing a soft underbelly.

Iz hung her head. "I'm a failure."

"You're not," I assured her, selfishly hoping she'd buy that and we could get this over with. "You made a national name for yourself reinterpreting myths and folklore and helping women craft new visions for their lives."

Iz nixed that with a scowl and a flick of her fingers.

"And you put in a lot of hard hours on those all-women building projects. Women and children who might have been on the street now have homes."

"Mostly thanks to Penelope," Iz muttered. "And plumbers and carpenters who know what they're doing. All I am is grunt labor."

"Grunt labor is important. Without—"

"Stop it," Iz ordered. "I know what you're going to say and I don't care. I want to have a life like everyone else, like you. But I'm no good at it."

*Wait!*

*Had my sister just said she wanted a life like mine?*

*Send up a flare! Alert the media! Stop the presses!*

Of course, all of that was only in my mind. What I said was, "Maybe you're not good at it because you haven't had much practice. Traveling, couch surfing, and inciting riots didn't prepare you for settling down."

It also didn't prepare her for finding or holding a job, committing to a relationship, doing her part as a partner and roommate, or a lot of other things. But, since Iz always claimed to be a big-picture person, I didn't pile on what she might consider to be petty and distracting details.

"I helped stage demonstrations," Iz grumped. "I didn't incite riots."

Maybe not on purpose, but riots were often the result. Just ask the cops who'd been called to corral angry crowds—crowds that came to join the protests Iz led, or came to protest against the protests.

"I tried to help women visualize their paths to whole lives, to get up and out of their comfort zones. Working up some anger can help free your mind."

In that case, since she often started from angry, Iz's mind should be as free as the breeze. Heck, forget about a breeze. Her mind should be as free as a gale-force wind.

"Have you tried that?" I asked in an innocent voice. "Getting mad to visualize your path?"

"Of course I've tried!" Iz reached for her plate and shot me a glare while puffing herself up like a toad. So much for showing her soft underbelly. "Do you think I'm a dummy?"

I didn't answer. What I did was fake a cough and duck my head to hide the smile twitching my lips. Maybe I'm a victim of Stockholm syndrome, but it felt good to have the old confrontational Iz back in the house. I might not like that version of my sister much, but I knew where I stood.

"Don't get me wrong. I love confrontation and shaking things up. Tearing down things that aren't working. But I was never there for the reshaping and rebuilding." Iz stabbed casserole with her fork. "I'm not sure I'd know *how* to rebuild what I helped tear down."

I seconded her statement. But in silence.

"Penelope doesn't want me to give up what I feel called to do, and she's been great about supporting me. She's cut me a

38

lot of slack with chores and cooking and other stuff I was never much good at."

I nodded, recalling an attempt at an apple pie that came out burnt on top and raw on the bottom.

Iz forked in casserole and mumbled, "I want to make a difference."

"You have," I assured her. "You've made a lot of difference."

"I mean a *real* difference. A difference I can see."

Not grasping the distinction, I kept quiet.

"I want to make a *bigger* difference on a *smaller* scale. No more faceless crowds. I want to help one person—or just a few people—at a time."

Ah. Now I got it. "How? Doing what?"

Iz set the plate aside again. "I have no idea."

Allison was at the movies with Josh and I was watching what passed for a sunset and throttling my urge to take just a quick jog along the river trail, sneak across Verna's deck, and peek in her window, when Dave returned. The huge paper sack in his arms gave off a powerful scent of garlic that set my salivary glands doing their best to create enough drool to make a Saint Bernard envious. He set the bag on the dining room table and called down the hallway. "Come on, girl, you can make it."

Lola limped into view, whining with each step.

Cheese Puff hurtled down the stairs and raced to her side. Standing on his hind legs, he licked her muzzle, then dropped and nudged her forward.

"Did you work her too hard?" I asked.

"No." Dave raised his hands in surrender. "We walked her into the house and through the rooms. And she sniffed around the perimeter. That's it. But, on top of the stroll you took earlier, maybe it was too much."

Lola flopped on the rug beside the sofa and Cheese Puff nuzzled her ears. I brought the water bowl from the kitchen and she lapped at it a few times, but showed no interest in the dog biscuit I offered. Cheese Puff, however, snatched it from me, bit off a corner, and shoved the remainder beneath the sofa, barking to show her where he hid it for later. After she barked in return, he snuggled against her chest.

I returned the water bowl to its place. "Other than being in pain, did she do okay?"

"Yeah." He pulled take-out containers from the sack. "She used to love what she did. She'd race around like a kid at an Easter egg hunt. Even after she developed allergies she was still ready and willing. But today I had to give some commands twice. She plodded like an old horse heading for the glue factory. And sneezed every ten seconds."

I set out plates and, after cursing the drawer that either stuck open or closed, and making yet another mental note to remind Jim to take a look at it, rounded up forks and serving spoons. "Did she at least find the drugs?"

"Yeah. They were under the house, inside outflow pipes that weren't connected to anything."

"So the day wasn't a total waste."

"No." He grinned. "At least not like it was for your ex."

"Jake?" My stomach clenched and I felt a headache ballooning behind my eyes. My philandering ex-husband had done jail time for his role in helping a steroid-pushing homicidal girlfriend promote her product, and was now working on paring down a massive amount of community service hours. The terms of his release called for him to avoid criminals and criminal activities, but his definitions didn't always mesh with those of the court. "Was Jake at the drug house? Is he dealing? Did you arrest him?"

"He wasn't *at* the house. He was driving by. He wasn't dealing. And *I* didn't arrest him." Dave sat and opened a container. "This is for you." He pushed it across the table as I slid into my usual seat. "He ran a stop sign and got cited by one of the patrol officers assisting us. He's looking at some huge fines. Maybe a few days in jail."

Jake had made a career of sponging off others—mostly women—and investing money that was seldom his own in ventures that only occasionally paid off. If he was facing a hefty fine, he could soon be knocking on my door begging for a loan. A loan he wouldn't get.

I leaned over the box and inhaled the aroma of eggplant parmesan, trying to drive the image of Jake from my mind. I was long past the pain of being cheated on, and he'd repaid the money he siphoned from my account before I divorced him, so I now found his exploits ridiculous and even amusing—in a sad kind of way. "He'll get jail time for running a stop sign? He must have a metric ton of previous violations."

"Nope. The moving violation was the tip of the law-flaunting iceberg he was floating on today." Dave chewed and swallowed a quarter of a meatball. "Jake's running a tour business."

"What? Jake's never been farther from Reckless River than Seattle. He knows as much about foreign countries as I know about advanced calculus. How can he run a travel agency?"

"It's not a travel agency." Dave wound spaghetti on his fork. "He bought a bus. He does narrated tours."

"Of what?"

"The seamy side of Reckless River."

I laughed. "Must be short tours."

41

"Longer than you might think." Dave gave up on winding and used the edge of his fork to cut sections from the mound of spaghetti on his plate. "There's a lot of sleazy here if you know where to look."

And Jake would have a great idea of where to look—especially if he used knowledge acquired behind bars.

"Wait." I paused with a chunk of eggplant mere inches from my eager lips. "Back up a few sentences. Did you say he *bought* a bus?"

"A small bus," Dave mumbled around a mouthful of spaghetti. "Holds maybe 20 people."

"Still. Buses don't come cheap. And Jake is low on funds."

"But apparently not low on female friends with spare change. He told me he has several investors."

I popped the eggplant in my mouth and sighed. Jake was scum, but he was charming scum. I felt sorry for the women who succumbed to his financial pitches. The only return on their investments might be "opportunities" to spend even more money on dates with my ex. At the same time, having once fallen for his pie-in-the-sky promises, I felt smugly delighted to know I wasn't the only fool in town.

Dave stuck his fork in a huge meatball, raised it to his mouth, licked off the sauce, and attacked it as if it was an ice cream bar. "Frankie DeMille came up with the idea," he said after he swallowed a chunk.

Frankie, a flamboyant woman of indefinite years, was the director of the Reckless River Amateur Theater Company. She'd been smitten with Jake when he turned up asking about community service, and gave him a role in their winter production. He'd never acted before, but Jake took to it the way a mosquito takes to sucking blood. He'd wowed female actors and audience members alike. As for male actors and partners of female audience members? Not so much.

"Did Frankie loan him money as well?"

"Don't know. But I doubt he would have hit her—or his other investors—up for much. The bus probably rolled off the assembly line about the time you got out of middle school."

That made it somewhere north of two decades old. How far north, I decline to reveal. "Still, to repeat myself, buses don't come cheap."

"This one looks like the previous owner might have paid Jake to take it. Cracked windows. Bumper wired in place. Balding tires. Squealing brakes. Exhaust spewing like a volcanic eruption."

"So the citation was for safety violations?"

"And failure to possess the proper insurance. Or license." Dave gobbled the remainder of the meatball. "But remember the law-flaunting iceberg I mentioned? Those issues don't even get us down to the waterline."

# Chapter 6

Dedicating myself to eggplant and a heap of spaghetti, I pondered that for a moment, considering what I knew of Jake and how he operated. The image of the iceberg faded and was replaced by one of a weasel. "Let me guess—he tried to talk his way out of the whole mess."

"*Bargain* his way out. Offered tickets for his bus tours in exchange for looking the other way."

Only in the inflated-ego universe my ex inhabited would that seem like a fair trade. "That explains the possible jail time."

"Yeah. Attempting to bribe a cop in front of other cops was a dumb play. Even for Jake." Dave dug into the take-out box for another meatball. "The folks on the bus loved it. They applauded when Jake got cuffed. They thought it was part of the show."

I started to laugh then caught myself. "Wait. They hauled him to jail? What happened to the bus? And the tourists?"

"They didn't follow through on the arrest." Dave grimaced. "I, uh, intervened. Not for him. For the poor saps on that rusting hulk of a bus." He winced. "Although, now that I think about it, they might have been safer walking back."

I felt Dave's pain. Doing something to benefit Jake always made me feel dirty, defiled, and disgusted with myself, a traitor to all that was ethical and fair and unselfish. "Maybe the

44

chamber of commerce will give you an award for assisting visitors."

"And maybe my fellow officers will hang me in effigy."

"Or not. You saved them some paperwork. And maybe the jail supervisor will take you to lunch because he won't have Jake on his roster again—at least not until the citations are processed and he's fined and doesn't bother to pay and gets hauled in."

I reached across the table and took Dave's hand. "I know it makes you feel like you've been slimed. But I think you did everyone a favor—including all those women Jake would have hit up for bail tomorrow morning."

"You can bet he'll find something to hit them up for." Dave gnawed at the meatball, a furrow between his eyes. Then he shrugged and the furrow smoothed out. "Anyway, it's done. I can't take it back."

Words to live by. Words I'd repeated many times when thinking about my brief marriage to Jake.

My cellphone rang. I glanced at the clock as I scooped it from the coffee table. "Everything okay?"

"She's mad," Sybil reported. "Really mad. She says if I bother her one more time she's done being friends. She says she'll take back the TV and stop paying my cable bill."

That qualified as a major threat in my league as well as Sybil's. "But she's still coming over to watch your Sunday night show?"

"Yes."

"All right, then you can stop calling. Unless she doesn't show up. Got it?"

"I don't call. But if she doesn't come over, then I do call."

"Right."

After a long sigh, Sybil disconnected.

"What was that about?" Dave asked.

Between bites of eggplant, I told him about Verna's condition, praised Lola for her protective instincts, and explained my instructions to Sybil and the reason for them.

"Have you gone sneaking across Verna's deck to peek in the window yet?"

I smacked my fork on the table. "Why does everyone around here think I'm nosy?"

"Not me." Dave raised his hands in surrender. "I absolutely don't think you're nosy. Consumed by curiosity? Perhaps. Allergic to secrecy? Maybe. But nosy? Certainly not."

I shot him the kind of substitute teacher glare I'd turn on a kid writing a lengthy text on his cellphone while I was giving instructions for a project. "And you, on the other hand, aren't the least bit interested in why Verna won't allow anyone inside her unit?"

"I'm interested, sure," he said in a smug tone, "but I don't have an itch I need to scratch with both hands."

The word "itch" made a spot between my shoulder blades tingle. You probably know where that spot is. And maybe, like me, you can't quite get your fingernails at it, no matter which hand you use, which angle you come at it from, or how you stretch and contort.

I gritted my teeth and willed the spot to stop itching. I wasn't about to give Mr. Smug the satisfaction of seeing how his words affected me.

But the minute he turned to carry his plate to the sink, I seized my fork, stuck it under my T-shirt, and went at the itch with all four tines.

"So Lola was protective?" He rinsed the plate and set it in the dishwasher rack.

"Extremely. She didn't want to leave when Verna went inside." I gave the itch one more scrape with the fork. "If they

46

retire her as a drug dog, she might have another career ahead of her."

Dave glanced at Lola who was emitting rumbling snores and twitching her legs. "Do you think she's smart enough to fake allergies and the limp?"

"She's smart enough to know she gets extra attention for being hurt. But I think it's more like she's exaggerating than faking." I set the fork on the table, closed the take-out boxes, and carried them to the refrigerator. "She's had a lot of time off the job to be the family dog. And, much as she loves you and wants to please you, I'm pretty sure she's had it with sniffing out drugs."

"Yeah. I get that message loud and clear." Dave liberated a bottle of beer from the refrigerator. "But our new HR czar doesn't. She says Lola and I should return to the drug squad darn quick. When I expressed concerns about her allergies and her injury, what I heard was she's a dog and I'm her handler and I should make her do her job."

"*Make* her do her job? How? Beating her? Starving her?"

Dave shuffled his feet. "No one used those words."

"Well I'm reading between the lines and it sounds to me like the HR czar doesn't know the first thing about dogs. Lola works for you because you're a team, because she loves and respects you."

"And because she gets treats."

Cheese Puff raised his head at the word "treats." When he saw nothing offered, he curled his upper lip in disgust and burrowed against Lola again.

"*Rewards*," I fumed, tossing silverware at the dishwasher basket. "Rewards for doing her job. Not penalties if she doesn't."

Dave nodded and waited until I'd loaded my plate and glass before he spoke. "And if a dog decides to go on strike?" He thrust his chin toward Cheese Puff. "And doesn't respond to rewards? How do you handle that?"

I kicked the door of the dishwasher up and gave the table a few vicious swipes with a sponge. When Cheese Puff refused to practice their dance routine with Mrs. B, she'd tried everything from special treats, to threats, to a multi-hour staring contest. All to no avail. My entitled mutt was 10 pounds of stubborn determination. Had Lola learned her recent behavior from him?

I tossed the sponge in the sink. Cheese Puff had come through in the end and turned in an award-winning performance. Would Lola suck it up and get on with what she'd been trained to do because of her bond with Dave?

"Sometimes we lose sight of the fact that Lola is a working dog," Dave said. "I don't know what the department shelled out to get her when the cop she was with retired, but I bet it was in the vicinity of five figures."

A big chunk of change. More than I had kicking around. But to Mrs. B it was a small drop in a large bucket. "Maybe we could buy her!"

"If the department was willing to sell."

The way he said it rang alarm bells at the back of my brain. Big alarm bells. Really loud alarm bells. "She's middle-aged in dog years. She's got allergies and can't move fast. So why wouldn't they sell her?"

"Because they'd have to get another dog. And there might be a training period. And a disruption in law enforcement. The HR czar is all about continuity." His gaze skittered away from mine. "And I need to toe the line because I've been operating fast and loose."

"I thought that was how the drug squad was supposed to operate."

"Yeah, well, she wasn't talking about that. See, I never got official clearance to take Lola on the search and rescue training where we got hurt. The chief let it slide, but then the medical and vet bills started coming in, and Lola's still limping and . . ."

I felt the eggplant parmesan turn to cement in my stomach. For a moment I was furious at him. Then I was furious at the HR czar. Then I was just plain furious because sweet, loving Lola was a pawn in someone's stupid power game. "If you don't toe the line, what happens? Would you be transferred to another division? Demoted?"

"I don't know." He grimaced. "I haven't thought about it."

"What happens to Lola if your assignment changes?"

Dave froze for a few seconds and then his gaze slid toward Lola. "I guess they'd match her with another partner."

"And she'd live with him? Or her?"

"That's the way it works."

Lola's legs twitched again. Cheese Puff snuggled closer and cast a baleful glance at Dave.

"Would they let her visit? Maybe come over for weekends?"

"I don't know. I'd guess not. At least not at first, not while she and the new handler are getting used to each other."

I imagined life without Lola around. I didn't like the images my brain manufactured. Some concerned Cheese Puff's behavior after losing his companion. My entitled mutt wasn't the type to simply mope. He was the type to exact some form of revenge. "But she'd have a good home, right? She'd have treats and walks and get lots of attention like she does here."

Dave got the fearful look of a goat staked out to lure a tiger. I'd seen the expression before. "What are you wishing you didn't have to tell me?"

"Um, some handlers keep their dogs in kennels." He took a step back. "Or have them sleep in crates."

"Kennels? Crates?"

Cheese Puff yipped.

Lola opened her eyes. I swear I saw tears in them.

"Not everyone treats dogs like we do, Barbara," Dave said in the rational tone I find so annoying. "Some people believe dogs should sleep outside."

"Outside? In the rain? In the winter?"

"Well, maybe in a garage."

Cheese Puff yipped again.

Lola grunted as if in pain.

"You say that like a garage is a palatial mansion." I crossed my arms and stood tall. "Just so you know, I will not stand by and watch Lola go off with someone who will treat her like . . . like a dog."

Dave blanched and his Adam's apple jerked as he swallowed.

To make sure he was good and terrified, I amped up my threat. "And neither will Mrs. Ballantine."

Dave and I didn't speak much for the rest of the evening. Or, rather, I didn't speak much. Silence, I thought, would underline my position better than any amount of clarifying conversation. After a few attempts to open a dialogue, he cleaned up the kitchen and hunkered in one corner of the sofa with a book about the *Titanic*. A fitting choice. If Lola ended up sleeping in a crate in a garage, he was sunk.

At 9:30, after a final check of the blank space on the website where subbing jobs would appear if there were any, I called for the dogs to make a trip to their latrine—the thick layer of bark mulch in the rose garden. Cheese Puff trudged to the door then set a new record crossing the deck through an icy drizzle. Lola grunted, but refused to move.

"She'll bark if she needs to go out." Dave said.

"Just like she'll have to do if she's in a crate," I sniped.

He shrugged and headed to the bedroom, pausing at the top of the stairs to rap on Allison's door and call out, "Turn off that sorry excuse for music and go to sleep. Finals start tomorrow."

"I knoooooow finals start tomorrow." Allison howled. "I'm not stuuuupid. But I can't study without music."

"And I can't sleep with it. Put your earphones on."

"I can't find them."

"That's the third pair she's lost since school started," I told Cheese Puff as he scooted inside. "I should advise Mrs. B to invest in the company."

"Don't make me come in there and turn it off," Dave said in his cop voice.

"I locked the door," Allison shot back.

"I kick in doors for a living," he reminded her.

"Allll riiiight."

Pounding bass, the backbeat for the soundtrack of Allison's at-home life, ceased.

Twenty minutes later, clinging to the edge of the bed, and as far from Dave as space and blanket width allowed, I fell asleep.

Two hours later, I woke up.

Something wasn't as it should be. There was, as they say, a disruption in the force.

I stared into the dark, trying to recall what I'd heard or felt.

Beside me, Dave emitted his usual snuffling, snorting, strangling snore. The vent in the floor made a shushing sound as it forced warm air into the room. A plane roared overhead.

All normal midnight noises.

Cheese Puff, who had burrowed beneath the covers, released a muffled yip and clawed at my thigh. I shook him, interrupting a dream of chasing the cat next door to Mrs. B, or besting the duck that sent him to the vet last year. He grunted and was still.

Also normal.

I strained my ears.

Rain spattered against the window.

The roof creaked.

And Lola whined.

# Chapter 7

I sat up, flipped the covers aside, toed into a pair of fuzzy slippers, and poked my arms into a yellow bathrobe that made me feel like a taxi. I hated it but, since it had been a Christmas gift from Allison, couldn't give it away. And I hadn't thought of a way to misplace it—at least not a way that would seem believable. There weren't many spots where an item could be misplaced in a two-bedroom condo.

Grabbing the cellphone I'd promised Dave I'd take along if I went out at night, I headed downstairs. Lola stood in the hallway, little more than a shadow in the faint light cast by the lamp above the stove.

"Need to go out, girl?"

She barked agreement.

I grabbed a jacket from the hall closet and headed for the door to the deck.

Lola barked again and limped toward the door to the parking lot.

Strange. We always went out across the deck unless we were driving somewhere.

"Come, Lola." I thumbed the latch on the sliding glass door.

Lola didn't come.

I called again.

And again.

I locked the door, trekked along the hallway, and gripped her collar. "Let's go. Out back."

Lola sat.

"Up. Come on, Lola. Out back."

Lola growled and twisted her neck, pulling against my grip.

"What's gotten into you, girl? We're not going to work. We're not going after drugs." I released her collar. "Come on. You don't have to walk any farther than the rose garden."

Lola turned, scratched at the door, and barked.

I hesitated for a moment. Bernina Burke, the condo manager and my archenemy, had recently taken a "no tolerance" position on the rules concerning the specific areas where dogs were allowed on the property at 90 Columbia Lane. Except for "necessary" trips to and from vehicles or to other units, the parking lot and tiny abutting lawns were off-limits.

But I'd only be in trouble if Bernina saw me. Right?

I cocked my head and listened. Still raining. Hard. And since it was past midnight Bernina, being at least 3,000 hours behind on her beauty sleep, was probably in bed.

Lola scratched again and barked.

The worst Bernina could do was bully and bluster and bloviate at a pitch designed to rupture my eardrums. Then she'd put another black mark on my record or complain to the condo board and demand tougher rules.

The worst Lola could do, however, involved an olfactory assault that would have me gagging for hours. Lola's worst would have me using up all the carpet cleaner and paper towels we had on hand.

No contest.

I lifted Lola's leash from its hook, checked to make sure I had my keys and a plastic bag in my jacket pocket, then opened the door a few inches and bent to clip the leash to her collar.

Lola jerked from my grip and shot into the rain, running as if she'd never been injured.

Remembering times in my life when the call of nature was more like a shout, I didn't fault her.

I lingered beneath the scant shelter provided by the small decorative roof above the door until I realized Lola hadn't stopped to squat beside the low hedge that separated my unit from the next. She reached the sidewalk along the edge of the parking lot, made a hard right, and streaked off.

"Come back," I called in a low voice I hoped wouldn't wake my neighbors—or at least neighbors likely to complain about a dog on the loose. "Lola, come."

Lola didn't come.

What she did was bark.

Repeatedly.

"Way to draw attention to your unaccompanied status," I muttered.

Adding a few select words I won't repeat here, I raised the hood of my jacket and plunged into the hammering rain. Hoping the spatter and slosh would cover me, I called for Lola to stop barking and come.

I could take yet another lecture from Bernina, but I wasn't sure I could take the sight of her sleepwear. Simply imagining what might be imprinted on her nightgown or pajamas—tanks, nuclear missiles, or perhaps likenesses of evil cartoon characters—gave me chills beyond what the January night could deliver.

I discovered Lola on Verna's front step, scratching at the door. When I reached for her collar, she growled, jerked aside, and scratched again.

Registering her determination and anxiety, I didn't make another attempt to drag her away. Instead I put my ear against the door and punched the doorbell. Even above the sounds of rain and wind and Lola's scratching and whining, I heard the chimes. Assessing the volume, I concluded that, as in my unit, the chimes were located in the hallway near the living room, beside the staircase to the bedrooms. If the TV wasn't blaring and Allison didn't have her music powered up to an intensity that could smash granite, we were able to hear our chimes in every room, and even out on the deck. If Verna was inside, she should be able to hear.

Unless Verna slept like the dead.

Or was dead.

I jabbed the button again, hammered on the door with both fists, and listened. Hard.

Unfortunately, all I heard was my pulse pounding like a bass drum at the bottom of a deep well.

Lola whined and scratched again.

Snatching my cellphone from my jacket pocket I punched in Verna's number and pressed my ear against the door. While I listened to my galloping pulse, I watched a mental slide show of images dredged from my imagination—Verna drowned in her bathtub, Verna electrocuted by a faulty socket.

I disconnected and dialed Sybil. "Is Verna at your place?" I blurted.

"Huh? Uh, no, I don't think so," she mumbled in a sleep-dazed way. "Want me to get up and look?"

I disconnected and called Mrs. B. "Is Verna with you?"

"No."

"She's not with Sybil. She doesn't answer her door. And Lola's scratching at it and won't let me pull her off."

"I'm on the way."

I called Dave. "I think Verna might be sick or hurt. Lola's scratching at her door and won't leave."

"Be there in a flash."

I rang the bell once more and pounded on the door yet again. Then I wondered whether I should wake Bernina Burke and see if she had a set of keys. It seemed like a long shot. If Verna hadn't shared keys with her best friends, no way would she want Bernina to have a set.

And, if Bernina had keys, did I want to listen to her cite the conditions under which she could use them? Did I want to listen to her imply I'd gotten her out of bed for no good reason?

Even if I had time to waste, the answer was "NO."

I was about to call Jim and ask him to get a pry bar or sledgehammer when two things happened: Dave sprinted up the short walk, and I heard the sound of deadbolts snapping on the other side of the door.

"Verna?" I called. "Verna, are you okay?"

Mrs. B opened the door. She wore a pale blue flannel nightgown so wet it dripped rainwater on her bare feet. One hand gripped a bronze pole lamp as tall as she was. The base was scratched and dented. "I broke the glass door to the deck," she panted. "I didn't see her on my way to let you in, but . . ."

She stepped aside and I saw why she'd paused. Boxes were piled to the ceiling on both sides of the hallway. Beyond them I saw towering stacks of newspapers and leaning heaps of magazines.

Lola barked and squeezed past Mrs. B. Dave flicked on a flashlight with a beam like a lighthouse and followed, his bare feet leaving wet marks on the dark gray linoleum. I went just far enough to close the door behind me and huddled against Mrs. B. "I don't know what to think," she said. "It's . . . I never imagined Verna was . . . I don't know what to say about this."

I didn't either.

"She's on the stairs," Dave called. "Looks like she had a stroke and fell. Call an ambulance. Bring me a coat or a blanket. And a pillow."

Relieved to have tasks to accomplish, we broke apart. I handed Mrs. B my cellphone and, after scanning Verna's living room, kitchen, and the small downstairs closet—all packed with what could best be described as junk—raced home for a quilt and a pillow.

I carried them up the cluttered staircase to Dave, almost forgetting I'd been angry with him. Uncomfortable as it appeared, he hunched on the landing beside a stack of boxes, stroking Verna's hair, explaining that help would arrive soon and she'd be just fine, assuring her she'd be shopping with Sybil again in a few weeks. Lola stretched out a few steps above, her neck across Verna's bare feet.

"She's responsive," Dave whispered, "but barely."

I passed that along to Mrs. B who had spread out a few magazines to protect her feet and was sweeping up bits of broken glass, all the time talking on her cellphone to Jim, giving him instructions for securing the broken door. When I took over the sweeping, Mrs. B called Sybil and told her to get dressed and ready to go to the hospital. Then she zipped home to change.

Alone in the living area—or, rather, the few square feet of living area that could be lived in, I listened to Dave murmuring to Verna. And I told myself not to begin cataloging what she had hoarded.

I might as well have told myself not to breathe.

The living room was filled with furniture, chairs piled on chairs piled on sofas. The heap was topped with paintings and mirrors and magazine racks and lamps. Except for the very end of the table, the dining room was stacked with boxes, books, newspapers, magazines, more chairs, and throw pillows. The space beneath it was filled with more of the same. It appeared Verna took her meals in an area large enough only for a tiny microwave and the plate she ate from. And the plate must have been dessert-sized because a mug with a teabag draped over the side occupied about a quarter of the space right now. A scruffy office chair, missing a wheel and possessing only one armrest, seemed to be her seat of choice. A large black leather purse hung by its strap from the back of the chair.

Narrow trails through mounds of hoardings led to the refrigerator and the stacking washer and dryer. The stove was almost invisible beneath a vast collection of bowls and platters and dead plants. One side of the double sink was filled with a collection of cookie jars and piggy banks, some broken. The other side contained a single plate—small, just as I'd figured—and a fork.

Feeling as if the heaps would avalanche down on me, I retreated to the path in the hallway. My chest constricted and my breath came in sharp puffs. My head spun and my knees wobbled.

And then someone knocked on the open door to the parking lot and two men made their way down the hall, walking sideways to get their gear through the narrow space. Neither rolled his eyes or shook his head. I wondered if they'd been on calls in places like this before, or if they were remarkably contained.

I pointed to the stairs. "Up there."

"It's tight," Dave called out.

"No kidding," one of the men said after a moment.

"I'll get the backboard," the other said.

Dave hung by Verna's side for a few moments, identifying himself as a police officer and talking with the paramedics. Then he squeezed down the staircase, led me to the tiny space by the dining room table, and wrapped me in a hug. "You okay?"

"Yes." I shivered. "No. Maybe. I don't know."

"That's normal." He kissed the top of my head. "This was a shock. For all of us."

"She was always so . . . so immaculate and organized. Her clothes. Her hair. The spreadsheets she made for the sandwich shop."

"I've heard it's like that sometimes. She separated the outside world from this. She didn't want anyone to know."

"But if we knew, we could have helped."

"Maybe she didn't want help. Or didn't realize she needed it. Maybe this developed slowly."

"But if she hid this, she must have known it wasn't . . . right."

"There are many levels of knowing." Dave tipped my chin and kissed me. "And many levels of right."

I returned his kiss, pushing what might happen with Lola into the future, and thinking how lucky I was that Dave had saved my life and worked his way into it.

"We better find her medical card," he said after a moment.

"Look in there." I pointed at the purse.

He unhooked it from the chair, set it at the edge of the table, and folded back the flap. "Huh."

"What?"

"No clutter." He tipped it so I could see the contents—a checkbook, wallet, pen, tissue pack, and a small makeup case. "I bet you have twice as much junk in yours."

This from a man who made a career of kicking dirty socks and shoes under the sofa.

I hauled in breath for a smart remark, but the crunch of broken glass announced Jim's arrival with a sheet of plywood and a toolbox. "How's she doing?"

"She may have a few broken ribs and she's disoriented," Dave said. "Didn't know who I was. Can't move her right arm and leg much."

I shivered once more and he held me closer.

"Probably stick in a stent or two," Jim said. "And whack her up with some drugs. Then there's physical therapy. If she works at it like she works at all her other projects, they'll have her back on her feet in no time."

It sounded like he was trying to convince himself more than trying to persuade us.

# Chapter 8

"The wild card is time," Jim went on. "No telling how long she was lying here."

"When did the mystery show end?" Dave asked.

Jim thought for a moment. "Ten. But they always settled their bet before she started home."

"Their bet?" Dave and I asked as a chorus.

"They bet on who would get killed and who the killer was." Jim chuckled. "Big money. Sometimes a dollar a bet."

"I think she had a cup of tea when she got home." I pointed to the mug at the edge of the table. "The tea bag is still wet."

"And she has a nightgown on," Dave added.

Jim checked his watch once more. "So maybe she was in bed. Maybe even asleep for a time. Maybe it hit her only a few minutes ago and they'll slap those meds in and she'll be up to snuff again soon."

"If she is, it's all thanks to Lola." I stressed her name. "She sensed Verna was sick this afternoon and didn't want to leave her. She woke me up around midnight and insisted on going out the door to the parking lot. She growled when I reached for her collar to lead her to the deck."

I gripped Dave's arm, half to make my point and half to let him know I remained in Lola's corner. "She'd never hurt me. She growled to let me know she had a mission."

62

"Where is she now?" Jim asked.

"Keeping Verna's feet warm," Dave said.

"Dog oughta get an award." Jim gathered a handful of his flowing white beard and used it to wipe tears from his cheeks. "Oughta get a statue in the park."

"I think she'd be happy with a good scratch behind the ears and a biscuit," Dave said.

"She'd be even happier with her retirement papers," I hissed, digging my nails into Dave's arm. "And a promise she'd stay with us, and never have to sleep in a crate in a garage."

Before he could answer, one of the rescue workers called out, "Could someone clear space in the hallway?"

"You bet," Jim said.

He and Dave got to work moving boxes from the hallway. I helped with wedging them into the space where Verna took her meals and the pathway into the kitchen. When they were finished, Dave grabbed Verna's purse and headed outside to hand it off to Mrs. B.

In a few moments, they brought Verna down the stairs strapped to a narrow backboard. Her skin was gray, her mouth slack, her eyes open but unfocused. I wanted to touch her cheek, but I couldn't move.

Jim stepped forward and patted her shoulder. "You'll be right as rain in a few days, Verna," he boomed.

"She'll be fine," I added in a choked voice. Closing my eyes, I wished that would be true.

I heard Dave assuring paramedics he'd see to it Verna's condo was cleared out so she'd have a safe place to return to. I felt Lola rub against my leg then lean against me as she sat. Then I heard Dave's bare feet slap against the linoleum and felt his arm around my shoulders.

Sooner than I thought possible, the ambulance engine roared to life and tires swished across the parking lot. A second roar and another set of swishes told me Mrs. B was in pursuit with Sybil riding shotgun. I felt lighter and more hopeful, the way I usually did when Mrs. B was on the job.

Jim wiped his eyes again and muttered something about hoping to go out with a wink instead of a whimper.

Dave dug in the pocket of his jeans, removed a set of keys, and offered them to Jim. "She had these clutched in her hand."

"Wonder if she was planning to drive to the hospital." Jim took the keys, opened his toolbox, and got to work securing the door.

"There's nothing else we can do here." With Lola trailing us, Dave steered me toward the door to the parking lot. "Let's go home."

It seemed wrong to leave. But it seemed even more wrong to stay in a place so far removed from the way I thought it should be.

"Mrs. B will call as soon as she knows something," he assured me.

And an hour later, while I was pacing a circle around the dining room table, she did.

"Stroke," she confirmed.

I took a breath before asking, "Will she be okay?"

"They won't say that, dear."

I gripped the phone tighter. "What *will* they say?"

"They'll know more in the morning." She adopted a brisk, in-charge tone. "Now you take tomorrow off from subbing, sleep in, and eat a good breakfast. I'll want you to help me move furniture."

"At Verna's place?" I tried to keep trepidation out of my voice, but couldn't. Even if there was space we could move furniture to, I hesitated to shift things more than Dave and Jim had last night. For all I knew, Verna had a method and reason for placing each item. I didn't want to disrupt the order. And I certainly didn't want to be responsible for accidentally breaking something she treasured.

"No, at my place," Mrs. B said. "She'll need light and air and space to have physical therapy and use a walker when she's ready. We'll set up my living room as a recovery room—like we did when your sister got shot at that rally last year."

I was onboard with her plan, but I wondered if Verna, strong-willed as she was, would agree.

Mrs. B seemed to read my mind. "I imagine she'll object, but it's not safe for her to be alone. And she can't go home until something is done to clean it out. I intend to speak with her doctors."

Meaning "lay down the law" to her doctors. "With the goal of undercutting her arguments?"

"Entirely for her own good, dear. She'd be miserable in a rehab facility, no matter how nice. And she'd make the staff miserable, as well. You know how she can be."

How Verna can be is pretty much how Mrs. B can be—opinionated, confident, and not wild about compromise. I had no doubt that, due to Verna's weakened condition, Mrs. B would triumph in the first round. But once Verna regained her strength . . . Well, fur would fly.

Concerned as I was, sleeping in was out of the question, but I had no problem with the "eat a good breakfast" part of Mrs. B's instructions. Dave was chowing on the leftover pasta, so I whipped up a mess of pancakes with blueberries and bananas, passed on the butter, but treated myself to several swirls of squirt cream on top. Sure, that added a lot of calories, but I figured I'd burn them off later. And, compared to the amount of cream Allison piled on, my heap was minimal.

(For the record, it's a well-known fact that comparison calories don't count as much as regular calories—at least not when you're on the low end of the seesaw and taking in fewer than others sharing the meal.)

While waiting for Mrs. B's call, I cleaned the kitchen, made the bed, and took Cheese Puff and Lola out for a brief walk between rain showers. Around 9:30, I got a text from Ardie. "Jerome Morrow still MIA. Didn't answer Chill's calls this weekend. Or today."

"Is she frantic?" I texted back.

"Passed frantic hours ago. Chewing nails. Hers."

That might not sound bad to you, but Big Chill, as I've mentioned before, is the queen of good grooming. She's famous for perfectly manicured nails, usually painted in vibrant shades of red. She's also the queen of dealing with stress without sacrificing her appearance. "Yikes."

Just after I sent that message, my phone rang. "I need you," Big Chill said by way of greeting.

Like I said before, finals were underway, and teachers were allowed few reasons for calling in a sub. "Someone get sick?"

"I'm afraid Jerome might be. No one's seen him since late last week. He doesn't answer his phone or return my messages. I need you to drive up there."

I glanced at the clock and then toward Mrs. B's unit. If I wasn't available to help move furniture, I'd be in deep doo-doo. On the other hand, if I turned down a request from Big Chill, I'd be in deeper doo-doo. And the Chillster's kind of doo-doo could affect my chances of landing a teaching position at Captain Meriwether. "Uh, drive up where?"

"To his cabin. By the Lewis River."

Dave and I had driven along the Lewis River in the fall. I recalled meadows and forests and waterfalls and winding road —a lot of winding road. I also recalled the river had two forks and the one to the north served as a county boundary. "Where up the Lewis River? And which side?"

"This side. That's all I know for sure." Big Chill's voice broke and I heard the kind of noise I make when I'm sucking back tears. "I don't think it's close to Woodland. But it's probably not as far as Lake Merwin."

Not much help. I had no idea of as-the-crow-flies distance. But I'd guess the as-the-road-runs distance was a heck of a lot more. And then there were side roads. I could be knocking on doors all day. And if Jerome Morrow had been as invisible to neighbors as he had to his staff, I might be knocking all night.

"Have you called the sheriff's department? Maybe they'd send someone to do a welfare check."

"I thought of that, but I didn't want to seem like . . . like a batty old woman."

No one who wanted to keep key body parts attached would ever refer to her as batty or old. But I didn't utter the words. Nor did I comment on the exhaustion and weakness I detected in her voice. "I'll call Dave," I said in a take-charge tone. "I bet he has ways of finding an address—from tax records or utilities or something. Once I know where I'm going, I'll head out."

Or, with any luck, Dave would volunteer for the job and leave me at the beck and call of Mrs. B. Perhaps he'd volunteer even before I reminded him about my concerns for Lola's future.

"I knew I could count on you to help."

Big Chill's voice was soft, but I detected a because-you-know-what's-good-for-you undertone. "I'll keep you posted. I'll call as soon as I know anything."

The Chillster made another snuffling, sucking sound and disconnected. I punched in Dave's cell number. Mostly he didn't answer when I called while he was working, but today—perhaps because of my position on Lola's future, or because he was concerned about Verna—he picked up after the second ring. "Jerome Morrow is missing," I said.

"Who's Jerome Morrow?"

So much for any illusion that he gave his full attention to my reports on the life and times of the crew at Captain Meriwether High School. "The invisible principal."

"If he's invisible," Dave asked with a forced chuckle, "how does anyone know he's missing?"

I clamped my teeth and let my silence speak.

"Okay. Not the time to be funny. How can I help?"

I unclamped and laid out the situation.

"Should be easy to get an address, but . . ."

"But what?"

"But if— Listen, I'm not saying you couldn't handle an emergency situation because you've handled plenty and done a good job, but you promised Mrs. Ballantine you'd be available to help her. How about I run up there?"

I pretended I needed convincing. "Well . . . I told Big Chill I'd call her right away if—"

"I'll call you if I locate him," he said in a patient voice. "Then you'll call her."

"I guess that would work."

"Then I'm on it. Have you ever actually seen this guy? Do you know what he looks like?"

"Um, the last time I saw him was about a year ago. He's average height and kind of round and soft and pale. And he has gray hair."

"Got it. Have you heard anything about Verna?"

I glanced at the clock again. The morning was wearing on. "Not yet."

"If the news was bad, Mrs. Ballantine would have called by now. I bet she's busy telling the hospital administrator how to run the place better. The poor guy will be reconsidering his career choice."

All probably true. But I was in no mood to chuckle. "I guess."

Dave abandoned attempts to lighten the mood. "All right. I'll get back to you soon."

He disconnected, leaving me to worry about Verna and about Big Chill's mental and physical state. Her job was stressful but, like a plate-spinner or a juggler, she'd always managed to keep things from crashing down. So far, she hadn't lost momentum. And so far, she'd faced down those who hinted it was time to retire. I couldn't imagine Captain Meriwether without her. But nothing—and no one—went on forever.

Before my mind could spin up a vortex of dark thoughts about mortality, my phone rang.

# Chapter 9

For a long moment I stared at the phone, willing the next bit of news to be good. Then I punched it on.

Without a greeting, Mrs. B issued a set of orders. "Jim and some of his friends will take care of the furniture at my place. He's over at Verna's now, taking out the garbage and clearing anything suspicious from the refrigerator."

I shuddered. If Verna had hoarded food the way she'd hoarded other things, Jim had a large, and potentially nauseating, job ahead of him.

"I need you to check her clothing sizes. Then get the credit card tucked in my nightstand under the tissues and prepare to melt it down. Start at the mall."

I suppressed a groan. Hit by a double whammy. Not only shopping, but shopping at the mall. I grabbed for what I thought was a lifeline. "Won't there be a problem with me using your card?"

"No. Your name is on the card along with mine."

A little factoid I hadn't been informed about. "What? Why?"

"For emergencies. Like this one."

I thought about mentioning that a card I wasn't aware of was as good as worthless in an emergency, and adding that a key to preparedness was communication, but Mrs. B rushed on.

"Verna will need soft and comfortable clothing she can get in and out of easily. We won't have time to order on the Internet, but if you check out some of the sites specializing in clothing for stroke victims, you'll get an idea of what to look for. Velcro. No tiny buttons."

I got about half of that because I was still processing the part about my name being on a credit card with Mrs. B's. If you've been keeping up with my life, you know Mrs. B decided —without informing me—that I would inherit the bulk of her estate. And you also know I hope she lives many, many years. In the meantime, my goal is to live within my means. Mrs. B's goal, however, seems to be to enhance those means with gifts of all sorts. I was concerned about sliding with the credit card down a slippery slope, expanding the definition of "emergency" to, say, finding I'd run low on socks or was $20 short of buying a new sweater.

"We can talk about the card later, dear. But now you need to get going."

I know an order when I hear one. "I'm on my way. Does this shopping mission mean they'll let Verna out of the hospital soon?"

"Probably. If we have everything lined up to care for her."

Meaning I'd better get it in gear. "If I can't find clothing that's exactly right, maybe I can get my friend Ardie to make alterations."

"Perfect. Remember Verna has style and flair all her own."

True. Her wardrobe ran to capes and scarves, hats and pirate boots.

"Although," Mrs. B mused, "that style may not be practical for her recovery."

Also true. "I'll aim for practical in bright colors. You said *start* at the mall. Where do I go afterward?"

"Grocery store. She'll need soft foods."

"Like baby foods? Or foods we can cook and smash up ourselves?"

"Choice number two, I think. But see what you can find. Check out recipes for stroke victims before you shop and see what they recommend."

"Got it."

"Good. Is everything all right there? Is Lola okay? And the little prince?"

"Lola's been asking to go out the parking lot door. I think she wants to check on Verna. Cheese Puff is in his usual spot."

If he wasn't with Mrs. B or out with a member of the Committee, my entitled mutt whiled away his days wedged between the cushion and arm of a chair in the living room.

"Well, give him a kiss for me and tell him I'll be home as soon as I've sorted out a few more things."

Or sorted out a few more medical professionals. I wouldn't want to be a nurse or doctor who didn't measure up to Mrs. B's standards.

While I was visualizing a typical confrontation, she signed off, saying she knew she didn't have to remind me about how much I had to do. Her way of saying "Get busy."

And I did.

I grabbed my purse and a notepad and zipped to Verna's unit where I found Jim armored in a pair of thick yellow kitchen gloves. Holding a sturdy black plastic bag, he stared at the open refrigerator the way someone with a fear of spiders might regard the mother of all arachnids heading his way at an eight-legged gallop.

(For the record, I'm pretty sure spiders have eight legs. Not that I've ever stopped to count before dealing with them. I've never seen one gallop, and have no idea if they do. That's just a figure of speech. As for what "dealing with them" involves, it all depends on the size, color, and location of the spider, how startled I am by its appearance, whether Dave is home, whether I'm in a live-and-let-live mood, whether I can close a door and put off dealing with the creature, and a host of other factors.)

"It's a wonder Verna didn't die of food poisoning years ago." Jim held up a jar of mayonnaise and one of sauerkraut. "These expired around the time you married Jake."

It seemed fitting Jim would equate my bad marriage with spoiled food, so I flashed a half-second smile. Then I explained my mission and headed upstairs.

The door to the small second bedroom opened only wide enough for me to squeeze through and realize I wanted to squeeze out again. Boxes had been piled to within a few inches of the ceiling. Each was labeled, but the labels were similar. "Clothes. Clothing. Shoes. Scarves. More clothes."

I crossed the hall to the larger bedroom and followed a trail between boxes to the bed, a tiny computer desk, and then on to the closet. No surprises there. Clothing was packed on the upper shelves, crammed on hangers, and stacked on top of shoes that were stacked on top of more shoes piled on the floor. I spotted a few things I'd seen Verna wear recently and noted sizes, then beat a hasty retreat—a really hasty retreat.

Jim had filled one trash bag and was starting on a second when I made it to the kitchen. "I'm off to the mall to buy recovery clothing."

He dropped a tub of yogurt in the bag. "First time I ever thought going to the mall was a better option than what I was doing."

I almost offered to trade. Then he pulled out something green. It kind of slithered into the trash bag.

I beat my second hasty retreat of the day.

And got as far as the rain-spattered parking lot where I found Stan Stewart slouching against the driver's door of my car. A reporter for the *Reckless River Roundup*, he likes to think of himself as Woodward and Bernstein rolled into one scruffy package, and he acts like he's too good for Southwest Washington. This morning, however, it appeared he'd left the act in his other suit. Not that he had another suit. In fact, I doubted he had even *one* suit. Whenever I saw him, Stan wore baggy slacks and a ratty jacket and appeared to have combed his hair with a spoon.

"Got anything for me?" he asked.

"Anything as in what?" I hunched my back against a blast of wind-driven rain and dug my car key from my purse. "Fashion tips?"

Stewart wasn't amused. But he didn't appear annoyed, either. The expression on his face—a just-the-facts-ma'am expression—didn't change. "News tips."

I laughed. "It must be the slowest day in the history of news if you came to me for a story."

Again, his expression didn't change. "You tipped me to the attempted swindle involving the community pool last year," he reminded me. "I'm up for a regional award for the series I did on that."

"Congratulations." I motioned for him to move aside.

He didn't budge. "You found those Bigfoot tracks last summer. You caught the woman who framed your friend Mrs. Ballantine for murder in the fall. You're always stumbling across dead bodies or finding the people who made them that way."

"I am not *always* stumbling across bodies," I insisted. Sometimes a few months went by in between discoveries. Besides, I stumbled only once. And that was in the vicinity of the body, not over it. The rest of the time I'd done a pretty good job of keeping my balance at crime scenes.

"Whatever." Stewart waved that aside. "I'm desperate. I'm stuck in this soggy excuse for a city and my brain is turning to

74

mush. I need a big story and I need it soon. You must know something about something."

"I know I have to get going. I know I need to buy clothing and food for a friend who had a stroke." I poked the key at his nose. "I also know I'm getting wet and that's making me crabby."

Stewart raised his hands in surrender and backed off. "You'll call me if you hear anything? If you see anything? Anything at all? Even if you think it's not much?"

"Sure. Right. You got it. Your number's in my phone."

I slid into the car, fired up the engine, and backed out of my space thinking that in addition to knowing I was busy, wet, and crabby, I also knew something else. I knew Jerome Morrow was missing.

An hour later I knew more. And I knew Stan Stewart would be interested. But I also knew it wasn't my story to tell.

My cellphone rang as a teenage clerk chewing a wad of gum and wearing more eye makeup than I'd put on in the past month was ringing up the damage for a mountain of fleecy sweats, socks, and slippers. "Have you got a grip on something substantial?" Dave asked by way of a greeting.

*Uh oh.*

A question like that seldom meant good news. Unless it was good news of the you-won-the-lottery variety. "I'm holding Mrs. B's credit card. Is that substantial enough?"

"It will have to do." Dave paused for a second. "I found someone I believe is Jerome Morrow." He paused again. Anticipating what he'd say next, I folded my hand around the plastic rectangle until it dug into my skin. "He's dead."

"Where? How?"

"I . . . uh . . . that's all I can say right now."

"But . . ."

"That's all I can say," he repeated. "Harvey Goodspeed is on the way up here."

That told me a lot. Harvey Goodspeed was the homicide investigator for the sheriff's office. Last fall he'd been sidelined by a heart attack and surgery during a case that cast Mrs. B as the prime suspect thanks to a devious woman who ended up behind bars. Jackie DeWill's arrest, mostly thanks to me and Paulette, was yet another reason why Detective Charles Atwell, my nemesis since the murder of high school history teacher Henry Stoddard, never sent me flowers. He took over Mrs. B's case when Goodspeed landed in the hospital, and had been standing around waiting for that pesky stuff called admissible evidence when we got Jackie to incriminate herself.

"But don't read anything into that," Dave added. "Don't make up your mind this is a murder case. I called it in and Harvey called back and said he was coming to take a look."

"So he's back from medical leave?"

"On a part-time basis."

The clerk blew a bubble and pointed to the sales slip curling out of the register. I relaxed my grip on the credit card and handed it over. She glanced at it, frowned, and then smiled. I figured the lift of the lips had a lot to do with Mrs. B's name. When you shop as much as she does, you attain legendary status.

"So, if it's a suspicious death, and Goodspeed needs help, Atwell might be called in?" I asked. "And you'd help him?"

"Anything's possible," he said. "But it might have to be on an after-hours basis."

I crossed my fingers, hoping that would come to pass because it would put me in a prime position to glean information. To my endless amazement, Atwell and Dave were buddies. During Dave's limited-duty time, he'd been flying beneath his buddy's wing, learning the ins and outs of homicide investigations. "What can I tell Big Chill?"

"You know we don't release a name—"

"—until you get a definite identification and notify the next of kin. Right. But if there's a next of kin, Big Chill will know who it is. And if there isn't, she'd be the one to identify him."

I heard a sigh, then Dave said, "Have you ever met a rule you didn't try to bend?"

I didn't dignify that with a response—mostly because we all know the answer. Unlike the average toddler, I realize there are reasons—often darn good ones—for rules. And I'm okay with most of the big ones. But sometimes I feel there should be more flex and bend in lesser rules and regulations.

Dave tossed silence right back at me.

The clerk tapped a small gray screen set at an angle on a bracket beside the register—an angle that required bending both my elbow and wrist. I signed with one of those non-pens, trying to approximate my normal signature and failing, creating something that looked like a forgery attempt by a flounder.

Tapping the pen against the OK button, I took another run at crinkling the rules. "When Big Chill keeps quiet about something, her lips are sealed tighter than an Egyptian tomb."

Dave said nothing.

I plunged on. "A tomb way out in the desert. Miles and miles from anywhere. A tomb no one has discovered yet."

"It's not my decision to make," he said with what sounded like more relief than regret. "Talk to you later."

*Drat.*

The clerk stapled my receipt to a bag large enough to make a Sherpa weak in the knees. I tucked the phone and credit card away, took a deep breath, and lifted. Fortunately it was bulkier than it was weighty, and in a few minutes I wrestled it into the trunk of my car.

Then I sat behind the wheel, facing a dilemma. Should I tell Big Chill what I knew? Or should I wait for the wheels of justice to grind?

If you recall, I hadn't actually told Dave I wouldn't pass along my knowledge. And he hadn't actually told me not to. Sure, he'd cited policy. But he'd said it wasn't his decision to make. Was that code for saying he wouldn't be mad if I motored over to the high school?

I decided I'd ponder the question on the way. After all, I needed to confer with Ardie about alterations. And Ardie was at the high school.

# Chapter 10

By the time I reached Captain Meriwether, I was confident I wouldn't have to say anything. Big Chill, being the sharpest pencil in the pack, would size up the situation and reach a conclusion a nanosecond after I crossed her threshold.

And she did.

"He's dead." She gripped the edge of her desk, fingertips blanching. Her nails were so ragged they could have been mine. "Isn't he?"

I closed the door to her office. "Unofficially, all I can say is Dave found a man, and that man is deceased."

"I knew it." She seemed to shrink and shrivel and pack on a decade's worth of years. Crossing her arms, she rocked, the chair creaking softly. "How? How did he die?"

I came around behind the desk and knelt beside her chair. "I don't know. Dave didn't give me any details."

"He didn't? Or he wouldn't?" she whispered.

"More like he couldn't. It's out of his jurisdiction. It's a county case." I stroked her shoulder, her cherry-red sweater as soft as a kitten's fur. "A detective is on the way, but it could be hours before he has any information to release to the public."

"But they know it's him? They know it's Jerome?"

"Not for sure. Not yet."

She sat up, shrugged off my hand, raised rhinestone-studded glasses, and blotted her eyes with a tissue. "He has no close family. Just an elderly second cousin in Georgia. If they need someone to . . ." She choked, folded in on herself, and rocked once more.

"I'll tell Dave." I stood and dug out my phone. To my relief, he didn't answer so I didn't get grilled about how much I'd revealed. I left a brief message saying Jerome Morrow had no family close by, and providing Big Chill's number.

When I finished, she blotted her eyes once more. "He was like an old farm horse, worn out from trudging across the fields and pulling a plow. He hadn't said, but I knew this would be his last year—one way or another."

Meaning, I guessed, the district would put him out to pasture if he didn't voluntarily go there himself. "We'll all miss him," I said.

"It's hard to miss what you hardly knew was there." She laughed and tossed her tissue in the wastebasket. "Did you ever talk with him?"

I shook my head.

"That's what I thought. How many times did you actually see him?"

"Three."

She narrowed her eyes.

"Okay, definitely twice. And possibly one other time. He was at the end of the long hallway in the science wing. He turned the corner so fast I didn't get a good look, but I'm pretty sure it was him because he was wearing a gray suit. Rumor has it he always wore a gray suit."

"The shades vary, but you're right, it's always gray. *Was* always gray." She got a faraway look in her eyes. "He had a knack for disappearing, didn't he? It was like he could fade into the paint on the walls or melt into the carpet. I'd look away for a second and he'd be gone."

"Was he always that way?"

"No. Not at first. He was a lot like Tremaine, always handling things face-to-face, doing a little more, a little extra. He wasn't a cheerleader for every new edict on how to teach handed down from on high, but he was a good soldier." Big Chill rolled her eyes. "Even after he lost respect for the edicts and the people who issued them, he tried to put a positive spin on things. But you can't keep that up forever."

"Unless you take massive amounts of mood-elevating drugs."

She smiled. "Or perfect the art of disappearing and get yourself a cabin out in the country where you can get away." Her eyes filled with tears. "You're sure you don't know how he died?"

"Positive. I'm not even sure the man Dave found is Mr. Morrow. But if I hear anything I'll let you know—even though I'm not supposed to."

"And I won't say a word until it's official." She wiped her eyes and put her right hand on her chest. "Although I know it's him. I feel . . . empty."

She drew in a long breath and pointed to the door. "Run along before gossip lights up the grapevine. If you're in here more than a few more seconds they'll have half a dozen stories circulating. You'll hear you had your pay docked, got a raise, or were drummed out of the district."

I snapped off a salute, checked the clock, and scampered to the math wing to find Ardie. Dressed in her usual color—black —she was at a table in the common area struggling to explain the wording of a test problem and the purpose of algebra to a boy with hair the color of ripe tangerines. His expression said she could talk all day, buy him a pizza, and offer a major amount of money, but he still wouldn't give a rip. She stared at me as if she'd been treading water for hours and I was rowing a boat her way.

"Why don't you go back into the classroom and give it some thought," she told the boy.

He didn't argue.

When the door closed behind him, she groaned, bent forward, and thumped her head against the textbook on the table.

"Could have been worse." I slid into the kid's chair. "You could have been trying to explain the problem to me."

(For the record, in case you don't already know, I am *not* in possession of the kind of brain that "gets" math. With great concentration and hours of study, I made it through the basic classes in high school and college with nothing higher than a C+. Since then, I've stuck with addition and subtraction with brief forays into the geometry involved in figuring square footage to determine the required amount of carpet cleaning solution.)

Ardie groaned again. "Explaining algebra to you? I'd have more success using a piece of cooked spaghetti as a tent stake." She smiled, her teeth bright against her dark skin and deep purple lipstick. "But thanks for the interruption. What's up? Did they call you in for someone?"

"No." I explained about Verna and Mrs. B's orders and wondering if Ardie could lend a hand. "Mrs. B would pay for your time."

Ardie brushed that aside. "I'm happy to help. Why don't I come over to your place with my machine this evening? We can assess what you bought and look through her closets for things I could alter easily."

"Better bring a compass or you may never find your way out again." I filled her in on what we'd discovered about Verna.

"The poor woman." Ardie scratched at her arms with fingernails painted a greenish black. It wasn't a color I would have chosen, but on her it worked. "Makes me itch just thinking about that much stuff. Makes me want to go home and toss half of what I've got."

I doubted Ardie had much, and I really doubted she could spare half of it. Her paycheck as a classroom aide probably wasn't robust. And, thanks to her generous heart, she spent a chunk of it on granola bars and fruit snacks to hand out to hungry kids. I'd make sure she was compensated for the alterations—well compensated.

Ardie closed the textbook. "Did you see Wilhelmina when you came in?"

"Who?"

"Wilhelmina Frost." Ardie rolled her eyes. "Big Chill."

Ah. Sometimes I forgot she had a real name.

"Uh, yeah. She was in her office." I stepped out on the tightrope between fact and fabrication. "She seemed upset, so I didn't hang around to chat."

Not exactly a lie, because I was pretty sure the definition of "chat" wouldn't cover the form or substance of our conversation.

"Her blood pressure must be off the charts. Hope Mr. Morrow turns up soon." Ardie tucked a stack of worksheets into a folder. "Gotta run. See you this evening."

I let out the breath I'd been holding and made for the exit with the butterflies-in-the-gut feeling I get when I float a lie.

Mrs. B fluttered in scant seconds after I lugged the last bag of purchases through the rain and set it on the dining room table. With Cheese Puff supervising, and putting his front feet on the table whenever I turned my back, she dug through the canvas grocery sacks, approving of the applesauce, soups, and packets of hot cereal. "Good, you got eggs. I meant to mention I have only a few left."

Cheese Puff nosed a bottle of cranberry juice, decided it didn't contain bacon, and retreated to his favorite chair wearing a look of doggie disgust. Lola, perhaps because she had a superior sense of smell, hadn't bothered to rise from where she'd flopped between the sofa and the coffee table. She'd been calm and quiet and hadn't made an effort to get to Verna's door. I wondered if she'd concluded Verna was elsewhere and being taken care of.

Moving on, Mrs. B tore into the giant bag from the mall.

"Those are mostly sweatpants and tops," I said. "Soft and loose. Nothing fancy."

"But you found bright colors. Turquoise. And chartreuse. And the socks are fun." She held up a pair with a wild zigzag pattern in pink and green and purple. "Oh, and look at the rubber gripper dots on the bottom. How clever."

She pawed through the remainder of the contents, commenting on slippers and a robe and passing along the latest on Verna's condition and speculation about how long it would take for her to regain full use of her arm, leg, and speech. "What about underwear?"

"I, uh, didn't get any." When I'd entered the lingerie department in search of front-closure bras, I'd realized I hadn't checked Verna's size. I also realized I hadn't checked the Internet for advice about panties. Getting them up and down with one good hand could be difficult. That's when I started to wonder if Verna would have to wear adult diapers—at least for a time. And that's when I headed for the register. No doubt I'd have to think about adult diapers someday. But not today. "I'll go back tomorrow. Or this evening if you—"

"No need, dear. Let's not rush." Mrs. B returned groceries to the canvas sacks, then folded the robe and socks and piled

84

them at the edge of the table before stuffing everything else back in the bag. "I'll look through her dresser later on. And the staff at the hospital may recommend . . . alternatives to panties."

It appeared Mrs. B didn't want to talk about adult diapers, either.

I folded the bag closed and set it on the floor beside Cheese Puff's favorite chair. "Ardie's coming over this evening with her machine and everything she needs to make alterations."

"Then I shall return later." Mrs. B gathered up the robe and socks. "Now, if you'll assist me in getting all this where it belongs, I'll take a long, hot shower and follow it up with a lengthy nap. Hospital chairs may appear comfortable, but I assure you they are not. And Sybil insists there's no reason for both of us to suffer."

Dave came home minutes before 6:00 with a tight-lipped expression that signaled I shouldn't ask about Jerome Morrow because I'd be wasting my breath. I'd been expecting that and was okay with it—partly because I knew he had to follow procedure, but mainly because I'd gotten a telephone update from Big Chill half an hour earlier.

"A man named Harvey Goodspeed called," she'd told me. "He wanted a more recent picture than the one on Jerome's driver's license. I e-mailed him the shot from the yearbook."

I recalled that candid snap of Morrow emerging from his office, phone clamped to his ear. How long had the student who took it had to lie in wait?

"He wanted physical details, too. Height, weight, hair color. Even asked if Jerome had tattoos. Visible and, uh, not."

I'd held myself back from blurting the obvious question.

"As if I'd know," Big Chill had fumed. "As if our relationship had been so . . . so unprofessional."

85

Question answered.

"Not that I'd expected to, but I didn't hear back from Mr. Goodspeed," Big Chill had muttered. "So I made a few calls of my own. Several of our graduates work for the sheriff's office. And many of them were not exactly model students."

See what I mean about knowing where the bodies were buried and where to apply pressure?

She'd paused then and I'd heard a sniffle and the soft crumple of tissue. "Anyway, there's no doubt it is Jerome. But no one would say that officially, and no one would say where he was found or how he died. All they'd say is it's under investigation. What does that mean? Is it good or bad? Does it mean he was murdered?"

I'd taken my turn at pausing before I told her, "It means they're doing a thorough examination of the scene. They don't want to jump to conclusions or release information until they know what they're releasing is correct."

What I hadn't said was that if Jerome Morrow had been dead for several days, and if he'd been inside a heated cabin, the cause of death might not be immediately apparent. Big Chill was what they call "a tough old bird," but she didn't need to be thinking about bodily fluids, bloating, and blowflies.

Neither did I. So I'd rushed on. "I bet they release something before long. Even if it's just his name."

I'd been willing to make that bet because I'd stacked the deck by calling Stan Stewart and tipping him to the body of a man found in a cabin along the Lewis River. If Jerome Morrow had been murdered, Stewart would have a front-page story. But no matter how Morrow died, he'd held a prominent position in the community and been principal for a long time. His death would create ripples in the educational community.

I'd promised Big Chill I'd call if I was able to wheedle information out of Dave, but told her not to get her hopes up. When he put his mind to it, he kept secrets as well as she did.

And I recognized he was in secret-keeping mode when he was two steps inside the door. How? Because he ducked inside the tiny office at the end of the hallway and parked his briefcase. Our two-bedroom condo wasn't exactly spacious, so we'd agreed to a no-peeking policy for the shared office. He never opened the drawers in my desk, and made an effort not to glance at mail or at the laptop screen. I did the same—although, as you can guess, having as much curiosity as the average cat, I wasn't as scrupulous about not checking out anything in plain sight. But even I wouldn't open Dave's briefcase.

So I bustled about the kitchen, making it clear I was busy cleaning and reorganizing cabinets, far too busy to pester him for details about the body he'd discovered. And all the while I plotted ways to make him spill the beans.

# Chapter 11

If the frown on his face was an indication, Dave seemed puzzled—both by my lack of curiosity, and by my actions. You see, thanks to Jim, the spices had already been alphabetized, the baking dishes and pans sorted by type and size, and the pantry turned into an example any home-organizing expert might use as a visual teaching aid. Fortunately, I'd thought of all that, and had an explanation ready. "Being in Verna's place made me want to clean and organize, but Jim's taken care of that, so I'm assessing."

"Assessing what?"

"What we can live without. I want to dump anything that lacks a purpose. And I want more space in between things."

He nodded, but I could almost see twirling pinwheels of confusion in his eyes. "Like this." I held up a jar from the array of spices I'd moved from their cabinet to the counter. "It's good for a few more months. But do we need cumin?"

Dave peered at the bottle. "Never used it. What does it go in?"

"Some types of Mexican dishes, I think."

"Toss it." He opened the refrigerator and grabbed a bottle of beer. "Except for the chicken casserole you make with hot green peppers, we order out for Mexican food."

True. And, to be honest, it was better that way. Way better.

Have I mentioned I'm not much of a cook?

I spilled the cumin in the trash and set the jar in the appropriate recycling tub in the pantry. Dave took a long pull on his beer, set it aside, and hugged me. "Are you worried about turning into a hoarder?"

"No." I snuggled against him, inhaling the scents of sweat and wood smoke and disposable gloves. Gloves like the ones he would have worn if he'd been asked to lend a hand searching Jerome Morrow's cabin. Or moving his body.

I swallowed and sent that thought to a dark and remote corner of my mind. I also unsnuggled a bit. "I don't want to get in the habit of hanging on to things I never use."

"Makes sense." Dave stroked my hair. "What else have you tossed?"

The answer to that was zilch. But I had a pretense to keep up. And it wouldn't exactly be lying if I mentioned a few things I was *planning* to toss. Or things I'd *like* to toss. "A few old T-shirts."

I felt his body tense. "*My* T-shirts?"

"No." I manufactured a high-pitched laugh. "Why would you even think that?"

"Because you describe them as ripped, ratty, and reprehensible."

"Well, sure, but I know how much they mean to you." I spotted the opening for a dig. "I've been doing a lot of research about hoarders today. Did you know that if someone tries to take away even a little of what they've saved, they can get violent?"

"If it takes fear of potential violence for you to hold back from tossing my T-shirts, I'm okay with that."

Dave chuckled, then released me and took a step back. "Wait a minute. Are you saying I'm a hoarder? Because I accumulated a few T-shirts over the years?"

*A few?*

*Try two dozen.*

I shrugged. "I don't recall saying that. You must be projecting."

"Hmm." He took another swallow of beer. "Where's Allison?"

"Upstairs. Studying for her English test."

"You sure?" Dave cocked his head. "I don't hear music."

"There's a reason." I pulled out a chair and motioned for him to sit. "She says she finds it distracting."

He did one of those cartoon-character reactions, a kind of head swivel and full-body twitch. The only thing missing was a balloon with the word "BOING" above his head. "Wait. Yesterday she couldn't study without it. What's going on? Is she laying the foundation for a major demand?"

I stuck spices back into the cabinet, careful to maintain alphabetical order. "Only time will tell."

(For the record, I hate that expression. And yet, here I was using it. I'd been four when I first heard it from an elderly neighbor who was babysitting me. I've long ago forgotten what I'd asked, but I remember clearly that after her response I spent many long minutes standing on a chair so I'd be closer to the cuckoo clock when the bird emerged to deliver the answer to my question. On that day, the experience had been the largest disappointment of my childhood. But after the death of my brother and the parental disassociation that followed, the clock incident became only a tiny sad blip on the radar of the past.)

Dave cast a hopeful glance toward the clock in the kitchen. "Will time tell me what we're having for dinner?"

"Probably not."

I paused, waiting for him to ask me to elaborate. Usually, being tired from teen wrangling, and feeling others should share the labor, making dinner wasn't on my daily agenda.

Besides, he hadn't offered even a sliver of information about the death of Jerome Morrow. And he appeared unlikely to do so. There would be no caving in and cooking this evening.

Dave winced. "Is this where I get the speech about being more proactive and more of a hunter-gatherer type?"

"No, this is where you get the alternate speech, the one about the benefits of calling with an approximate arrival time so we can discuss plans for dinner. Since I didn't hear from you, and since you ate the leftover pasta for breakfast, and since we were hungry, Allison and I had brown rice and roasted vegetables an hour ago. We left plenty for you. You can heat it in the microwave."

"Vegetables and rice? No meat?"

"No meat. I tossed chopped walnuts in with the rice."

"Nut meat," he said in a scornful tone. "I need real meat."

"I bet you had real meat for lunch."

"So?"

"So how much meat does your body need in one day?"

"I don't know what my body needs, but my mouth needs a burger. Or a chunk of fried chicken. Or a pork chop."

"Then your mouth better get your fingers to dial for takeout. Or get your hands and feet to drive you somewhere. All we have is sliced turkey and a few rounds of salami."

He studied the phone on the edge of the kitchen counter and the pink, green, and blue menus stuck behind it. Then he glanced at the clock, toward the door, and then at the refrigerator. "How would salami taste in rice?"

"I have not the slightest doubt it would be a gourmet treat right up there with pigs' feet, jellied tripe, or fried ants."

Dave sipped beer and regarded me with narrowed eyes. "Are you being sarcastic?"

"Are my lips moving?"

He drained the bottle and we waited each other out. Well, to be exact, he waited. I removed my mall purchases from the bag and stacked them on the table. "Whatever you decide, please don't eat it at the table unless it won't crumble, spatter, or spill. I'm skipping water aerobics because Ardie's coming over in a few minutes with her sewing machine to alter recovery clothing for Verna. She's doing well, by the way."

"Verna or Ardie?" Dave raised his hands. "Kidding. I should have asked about Verna the minute I came in." He pulled a plate from the cabinet. "It's been a rough day. How about we reboot our relationship system?"

"Does rebooting mean you'd expect me to cook up a large pig or a side of beef?"

"No. I probably eat too much meat as it is." He loaded vegetables and rice on the plate and slid it in the microwave. "But don't tell the guys I said that."

*Seriously?*

I folded the bag, stashed it in the pantry, and grabbed an extension cord from the hall closet in case Ardie needed it. "What will happen if I blab to your buddies? They'll insist on seeing proof you possess a Y chromosome? Make you eat lunch all by yourself? Have me locked up?"

"Anything's possible." He glopped sour cream and salsa on top of his steaming heap of healthy food, sprinkled on shredded cheddar, squirted barbecue sauce on top, and carried the plate to the coffee table.

Lola raised her head, sniffed, and snorted as if to clear her sinuses. Cheese Puff popped out of his chair crevice and leaped to the coffee table. When Dave turned his back in pursuit of a fork and napkin, my entitled mutt circled the plate with the same intensity he displayed on the riverfront trail when he encountered something aromatic in a decomposing kind of way, something worthy of being rolled in. In the interest of saving myself from spending the next half hour washing a dog that fought baths like a cat, I took action.

"Ack. Ack. Ack."

Don't ask me why, but that particular sound, emitted at volume, never failed to get Cheese Puff's attention. He halted, body half turned for a flop onto the plate.

"Get away from there."

Dave spun from wrestling with the recalcitrant silverware drawer. "Don't eat that, you stupid dog. It will make you sick."

With a yip of disgust, Cheese Puff leaped for his chair and burrowed into the crevice. I smothered a laugh and decided not to mention Cheese Puff had entertained other plans for the pile on the plate.

The doorbell rang as Dave sprawled on the sofa, fork in one hand, TV remote in the other. The sound of sports talk and the pungent odor of barbecue sauce followed me along the hallway.

Ardie stood on the step, the handle of a sewing machine case gripped in one hand, the strap of a canvas satchel over her shoulder. Raindrops glistened on the hood of her black rain jacket and on her nose and high cheekbones. I swung the door wide. "Come in."

Ardie pushed back her hood and wiped her feet on the mat. "Have you heard anything new about Jerome Morrow?"

The key word "new" in that question enabled me to lie without a second thought. Technically, when I'd talked with Big Chill, I hadn't learned anything I didn't already know or could have assumed. "No, nothing new."

"Poor Wilhelmina." Ardie stepped inside, cocking her head as she did. "Is your kitchen on fire, or are you roasting a skunk?"

I sniggered. "Dave has an aversion to plain food. He does all he can to keep condiment companies in business."

"That's right." Ardie smiled. "He was the one who mixed the clam and bacon and guacamole dips at the Christmas party." She handed me the satchel, set the sewing machine down, and shucked her jacket. "This smell makes me feel I'm back in the teachers' room, playing name-that-ingredient with Gertrude, while we try to figure out what's in Brenda's lunch."

I hooked the jacket and pointed along the hallway. "It won't take Dave long to eat. In the meantime I'll turn on the exhaust fan over the stove and see if we can clear the air a little."

"Don't go to any trouble. It will help me build up a tolerance for whatever Brenda brings tomorrow." Ardie hefted the machine and started along the hallway. "Speaking of tolerance, who's the woman patrolling the parking lot? The infamous Bernina Burke?"

"Yes." My fingers furled into fists. I'd accepted taking crap from Bernina as a fact of my life, but I wouldn't accept her dishing it out to my friends. "Did she harass you? Insult you?"

"Insulted my intelligence by assuming I couldn't read the sign about visitors' parking slots." Ardie nodded to Dave, hoisted the machine to the table, and removed the cover. "Insulted my good taste with that outfit she had on. Looked like an orange pup tent with sleeves."

"She's a fashion icon," I agreed. The next time Mrs. B was bored, perhaps she should take Bernina shopping again. Our condo manager was still best described as "hefty," but she'd lost significant poundage since the style makeover Mrs. B undertook last year. The clothing purchased at the time now flapped around her when she moved. So did loose skin in need of toning.

That thought made me feel the far-from-firm backs of my arms. I vowed to make up for skipping water aerobics tonight by working out with my hand weights tomorrow.

"I hope you didn't take any guff from her." Dave scraped the last grains of rice from his plate.

"No more than I take from high school students all day long." Ardie plugged in the machine. "Not to worry. I've grown a thick skin. I've learned not to take people like her seriously."

As I was wondering exactly what she meant by that last sentence, she continued. "Some people get a little power and they get all swelled up with it and make sure the rest of us know we're not on the same rung of the ladder. Lots of times it's got nothing to do with color or creed or education or money. It's all about the little kid inside, and how much that kid yearns for respect."

"The little kid inside Bernina may yearn for respect," I muttered, "but she also enjoys bullying the children inside everyone else."

"Little kids often do whatever it takes." Ardie unpacked her satchel, setting out scissors, thread, pins, and thin strips of Velcro. "And they're quick to get a taste for what makes them feel good."

Dave nodded as he rinsed his plate and racked it in the dishwasher. "At least Bernina's taste hasn't led her to a life of crime."

"That we know of," I said.

"I bet she has strong feelings about lawbreakers." Ardie separated sweatshirts from pants. "Wants them prosecuted to the full extent of the law."

"Prosecuted, persecuted, and then some," Dave agreed. "She's still carrying on about the person who stole the condo Christmas decorations and ruined her vision for the citywide competition. Still bugging me with theories about the crime. Says she's investigating herself because the police force isn't doing enough."

*If the police were doing anything at all.*

95

If you've been following the story of my life, you know Mrs. B and Jim were behind the theft. And you know that since Jim had the key to the storeroom and the decorations were tacky, the incident was actually less a theft than a removal in the name of good taste. It was unlikely Bernina would catch the culprits unless someone ratted them out.

"If anything happens to my favorite T-shirts," Dave warned me with a gloating laugh, "maybe I'll bypass law enforcement channels and report the theft to Bernina. Name you as the prime suspect."

"What's with the T-shirts?" Ardie paused, a seam ripper in one hand, a turquoise sweatshirt in the other.

"They're a little old," Dave said.

"They're faded and ripped and bagged out," I elaborated.

"They're classics. They represent years of rock and roll culture."

"Little-known culture."

"That's why they're so valuable. They're collector's items."

"I get the picture," Ardie said in a tone that made it clear we should stop bickering. "I'd like to see those T-shirts."

I groaned.

Dave shot me the kind of smug look you seldom see outside of an elementary school classroom, and headed for the stairs. "Back in a flash."

Ardie patted my head. "It will be fine."

That, I thought, depended on your definition of "fine."

# Chapter 12

"I don't care what he wears. At least I try not to care," I told Ardie. "But . . . Well, you'll see when he brings the T-shirts. In the meantime, I'll get Mrs. Ballantine. She's interested in your alteration plans."

When I told Mrs. B that Ardie was in the house, she decided the alteration process would go better with a pot of coffee and a platter of cookies, tartlets, and a dozen mini cupcakes. A quarter of an hour passed before we got back to my condo and found T-shirts displayed on every available surface and Ardie asking Dave a series of pointed questions.

"Do you want to preserve these? Or wear them? Because every time they go through the wash, you lose color and definition."

Dave glared at the washer and dryer.

"Do you want to be able to see the art and remember the good times?" Ardie asked. "Or do you want others to see it and be impressed that you were part of the scene? If they're familiar enough with the scene to be impressed."

Dave pondered while Mrs. B offloaded a carafe, cream, sugar, napkins, and a platter of goodies from the enormous tray I'd lugged over. He pondered on while I wrestled with the silverware drawer Jim hadn't fixed yet. "Well," he said with a sidelong glance at me, "I guess it's hard to impress people who don't remember these groups."

"Or knew about them in the first place," I whispered to Mrs. B.

She twinkled a smile and pressed a finger to her lips.

"So I guess I'm wearing them for myself. To relive the glory days." He cast another glance my way, this one sheepish. "And to annoy Barbara."

"Aha." I pointed a finger. "You admit it."

"Yeah. But that doesn't mean I'll toss the shirts."

"How about letting me make the shirts into art?" Ardie asked. "Like a quilt. Or a wall hanging."

Dave clutched at the nearest T-shirts and held them against his chest. "You mean, cut them up?"

"That was my original thought," Ardie confirmed. "But there's no reason I couldn't fold them instead."

Dave's sigh of relief wasn't as powerful as the wind in a young tornado, but it was in the vicinity.

"I'm leaning toward a wall hanging," Ardie said, "because the dogs wouldn't get on it like they would on a quilt."

Dave's glance swept across Lola and settled on Cheese Puff who was notorious for pawing sheets and blankets into a nest.

"I'll let you think it over." Ardie gathered the T-shirts strewn on the table. "Take your time. And don't forget the part of the process where you and Barbara talk about where you'll hang it."

Mrs. B responded to Dave's look of surprised confusion before I could. "And of course, depending on where you want to hang it, you both may need to confer with Paulette."

*Good one.*

Paulette had hung each of the few paintings on our walls and consigned many others to the back of the hall closet. She'd have a lot to say about a wall hanging crafted from Dave's old T-shirts—no matter how professional the crafting might be.

Dave seemed to recognize that fact. He cringed as if expecting a blow.

"Perhaps your office would be an appropriate place," Mrs. B suggested.

I nodded. Except for two small bulletin boards and a calendar, the walls of the office were bare.

"Not the hallway?" Dave asked in a small voice.

"Would you hang a Monet in a hallway?" Ardie asked. "Where you had to stand so close you couldn't see the big picture?"

"You need a little distance," Mrs. B added.

*Say, a mile or two.*

"Maybe the bedroom?" he asked.

"The windows and closet take up two walls, and the door to the bath breaks up the other one," I said. "That leaves only the space above the bed."

"Where you couldn't see the wall hanging if you were *in* the bed," Ardie pointed out.

"The office is much better." Mrs. B poured coffee. "We can rearrange the desks. Or perhaps buy smaller ones and make room for an easy chair and a lamp."

I spotted the let's-go-shopping gleam in her eye and decided not to dampen it. Our desks, purchased from secondhand stores years ago, were rickety breeding grounds for finger-jabbing splinters. They were also too large for our needs. After maneuvering them through the doorway, we'd angled them against each other without even a fleeting thought about *feng shui*. Paulette, apparently having exhausted herself on the other rooms, had raised no objections to our arrangement. Nor had she, on subsequent visits, nagged at us to empty the boxes of books and old financial documents piled in a corner.

The fact was that we'd lost momentum on the office. It was time for a change. If Dave could abandon the T-shirts as apparel, perhaps I could abandon my share of the office so he could have a man cave. That might also pay off in terms of a living room without smelly socks and shoes beside the sofa or "stored" beneath it.

"I probably don't actually need a desk," I said in what I hoped was a hesitant tone without the least sign of eagerness. "I can use my laptop anywhere. And if we got a couple of bookcases, and if I moved the older documents to the storage unit, then a small cabinet with a large file drawer and a couple of regular ones for stamps and rubber bands and stuff would do."

Mrs. B seemed to read my mind. "I've seen some very attractive oak cabinets. You could slide one in beside your dresser in the bedroom. Or place it beside Cheese Puff's chair. With a lamp on top, it would look more like an end table than a file cabinet."

Cheese Puff raised his head and shot Mrs. B a look that said he'd retain veto power on the plan unless a significant number of dog cookies came along with the cabinet.

"We'd have to run it by Paulette," I reminded her.

"That's right." Mrs. B tapped her chin with a forefinger. "But since she's so busy, the best course might be to act first and explain or make amends later."

"I'm already dreading her reaction when she sees the few inches Jim shifted the furniture. The word 'explosion' leaps to mind. But I'll go along if you do the explaining and make the amends."

"Done," she said.

"So I get the office?" Dave asked with a tone of wonder. "The whole office? All for myself?"

"I'll need a little of the bookcase space." I measured air with my hands. "Maybe two shelves worth." Sadly, following a series of keep-myself-afloat yard sales in the wake of Jake siphoning off my savings, my book collection now filled only a single carton.

"And the rest is all mine?" The tone of wonder was more pronounced.

"All yours," I confirmed. "A man cave."

"Can I get a big TV for the wall? And put my trophies on the bookshelves?" He tossed the armful of T-shirts at Ardie, jerked open the kitchen junk drawer, seized a tape measure, and headed for the office. "Maybe there's room for a dartboard. And a little refrigerator. And a recliner that vibrates. Gotta check prices. Talk with some of the guys."

Ardie folded shirts into a neat pile. "You'd think he never had a room of his own before."

I recalled the cramped apartment he'd shared with Allison, its living area half of what we had now. He'd given her the larger bedroom and taken the one that allowed for only a nightstand, a small dresser, and a narrow bed.

"You won't regret this, dear. You'll have relationship points to spare for months to come." Mrs. B patted my arm and turned to Ardie. "Now let's get to work. What can we do to help?"

"Grab a sweatshirt and rip out the seam from the wrist to the waist on the right side so she can use her good arm to close the Velcro I'll sew on." Ardie nodded at the satchel. "Should be another seam ripper in there and a pair of small scissors. And check out the bling."

"Bling?" Mrs. B stared at the satchel as if the term referred to a something living, something that might bite.

"Sparkly stuff. Ribbons. Fake jewels. Barbara got some knockout colors, but it seems like your friend has a flair for, well, a flair for flair."

"Ah." Mrs. B peered into the satchel, then tipped it and spilled the contents, a host of plastic containers of varying sizes. She attacked them like a kid on Christmas morning, popping the lids to reveal glittering contents.

"Just bits and pieces from when my nieces were small and wanted to dress like princesses." Ardie laughed. "I used to worry about the rude awakenings in their futures, and how many frogs they'd kiss—or much more than kiss—before they realized those frogs would still be amphibians in the morning. But now one is a biology teacher and the other is a stockbroker and they're engaged to guys who . . . well, treat them like princesses."

Mrs. B fingered her three-strand necklace of pink pearls. "Never underestimate the power of jewelry."

I bit a cookie to stifle a laugh. If some women thought of makeup as war paint, Mrs. B thought of pearls as both body armor and weaponry. When she sallied forth to do battle with bankers, bureaucrats, or Bernina Burke, she decked herself out with necklaces, bracelets, earrings, rings, and even pins—depending on how she measured the strength of her opponent. In the nearly two years we'd been neighbors, I'd never known pearl power to fail her.

Mrs. B popped open a container of plastic rubies, diamonds, sapphires, and emeralds. "What fun! Verna will love these. If you girls do the rest, I'll sew them on."

So we got to work, me ripping seams, Ardie stitching on strips of Velcro, and Mrs. B sewing fake jewels in clusters here and there. Now and then sounds leaked from the office—the metallic twang of the tape measure, the scrape of desk drawers, the slide and slam of boxes shoved aside, and the clicking of computer keys. A couple of times I caught bits of phone conversations about mounting brackets, and amazed comments about recliners providing heat as well as massage. I was on my final seam when the doorbell rang.

Since I was expecting no one, and since friends used the door to the deck or knocked, a chime of the bell could mean a solicitor, my sister, or, worse, Bernina Burke.

Lola gave me a look that said she'd get up, but only if I really needed her. Cheese Puff barked from his chair crevice, the sound muffled. And Dave shouted, "I'm on the phone with a guy who's got a recliner to sell."

"No problem," I snarked. "I'll get the door. It's probably only an ax murderer."

"Take the seam ripper," Mrs. B advised.

Great idea. But it would be useful only if the ax murderer was the size of your average inchworm.

I set the final sweatshirt aside, trotted down the hall, stood on tiptoe, and turned my head so I could peer through the peephole. I squinted, getting a fish-eye view of a bulky figure. It wore a trench coat and a slouchy hat like the one my sister had on the other day. But it also had a mustache. Unless Iz was having one more go at being a private investigator and had slapped fake hair on her upper lip as a disguise, this was a stranger. And I didn't open the door to strangers. Not even with Dave just a few feet away. Not even when I was holding a weapon with the destructive power of a seam ripper.

# Chapter 13

"Who is it?" I called in what I hoped was an authoritative voice.

"Harvey Goodspeed," a gruff voice answered. "Sheriff's department. Homicide. Is this Dave Martin's place?"

"Uh, yes."

From what I'd heard about Harvey Goodspeed, no one would want to impersonate him, so I opened the door halfway. A gust of wind delivered the stench of stale cigar smoke and cologne sharp enough to cut paper. Assessing Goodspeed's bulk, I swung the door wide, and called out for Dave. He burst from the office as our visitor wrestled himself free of his overcoat and flung it my way. He didn't remove his hat, but shoved it back a few inches, revealing a dozen well-oiled hairs straggling across the pale dome of his head.

"If this place had bigger and better signage," he grumped, "that woman wouldn't have to stand out in the rain laying down the law about parking."

"It's kind of a hobby with her," I said.

"Sorry if she annoyed you," Dave added.

"No need to apologize. I understand someone who respects the rules and believes others should do the same."

Dave and I exchanged glances of disbelief.

"Came to give you a heads-up," Goodspeed said. "Got a place we can sit?"

"My office is, uh, in transition."

Dave closed the door to the future man cave and led the way to the living room. Goodspeed trundled behind like an overloaded hay wagon with wooden wheels.

I freed myself from the grasp of the damp coat and snagged it on a hook. "There's coffee in the kitchen if you'd like some. And cookies."

Goodspeed grunted.

I mulled the volume and duration of the grunt for a moment, but couldn't decode it. Deciding that if he couldn't manage an actual word in response, I couldn't be bothered with further hostess duties, I followed, swatting air to try to dispel a noxious cloud of cologne.

By the time I reached the living area, Harvey Goodspeed had a mini cupcake in one hand and a cookie in the other and was casting the kind of glance at Mrs. B that an entomologist might cast upon a red and yellow beetle with its fangs embedded in his thumb. "I know you," he said in an accusatory voice.

Not intimidated, Mrs. B extended her right hand, a large diamond flashing, a pearl and diamond bracelet sliding on her wrist. "You certainly do," she said with a smile. "I'm Muriel Ballantine. Last year you suspected me of killing Big Shiny."

Goodspeed grunted and popped the cupcake in his mouth, leaving his hand free for a shake so quick a politician facing a mammoth crowd of supporters would be envious. A second after he released, he scooped up a custard tartlet with a swirl of whipped cream on top. Not what I'd call recommended eating for a man with his medical history.

Mrs. B seemed unfazed by his lack of good manners. Sizing up his girth she asked—with only a faint trace of sarcasm—whether he took both cream and sugar in his coffee.

Goodspeed grunted an affirmative reply—the man was as long on grunts as he was short on social skills—and settled his gaze on Ardie. "I know you?"

"Haven't had the pleasure." Ardie went on attaching Velcro.

Goodspeed didn't seem bothered by her failure to extend a hand, or by the slight pause before the word "pleasure." He stuffed the tartlet in his mouth and snatched the coffee Mrs. B offered. Then, dunking the cookie he'd held in abeyance, he surveyed the living room seating options and headed for Cheese Puff's chair at ramming speed.

Lola lurched to her feet, barking.

Cheese Puff popped from the crevice, levitated like a cartoon character, and hurtled across the chair arm, feet flailing. He hit the floor with a yelp and raced for the stairs.

A second later, Goodspeed's *gluteus maximus* hit the cushion.

The cushion gasped like a landed fish. The chair legs bowed and the frame groaned.

I winced.

Ardie sucked air.

Mrs. B turned aside.

Dave covered his eyes.

The chair held.

Goodspeed, who seemed to have noticed none of that, ate his soggy cookie in two bites, wiped his fingers on a tie the color of moldy pea soup, and said, "Paperwork won't come through for a couple of days, but the brass are all on board. Starting tomorrow you're on loan to me."

"Me?" Dave uncovered his eyes. "Tomorrow? On loan?"

"What part of what I said didn't sink in?" Goodspeed scowled. "It was a simple, easy-to-understand statement."

"Oh, it was. It was," Dave confirmed in a voice filled with both excitement and trepidation. Much as he wanted more homicide experience, working with Harvey Goodspeed wasn't the way he'd envisioned getting it. "Starting tomorrow I'm on loan to the sheriff's department and working with you."

"You got it."

"For how long?"

"Depends on the twists and turns of the case."

"What case?"

"The case you stumbled on this morning."

Dave didn't argue with the verb in that sentence, didn't insist he'd been searching for Morrow, not stumbling around at random. I wondered if he was biting his tongue like I was. Then I wondered if the word "case" meant Jerome Morrow's death had the marks of a homicide. I glanced at Ardie, trying to recall what she knew and didn't know. She was stitching away, seemingly focused on the fabric sliding beneath the jabbing needle.

Goodspeed slurped coffee and, using one hand to assist, brought his right ankle to rest on his left knee. "Bring that platter of goodies over where I can reach it, and let's talk about how I expect our arrangement to work."

Dave, ignoring my eyes rolling almost to the back of their sockets, complied. As he lowered the platter to the table, Goodspeed plucked up another tartlet, licked off the whipped cream, made a face, and dropped the remains on the coffee table. "Ugh. Peaches. Sorry excuse for a fruit."

"I believe I need to call Sybil and then get some rest." Mrs. B scurried to the door to the deck. "I'll leave the desserts." Her frosty tone of disgust implied that she considered them contaminated by their proximity to Goodspeed, and I should consign to the trash any remaining when he departed.

"And I believe my eyes are tired and I'm about to start sewing my skin to the seams." Ardie unplugged her machine and gathered up bits and pieces. "But my part is all finished except for anything that doesn't look right in the light of day. Why don't I leave everything here for now?"

"Perfect." I rushed to help her, thanking her while attempting to listen to the conversation on the other side of the room. If, that is, a gripefest about the complications involved with getting two HR departments involved in "a simple temporary transfer" could be considered conversation.

I lost a few minutes while walking Ardie to the door, but it was easy to pick up the thread. Dave caught my eye and pointed to the stairs, signaling I should give him some space. I nodded, tipped a thumb up in agreement, and then stretched out the tasks of loading the dishwasher and wiping the counters. After all, Dave's future affected my future. Plus, his future affected Lola's future, and that also affected my future. Besides, I rationalized, Goodspeed either hadn't noticed I was hanging around or else wasn't bothered.

With much restating and overstating, he informed Dave that he wanted to stay on the job even though everyone concerned about his physical condition wanted him to retire immediately if not sooner. Goodspeed acknowledged he'd never set records solving cases, but claimed he was a methodical double-checker who built water-tight cases prosecutors loved. He added he knew the county inside and out and had sources and snitches everywhere. He contended the justice system would be compromised if he was given the gate. So a deal had been hammered out. Goodspeed would stay on for another six months on a part-time basis, working side-by-side with his replacement, showing that person the ropes and sharing his knowledge.

And there, to paraphrase Hamlet, was the rub.

Harvey Goodspeed had been on the job a long time. And in all those years, he'd never been noted for working and playing well with others. He'd also never been noted for keeping his opinions to himself. Consequently, no one in the sheriff's department wanted to work with him. Neither did those serving in nearby counties. Regional advertising had netted only a few candidates, all of whom disqualified themselves after phone conversations with the man who would supervise them. Networking hadn't helped either.

From what little I'd heard about him, I wasn't the least bit surprised. Goodspeed, however, apparently had been stunned.

"I heard one excuse after another," he groused. "Sure, the pay isn't up there with New York and California. And, yeah, it rains all winter. Except when it snows. And of course the moving allowance doesn't cover squat. And, darn right, if I'm training you, I'll watch you like a hawk."

*A fat hawk with its talons wrapped around a chocolate cake.*

To his credit, Dave's grave expression didn't slip, and he continued to nod at the end of every sentence.

"Gotta find little mistakes before they get big." Goodspeed brushed crumbs from his tie. "You and . . . uh, Atwood, did an okay job last fall."

"Atwell," Dave corrected.

Goodspeed flicked that aside. "With a little more time you would have got all the pieces to fit and made the case before a bunch of idiots jumped the gun with their theatrics. But at least you were there for the arrest."

*Thanks to the idiots who jumped the gun. Me and Paulette. And my sister.*

Having run out of counter to clean, I moved on to the stove, ignoring another hand signal from Dave.

"You're young, and you've got a lot to learn, but you have good instincts. And your handwriting is better than Atwad's."

"Atwell's," Dave corrected.

"At-whatever." Goodspeed reached for the last cookie. "Can't smoke. Not supposed to eat anything worth chewing. But who wants to live forever?"

*Obviously not Harvey Goodspeed.*

He held the cookie close to his nose and inhaled, his rubbery lips lifting into a smile. "Heard you're tired of working drugs. Thought you would have applied for this."

"I wasn't aware of the opportunity."

That was possible. We'd been out of town for a week in November, Dave had been focused on the murder of a homeless actor, and he was notorious for deleting unopened e-mails in a random manner. But he also could be dodging Goodspeed's presumed question.

"Well, how about it?" Goodspeed gazed at the final cookie with a mix of anticipation and regret. I swear I spotted a tear glimmering in the corner of one eye. For a few brief seconds, recalling moments of sadness brought about by realizing I was down to the last bits at the bottom of an especially good bag of cheesy snacks, I felt myself warming to him.

"How about what?" I heard more than a single note of impatience in Dave's voice. In fact, I heard a complete song of impatience, a catchy little number entitled something like "Get to the Point Before I Break Your Face."

"How about working with me?"

"I thought that was a done deal. When you came in, you said I was on loan to you."

"You are." He slid the cookie between his lips, chewed exactly three times, and swallowed. "Temporarily. For this one case. What I'm talking about is the long haul. Taking over when I retire."

If Dave's mind was working like mine, it was now balancing opportunity against aggravation, change of career against collateral damage. Lola, for example. I held my breath, waiting for his response.

Goodspeed brushed another batch of crumbs from a shirt that had been improved by their presence. "Well? You interested or what?"

"Yes. I'm interested," Dave said with pauses between words. "But I need time to think it over."

"How much time?"

"Well, maybe—"

"A week," I said in my no-nonsense-substitute-teacher voice. "He'll need at least a week."

If thought bubbles appeared over the heads of non-cartoon characters, Dave's would have been filled with question marks. Goodspeed's bubble, on the other hand, would have been filled with exclamation marks. He gaped. "A week?"

"A week," I confirmed. "As methodical as you are, you should understand he needs time to consider the evidence and, uh, get all the puzzle pieces together and see how they fit."

Goodspeed's gape morphed into an expression of pressed-lip consideration. He checked his watch, shoved his ankle off his knee, and got to his feet, staggering the way weightlifters do when they try to hoist their limit. "A week it is."

# Chapter 14

"I'm perfectly capable of speaking for myself, Barbara," Dave told me a few minutes later out on the deck. His voice was a gritty whisper, and even in the dim light from the lamp beside the door, I could see his eyes flashing fire. "I don't need someone butting in and blathering about puzzle pieces."

Blathering? Really? I'd never blathered a day in my life. Well, not a full day, anyway.

I set my fists firmly on my hips—something that's easier to do when you're carrying extra poundage. "I'm sorry if I embarrassed you in front of Harvey Goodspeed, but as one of the puzzle pieces involved in your career-change decision, I felt I had the right to some input."

Dave mimicked my stance. "You could have had all the input you wanted later on."

"Later on when?"

"When we sat down and had a discussion the way adults do."

"Would that be *after* you promised to have an answer for him in the morning?"

He hesitated just long enough to tell me his next words would be a lie. "I would nev—"

"Ha! And what about Lola?" Seething, I pointed toward the rose garden where the dogs were doing their thing. "She's another piece of the puzzle. What happens to her physical and mental health if you take a job with the county and she gets a new handler and has to sleep in a crate?"

"We'll figure something out. She'll be okay."

"Okay isn't good enough."

My simmering anger came to a boil. This wasn't us bickering or even having a heated argument. This was a fight.

I braced myself against the deck railing. A fight with Dave was new territory. I could almost feel the ground shift beneath my feet. "So help me, if she has to spend even one night in a crate in a cold garage, I'll . . ."

"You'll what?" Dave said with a combative sneer.

I thought about that as the dogs came up the stairs and hustled through the drizzle toward the door. "I don't know. But I guarantee it won't make you happy. I guarantee it will be way more painful than spending tonight on the sofa."

"Me? Why am I on the sofa? You're the one who's butting in on something that affects the rest of my life."

The dogs skidded to a halt and stared at us.

"You're on the sofa because the bed was mine before we met. And because the possessive pronoun you used makes it sound as if *your* life has nothing to do with *my* life."

Lola whined and pressed against my legs. I reached for her collar. Our lives were diverging. It felt like I'd been stabbed in the heart.

"Pronoun?" Dave sputtered. "What are you talking about? A pronoun is some kind of English-class thing. What does that have to do with anything?"

"It has *everything* to do with *everything*!" My voice cracked on the last word and I stumbled for the door, Cheese Puff circling, Lola guiding me when tears blurred my vision. "Everything!"

113

I was tempted to slide the door closed behind me, but decided that would be childish, so I left it open and followed the dogs upstairs. Flinging myself on the bed, I clutched a pillow to my chest and waited for an eruption of sobs.

They didn't come.

Anger, it appeared, had overwhelmed other emotions. Or perhaps fury, like a flamethrower, had torched loss and sadness to cinders.

Lola and Cheese Puff stretched out on either side of me. Abandoning the pillow, I cuddled with them.

If this was it—if Dave's attitude toward Lola could be summed up as "she'll be okay"—then we'd reached the deal-breaker point in our relationship. Granted, that deal-breaker point wasn't the same as discovering my ex-husband's cheating and stealing, but it was every bit as gut-wrenching. Lola was obedient and loving and loyal. She was part of our family. And I wouldn't stand by and see her shunted off to someone who would treat her like . . . well, like a dog.

"Can we talk?" Dave called softly from the doorway. "I'm not sure what I said, but it seems like you're blowing this out of proportion."

*Blowing it out of proportion?*

No one involved in a potentially life-altering argument wants to hear that he or she is blowing things out of proportion.

Fury flamed in my brain.

I considered a dozen responses.

Instead, hugging the dogs tighter, I played the silence card.

"Okay," Dave said after what seemed like an hour.

I heard him pull blankets from the linen closet, heard the whisper of fabric as he drew his pillow from beneath the bedspread.

"We'll plan to talk in the morning."

*We'll* plan? As if he set the agenda. As if I had no say in the matter.

Well, he was about to find out that I wouldn't participate in any agenda set by a man who couldn't be bothered to return the loyalty of his dog.

So we didn't talk in the morning.

Or, to be exact, I didn't.

Allison was heading out the door when I came downstairs after a night of tossing, turning, and replaying every word of our dispute. Dave, his jeans and T-shirt even more rumpled than they'd been last night, kept up a running commentary on the newspaper headlines as he drank coffee and ate something that looked like a peanut butter and salami sandwich on raisin bread. I hummed to myself to make it clear I wasn't listening, took the dogs out, fed them, poured a cup of coffee, and went to the office to clean out my desk drawers and assess the contents. However things played out—whether Dave stayed and the office became a man cave, or whether he left and I turned it over to the roommate I'd have to recruit to help with the mortgage—I'd be a step closer to prepared to cope.

Dave trudged up the stairs and I heard the shower start and then the whirr of the hair dryer and the slide and thump of dresser drawers. When I heard him start down the stairs, I vacated the office so we wouldn't be in close proximity when he retrieved his briefcase. Our condo—perhaps soon to be *my* condo—isn't palatial, so I took refuge in the tiny washroom, scrubbing the sink and making as much noise as I could with a sponge, cleanser, and running water.

"See you later," Dave called through the door.

I stuck with silence.

"I hope Verna's still improving."

Silence.

"I'll fend for myself, so don't worry about dinner."

*As if.*

His footsteps retreated and the front door closed with what was not quite a slam.

I lingered another minute and then, fearing he might have crept back to confront me, opened the door by inches. And spotted the dogs gazing up at Mrs. B.

"Good morning, dear," she said in a voice just this side of a chirp as she poured herself a cup of coffee.

"Morning."

She studied me for a few moments, taking in my slippers, frayed jeans, water-spattered T-shirt, and bed hair. "No subbing jobs today?"

I dumped the cold coffee I'd left on the table, rinsed the cup, and refilled it. "Guess not."

She raised one eyebrow. "You do remember, don't you, that I open my bedroom window a crack before I go to bed?"

Meaning she'd overheard last night's argument on the deck. I felt both violated and relieved. Relief opened the emotional floodgates. I wobbled to the dining room table, sat, and burst into tears.

Mrs. B sat beside me, patting my back. What she didn't say spoke volumes. She didn't say Dave was a good man. She didn't remind me that he loved me and, just two months ago, asked me to marry him. She didn't say men and women often came at problems from opposite directions. She didn't say we might have misinterpreted each other. Most of all, she didn't say I'd blown things out of proportion.

All that, of course, didn't mean she was 100% on my side.

Mrs. B was a loving and loyal friend, but she cared for Dave as well. And she didn't wear blinders.

"I got so mad," I blubbered. "About Lola. And other stuff. But mostly about Lola."

Lola whined and licked my elbow.

"Yes, dear, Lola's future concerns me as well."

I waited for her to say, as she had many times before, that she would deal with the issue. But she said nothing. And she topped that with more nothing while tucking tissues in my hands.

I wiped my eyes and blew my nose. "Do I have to apologize?"

"No, not if you search your soul and find you don't love Dave and you don't want to work through this and mend your relationship."

I wadded the tissues, thinking of all the fun we had together, the way his kisses made my toes curl. I thought of how he'd accepted my entitled dog and the quirky characters in my life. And my sister.

"If you break up," Mrs. B mused, "and he has to move to an apartment like the one he had before, that won't be ideal for Lola."

Right. Unless she was reassigned, Lola would go with him. Something I hadn't considered.

I ripped the wadded tissues apart and wadded them back together.

"And, of course, if Dave moved out, you wouldn't be on the spot to advocate for Lola. And, frankly, you wouldn't have the right."

As if she knew what that meant, Lola pressed against my knee and whined louder. Cheese Puff flopped across my feet and joined in. I tore the tissues and wadded them once more.

"So, if you want to mend your relationship," Mrs. B went on, "an apology would certainly be a way to open a dialogue."

I resisted for a few seconds. And then I had a flash of genius. Okay, maybe not genius, but a flash of craftiness. An apology would throw Dave off balance. He'd never expect me to back down. Rattled, he might take the blame on himself. He might also let slip details of the Jerome Morrow investigation.

(For the record, although my hobby seems to have become dabbling in murder, getting the scoop on what could be a homicide wasn't the prime reason for making up with Dave. There were those toe-curling kisses mentioned earlier. There was Allison's emotional well-being. There was all the explaining I'd have to do to our friends. And there was the possibility I'd lose a few of them should side-choosing ensue as it often does when a couple breaks up. But there was also the possibility meeting him more than halfway would help strengthen the case for keeping Lola out of a crate.)

The child inside me moaned that being a grown-up was no fun.

I groaned in agreement.

Mrs. B patted my back once more.

"Do I have to apologize in person? Can I send him a text?"

Mrs. B fingered the triple strand of pearls encircling her neck. They made a soft clicking sound I found comforting. "Twenty years ago I would have said you needed to apologize in person or, if that wasn't possible, write a note on high-quality paper. But the world has changed, and the way we communicate now is nothing like it was."

She paused and I could almost see her mind reviewing the rules of etiquette and updating them. I bit the bullet and said, "I'll do whatever you think is right."

She stood and paced a circle around the table. "Well, I still prefer the old ways, but perhaps you could start with a text and follow up with a face-to-face apology and perhaps cook his favorite dinner."

Dave had clearly told me he'd fend for himself this evening, and he might be angry enough—even after an apology—to stick to that. But fortunately his favorite home-cooked dinner was my chicken and tortilla casserole served with salsa, guacamole, and sour cream. It was easy to toss together, kept for a few days, and warmed up well. Plus, I had all the ingredients on hand.

Figuring that amounted to a positive sign on the scale of a planetary alignment, or at least of the magnitude of a shoe sale coinciding with my tax return check, I decided to go with Mrs. B's plan. But first, I had a few conditions.

"I don't have to say I over-reacted or blew things out of proportion, do I?"

She poured a refill on coffee, mulling my question. "I suppose that's subjective. A matter of perspective. If you don't think you—"

"I didn't." I tossed my wadded tissues in the trash can in the cabinet under the sink. "I definitely did not blow it out of proportion."

Mrs. B cocked her head and raised one eyebrow.

I raised my chin and stuck to my guns. Well, pretty much I stuck to the one gun in my possession—a model noted for shooting hot air.

For a few moments we froze. Then I snatched my cellphone from the counter and thumbed in a message: "I'm sorry. Let's talk."

"That's it?" Mrs. B asked. "Nothing about how much you love him? Nothing about hoping he understands and forgives you for lashing out when you were upset?"

That first part was a good idea. The second seemed like me marching the extra mile across burning sand in my bare feet. Especially since it appeared clear that if Dave understood how I felt, we never would have had a fight. I tapped in "I love you. Hope we can talk soon." Then, before Mrs. B could make further suggestions, I sent it off and changed the subject. "When are they letting Verna out of the hospital?"

She narrowed her eyes for a second, apparently to let me know she was well aware of what I was up to. "Hopefully very soon." She clicked her pearls. "I'm headed over there in half an hour to confer with the medical staff."

I wondered if staff members were aware of what was in store for them should their plans for Verna's release not mesh with Mrs. B's. Talk about the iron fist in the velvet glove. "Can I do anything else? Besides finish the clothing project?"

"Well, Jim has all the furniture in place in my living room and I lined up a physical therapist. The only thing I can think you might do is go to the library and borrow a few DVDs. Classics would be good. And some of those small-town British whodunits Verna and Sybil love. Don't stress about what she may have seen. The stroke might have affected her memory. Verna's, I mean. Sybil's memory is . . ."

She didn't have to complete the sentence. Sybil's memory had more craters than the moon.

"Consider me on it."

"Nothing too noir or violent," Mrs. B cautioned. "Nothing with gushing blood in living color."

"I'm all about black-and-white classics," I assured her. "And Agatha Christie."

"Thank you, dear." She bent to give Lola a good ear scratching, patted Cheese Puff's scruffy orange head, and was gone with a final click of pearls.

Deciding a shower would provide a fresh start on the day, I was heading for the stairs when the phone rang. "Captain Meriwether" the display read. I snatched it up. "Hel—"

"That man should be shot," Big Chill raged.

# Chapter 15

Over the past year Big Chill had threatened violence against a number of men, so I felt justified in posing a question to narrow the field. "Which man are you talking about?"

"The fool on the radio."

That narrowed it down significantly. But, depending on your viewpoint, choice of sport and team, capacity for bad taste, or political persuasion, it still left a long list.

"Rick Rivers," she stormed.

Ah. *That* fool. The fool who downsized me from my role as a talk show producer and sent me into an economic tailspin. Well, in the interest of brutal honesty, make that a *faster* economic tailspin. Thanks to Jake I was already falling toward an ocean of red ink and the tide was coming in. "What's he done now?"

"Only told the whole world Jerome Morrow is dead and implied if he didn't kill himself, he should have."

*Yikes.*

I flipped through the morning paper to Stan Stewart's article. As I recalled, it didn't include Morrow's name and referred only to "an unidentified male" found at a residence in the north part of the county. But perhaps the sheriff's office had released more information after the paper went to press.

"I didn't hear it myself—I wouldn't listen to that sorry waste of space if you held my hand on a hot stove," Big Chill raged. "One of the aides heard it and asked a couple of others if he was the only one who hadn't gotten the official memo about Jerome's death. In five minutes it was all over school and everyone was in an uproar. Might as well tear up today's finals and send everyone home."

My mind went to work conjuring up images of distraught teachers and students as I fired up my laptop. "If you need me to come in to relieve someone, I'll be glad to help out—without pay."

That last bit, just so you know, was a spontaneous offer, not one made in order to suck up with an eye toward the future.

"Thank you. We've got counselors coming from other schools, but I'll call if I need you. And, if you come in, of course you'll be compensated."

"Deal."

While she sniffled and ranted, I scanned the newspaper's website and then zoomed on to see if the Portland TV stations had Morrow's name. They didn't. The most recent news release from the sheriff's department concerned a traffic fatality a week ago.

How had Rivers gotten Morrow's name? And what did he have against him? The Captain Meriwether principal seldom stuck his head above the educational parapet. He'd been about as visible in the community as . . . well, as he'd been in the halls of the high school.

"Did Mr. Morrow ever call in to Rick Rivers' show? Or complain to the radio station manager about something he heard?"

Big Chill snorted. "If Jerome listened to the radio, it would have been swing music or hits from the 50's. He was as out-of-date as dial phones and chalkboards. No, a report on public education graduation rates came out and it wasn't glowing. Not all that bad, considering changes in requirements, but Rivers made it sound like the school was in complete failure mode, and put all the blame on Jerome. And then he made that hateful insinuation."

While she talked, I did a search for Morrow's name. Nothing more recent than 14 months ago when he commented on the murder of Assistant Principal Jessica Flint and the loss to the school.

Somehow, Rick Rivers had information that had yet to be officially released. I wondered if Dave knew. I decided that under the unwritten rules of relationships, because we hadn't made up yet, I didn't have the "right" to call and ask.

"I called the radio station to challenge him," Big Chill said, "and got a recording. It told me I was caller number 12."

In all my time as a producer for his show we'd never had 12 callers waiting. In fact, it had been a big day if we had two calls on hold.

"I waited for five minutes and I was still number 12. So I hung up and called back after ten minutes and—"

"You were number 12 again."

"Yes! So I called the main number and I got into one of those endless loops where you push one or two or whatever and you never get to a real person."

No surprise there. Like many radio stations, my former place of employment was on the financial rocks. The budget was slashed on a monthly basis. The receptionist had been laid off, and I imagined the only person checking messages was the lone salesman.

"I'm tempted to drive down there and give that horse's patootie a piece of my mind, but Tremaine needs my help here."

That sounded like a hint that I volunteer. I nipped the idea in the bud. "The building will be locked and I bet the combination's been changed six times since I was downsized. There's an intercom, but Rick won't open the door for someone he doesn't know. Or for me. Especially not for me."

"That's what I was afraid of." She sighed. "Thanks for letting me vent."

"Happy to serve."

She disconnected and I took a page from Mrs. B's book and paced around the dining room table, considering my options. As I'd told Big Chill, going to the radio station was a waste of time. But something needed to be done to muzzle Rick Rivers, and I wanted to help cinch the muzzle in place. Not because he laid me off. And not because I didn't agree with him on many issues. Okay, *most* issues. And not because he was a blowhard and always out for himself—although those were certainly factors in my decision. But mainly I wanted him to shut up because he used his power and position to foment prejudice and social divisiveness.

And although I wanted his silence, I *really* wanted to see him smacked down.

Coincidentally, I knew someone who was longing to throw a punch—a journalistic punch.

I clicked on the *Reckless River Roundup* website, found the contact button for Stan Stewart, and hammered away at the keyboard. Stating I was to be considered an anonymous source, I told him about Rick Rivers' on-air bad-taste bomb and the impact on teachers and students at Captain Meriwether High School who learned about Jerome Morrow's death that way. I explained that procedures were in place for notifying teachers, staff, and students of deaths or other incidents that could affect them. I told him how the school provided counselors who were trained to deal with shock and grief, and had them ready when an announcement was made by teachers in each classroom. I suggested he call the district information officer and request an interview with Tremaine Scott who could explain all this in more detail. I also suggested Big Chill could give him background on Morrow of the warm and personal variety. And, finally, I suggested he try to find out how Rivers got information about Morrow's death that didn't seem to be available anywhere else. In a final note, I strongly suggested he ask whether the radio renegade realized—or cared—what the impact of his comments had been.

Feeling empowered after I sent my message, I showered and headed for the library, the radio in my car set firmly in the "off" position. I'd found listening to Rick Rivers did nothing for my blood pressure—at least nothing good. Plus, the seething that followed an angry eruption only encouraged me to stuff my face with snack food. And, as you well know, I needed no encouragement in that department.

When I returned from the library, alert amateur sleuth that I am, I spotted a trail of wet footprints in the hallway and surmised I had a guest. Since the door wasn't damaged and there were no scratches around the lock, I deduced said guest was most likely one in possession of a key. That meant the guest was not my sister. Instead of running for cover, I made for the living area.

Sybil, looking like the last daisy clinging to its stem after an autumn hailstorm, sat at the dining room table. Her blond hair was plastered to her head, and her normally pink skin was sallow. She wore a screaming orange raincoat and bedraggled brown bunny slippers. One trembling hand grasped a steaming mug and the other stroked Lola's head.

"Verna yelled at me. Yelled. Really loud. And Muriel told me to go home and rest," she wailed, "but I don't want to be alone."

Pretty much the opposite of how I felt. After the stress of the past two days, I craved a little alone time, perhaps followed by a nap. But it appeared that wasn't in the cards. Or in the stars. Or anywhere.

"I wanted to cuddle with Cheese Puff." Sybil blew her nose into a fresh napkin and added it to the heap on the table. "But he's in one of his moods."

I glanced at his favorite chair. He'd burrowed so far into the crevice only his tail and the tips of his ears were visible. For a moment I thought about apologizing for his behavior, but Sybil, as a member of the Cheese Puff Care and Comfort Committee, was one of those who had created this miniature monster by catering to his every whim. Even if I pried him from the chair, and even if I spoke sternly to him, and even if I paddled—gently, of course—his entitled orange bottom, he wasn't likely to change his attitude.

"Lola's there for you," I pointed out.

Sybil seized another napkin and released a torrent of tears. "All I wanted to do was help. And she yelled at me."

I got a caffeine-free diet cola from the refrigerator, glanced at Sybil, then put it back and went for a can with both caffeine and sugar. For good measure I got out a fresh bag of cheesy snacks. And cadged a box of tissues from the stock in the pantry. Tissues with lotion.

"Her speech is all messed up, so I don't know what she said. But she was definitely yelling."

After popping the top of the cola and managing to open the cheesy snacks without having the bag explode or rip down the side, I took a seat and waited.

Sybil snatched a tissue from the box and blew a nose red enough to make that famous reindeer green with envy.

"Do you want to tell me about it?" I asked.

(For the record, even though I hoped beyond reason that the answer would be "No," I think I managed to muster a tone of sympathy, concern, and interest.)

"I was only trying to plump up her pillows and she . . . she yelled . . . no, she *shrieked* at me. And her words were jumbled, like I said. But I got it. She wanted me to leave her alone and get out and never come back."

Yelling I could see, but shrieking, even given the bickering nature of Verna's relationship with her airhead friend, seemed a little extreme. I checked to see if Sybil was exaggerating. "Shrieked?"

"Shrieked," Mrs. B confirmed as she came through the sliding door to the deck—a door I'd neglected to lock when I took off on my errand run. "It knocked us all back on our heels, I can tell you. Especially because we couldn't see the reason."

She pulled a mug from a cabinet, filled it with water, and set it in the microwave to heat. "Sybil is *always* fussing."

"I am," Sybil confirmed. "Verna's always telling me to stop fussing when she comes over to watch television. And I say she's my best friend and I enjoy making her comfortable. And then she clicks her tongue and kind of sighs, but she tells me to go ahead and fuss because she knows she can't change me."

Mrs. B sat beside Sybil and gave her a hug. "And you never fuss in a bad way. You do it to try to make things better."

"And that's all I wanted to do. Make her pillows better. They were all squashed down." She yanked another tissue from the box and blubbered into it. "And she shrieked at me."

"It's probably no consolation," Mrs. B said, "but after you left she shrieked at me."

Sybil's eyes widened and I felt mine do the same. Unless my memory was faulty, even Bernina Burke had never shrieked at my wealthy neighbor.

Mrs. B removed the mug from the microwave and dropped in a tea bag, filling the room with the scent of oranges and cinnamon. "I left the room, of course, and conferred with a nurse. Apparently this kind of thing isn't unusual. Even though she's bouncing back at an amazing pace, she must be frustrated by what she can't manage on her own."

Sybil nodded slowly. "And she's proud. Very proud. She hates to ask anyone for anything."

"And now she has to." Mrs. B squeezed the tea bag and tossed it in the trash. "Until she's better, she has no choice."

"So what can we do to make it easier?" I asked. "On all of us?"

Mrs. B sat beside Sybil again and sipped her tea. "My thought is we stop fussing and coddling."

"You mean, not help her?" Sybil's face pinched into a frown. "How will she eat? And change her clothes? And . . . other things?"

"Of course we'll help her with all those things, but we'll do it in a professional, workmanlike, no-frills way."

"What does that mean?" Sybil's face pinched tighter.

"It means we give her space. We don't hover."

"But she's my friend. My best friend." Sybil clutched another tissue and unleashed a fresh torrent of tears.

Mrs. B sighed.

I did likewise, sliding my gaze toward Sybil. "I'm not sure she gets it. And I'm really not sure she can keep from crossing the line between helping and annoying."

"I'm not sure I can, either." Mrs. B sipped tea and gazed out the glass door and across the rain-washed deck. "I thought it would be best if all Verna's friends pitched in. I thought she'd be comforted by having us close. But now it seems we need someone less involved, someone with a no-nonsense attitude."

128

She shot a meaningful glance at Sybil who was soaking yet another tissue. "Someone who won't fuss and hover."

"Like a professional caregiver?"

"Not exactly. Not a professional."

"An *amateur* caregiver?"

"More or less."

I was confused. No, I was beyond confused. I was cruising past bewildered, puzzled, and perplexed. "What does 'more or less' mean?"

"It means we know someone who needs a job, someone I think would be perfect for this one, and someone who would be delighted to make, say $200 a day."

"We do?"

Sybil looked up from the tissue and we exchanged shrugs.

"We do," Mrs. B confirmed. "We all know someone who has the strength to lift Verna and could see to her basic needs without doing more than necessary, and without pampering her. Someone who is short on patience and long on opinion and, through her general lack of interest in others' problems, would encourage Verna to do more each day so she could return to independent living quickly. Someone who doesn't accept excuses from anyone but herself and wouldn't allow Verna to slack off on physical therapy."

Maybe you already saw where this was going and are wondering why I was so slow. My only defense is that there are people I make an effort NOT to think about unless I have to. Unfortunately, right now it appeared I had to.

I crossed my index fingers in a feeble attempt to ward off what was coming. "Don't utter her name. Please. Don't."

But Mrs. B did.

# Chapter 16

Within an hour, my sister was sitting at the table with us, demolishing my cheesy snacks and complaining because they were too salty, while Mrs. B summed up the job requirements. "Essentially, you'd need to help her in and out of bed, to a chair, and to the bathroom for sponge baths and, uh, other needs. You'll see that she does her exercises, make sure she drinks plenty of liquids, and eats what we prepare for her."

"She'll say she's not hungry," Sybil said. "She'll say she's watching her weight. She'll try to tell you she'll eat later or maybe claim she's allergic."

Iz nodded, up-ended the bag, and dumped the crumbs into her mouth. "When Barbara was little, the rule was no TV until the green beans were gone. She cleaned her plate every time."

And I had, I'd cleaned those disgusting canned green beans into a napkin and smuggled it out to the trash can under my T-shirt. But I'd kept a smug smile off my face and bottled my laughter inside, so Iz believed she was a master of child psychology. I imagined Verna would also have ways of getting around my sister's edicts. On the other hand, hooked as Verna was on British mysteries, if Iz confiscated the remote, she might cave and take the quickest route back to finding out whodunit.

"We have all the medical equipment the hospital staff suggested, but she'll say she doesn't need it, doesn't need your

130

assistance, and can manage on her own," Mrs. B said. "Some of her insistence may be because that's the way she always operated, and some because her mind is muddled and she honestly believes she can function as well as she did before. At any rate, don't argue with her, just stay beside her and make sure she doesn't fall or spill hot coffee on herself or—"

"I got it," Iz said in the cocksure voice I found so annoying. "Let her think she's in charge. Let her find out for herself what she can and can't do. Push her to do what will help her recover, but don't criticize or micromanage small details. Don't fill in the blanks in her conversation or correct actions or statements that seem weird."

I gaped. This was my sister talking. This was my sister exhibiting more awareness of human interaction than I'd thought possible.

"Exactly," Mrs. B said. "If she insists her left shoe goes on her right foot, don't argue. Let it stay that way until she notices. If she says the sky is green, ignore it. If she thinks Nixon is in the White House, let it go."

"Got it." Iz crumpled the cheesy snacks bag and tossed it on the table. "But I'll need a bonus if I have to pretend Nixon is still around."

My jaw dropped lower. Was that a joke? Was my sister making a joke?

Mrs. B twinkled a smile in my direction.

I shut my mouth and managed a sickly smile.

"Well, I think this will work out just fine." Mrs. B handed my sister a fat white envelope. "You'll find enough in there to cover the first five days and, of course, your meals will be included."

Iz narrowed her eyes and opened her mouth, but Mrs. B jumped in before she could speak. "I'm aware you have specific tastes in food, so I'd like you to make a list of what I should stock. And, should you want to order out for something not on hand, I will provide a supply of petty cash."

Given Iz's appetite, Mrs. B might need to cough up a lot more than what I think of as petty cash. And she'd undoubtedly find herself replenishing the cash supply often.

"There's a key to my unit in the envelope and Jim set up a bed in the office for you. We expect Verna to be released in the morning and hope to have her back here before noon. Jim and I prevailed on Bernina Burke to bend the rules and allow him to build a ramp to my door."

Knowing Mrs. B and Bernina as I did, I bet the prevailing involved raised voices and the citing of laws covering the elderly and disabled. Prevailing may also have escalated to include threats of protests by senior activists and extensive media coverage of said events. Bernina, as you well know, was prone to cling like a barnacle to condo rules and regulations and the authority those gave her. But since she'd set her sights on being hired to manage a larger and more prestigious condo complex, we'd been able to play on her concerns about anything that might torpedo her plans—such as bad publicity.

"You'll be here to help Verna get settled?"

You may see a question mark at the end of Mrs. B's sentence, but I assure you I didn't hear one. I glanced at my sister who was tucking the envelope in a pocket of her cargo pants. She also seemed to recognize the order and accept Mrs. B as the boss. "I'll read up on caring for stroke victims tonight. Call me when she's ready to leave the hospital and I'll be waiting here in the parking lot."

After a perusal of the contents of the refrigerator, pantry, and cabinets, and a few snide comments about my grocery purchases, Iz ate a chocolate bar I'd hidden beneath a stack of dish towels in the pantry, and departed. Sybil hugged Mrs. B, called her an angel, and toddled off to take a nap. Mrs. B sifted through the videos I'd borrowed from the library and asked, "What have you heard from Dave?"

I hesitated for a few seconds. "Nothing."

She cast a disdainful glance at my cellphone on the counter. "I feared that text was an ill-conceived idea. Have you called him?"

Feeling like an elementary school student summoned to the teacher's desk, I hung my head and scuffed my shoe on the carpet. I didn't attempt the ball-is-in-his-court argument or suggest he might have been too busy working a possible murder case to respond. I gulped air and whispered, "No."

"Well, I strongly suggest you—"

The doorbell chimed.

*Reprieved!*

I raced along the hallway. Even if Bernina Burke was on the other side—heck, even if a slavering wolf was outside—it was better than getting a relationship lecture from Mrs. B.

Flinging the door wide, I spotted Ardie and Big Chill sheltering under the skimpy overhang. Big Chill wore a bright red raincoat and carried a white umbrella decorated with multi-colored butterflies. Ardie wore her trademark black, in this case a leather jacket with the collar turned up to meet the broad brim of a black leather hat. Without a word, the Chillster furled her umbrella, stepped past Ardie, and made her way down the hall, her high heels clicking. I glanced at my watch, tapped the crystal, and checked again.

"You're right, school isn't out yet, but she's on a mission," Ardie said in a low voice. "She called me out of class and ordered me to drive her here. Hope we're not interrupting anything."

"Only another interruption." I laughed in a manic kind of way.

Ardie eased in beside me and closed the door. "You okay?"

"Never better."

She leaned close and looked into my eyes. "You sure?"

"Positive. It's just that I'm starting to think my life is nothing more than a long chain of interruptions."

"Might as well get used to it." She gave me a sidearm hug. "As long as the links in the chain hold, you'll be fine."

And if the links didn't hold?

If I pondered the question too long, it would surely tie my brain in knots.

Ardie seemed to sense that. She took my arm and ushered me to the living area.

Big Chill and Mrs. B hadn't waited for me to perform introductions. They'd apparently taken care of the preliminaries and made the leap to common ground—their hatred of Rick Rivers.

"He's a horrid man." Mrs. B plucked a box of tea bags from a cabinet. "No, he's a horrid *excuse* for a man. I still haven't gotten over the way he treated me last year. Calling me a stripper. Implying my success was based on trading sexual favors. But this—traumatizing teachers and students—this is far worse."

I waited for her to say the magic words, to say Rivers would be dealt with. I waited for her to say she had a plan for putting pressure on the radio station owner or, better yet, that she intended to buy the place.

But no.

She said nothing as she went about nuking water for tea while Big Chill listed what she'd like to do to my former boss. The list included drawing and quartering, water torture, toothpicks driven beneath his fingernails, and creative uses for a melon baller and a basketball pump.

Have I mentioned that Big Chill isn't a pacifist?

134

"I hope the newspaper reporter who called hangs him out to dry." Big Chill sat and kicked off her shoes. "But I bet Rivers won't care what anyone says. And I bet it won't make a bit of difference to his so-called career. He might have to make an apology, but he'll still be on the air spouting hate and BS, riling people up, dividing the community."

"I guess that's what the people running the place want him to do," Ardie said. "They've let him play the blame game for a long time now. And today Jerome Morrow got the tail pinned on him."

"Poor Jerome. He wasn't perfect, but he didn't deserve the blast of crap he got." Big Chill aimed a ragged fingernail at me. "What have you heard from Dave?"

At the mention of his name, Lola lurched to her feet and limped to my side. I leaned to stroke her head. "Uh, nothing."

Both Big Chill and Mrs. B scowled at me. The reasons were different, but the scowls were identical. If I didn't know better, I'd think they were sisters.

"He's, uh, probably, busy following up leads and, uh, logging evidence, and—"

"Call him," Big Chill and Mrs. B ordered in harmony.

"I don't think that's a good—"

"Fine." Mrs. B snatched up my cellphone. "I'll call him."

Was I okay with that?

No.

Did I want to make the call myself?

No.

Was I a coward?

You bet.

Mrs. B tapped the phone and put it to her ear. In a moment she said, "Dave. It's Muriel Ballantine. Wilhelmina Frost is with me. She's the secretary at Captain Meriwether High School. It's an imposition, but I hope you can provide us with some information about Jerome Morrow's death in light of what Rick Rivers said this morning."

She listened for a moment, an index finger in the air. "Tissue samples. Toxicology. I see. No sooner? Of course I understand. Of course, you can't compromise the investigation."

Just when I thought she was about to disconnect, she lobbed a question. "Will the sheriff's department respond to today's unfortunate radio broadcast?"

The finger went up again and she smiled at me. "I see. That should be an interesting article. I'll read it first thing." She gave me an appraising glance. "Yes, I also wonder how Stan Stewart got onto the information leak so quickly. Thank you, Dave."

She aimed her index finger at the phone and paused. "Oh, of course you can. She's right here. Hang on."

And she handed the phone to me.

# Chapter 17

Since I'd figured I had several more hours to consider conversational options with Dave, I was far less than prepared.

I stretched my greeting to three syllables and put a huge question mark on the end. "Hel-lo-o?"

"I'm sorry, too," he said in a brisk voice.

I waited for more, but heard only a faint hum on the line. "I hope we can talk later," I ventured.

"Talk? Or argue?"

I gritted my teeth. "Talk."

"Good. But I have to tell you there may not be much I can do about Lola. The HR czar isn't happy with me being loaned out and she's making it clear Lola is department property and has to return to work. One way or another."

I felt a green wave of despair crash over me.

"I have to go."

He disconnected, leaving me feeling sick and angry and exhausted and energized all at the same time. I felt like making a supreme, ridiculous, or futile gesture. Or all three at once. I wanted to march to the cop shop and punch out the HR clown. I wanted to stick Lola in my car and drive until I had three states between me and Reckless River. I wanted to scream "This isn't fair!" for about a week. And I wanted to stuff my face with cheesy snacks.

Except the cheesy snack bag, crumpled on the table, was empty.

"Everything all right?" Mrs. B asked.

"With Dave? I guess." I set the phone on the table and knelt to hug Lola. "But I'm worried about Lola."

For the benefit of Ardie and Big Chill, I started the saga at the beginning with Lola's allergies, the unauthorized search and rescue training, their injuries and recuperation, Dave's forays into homicide, and his temporary transfer to the county. Then I poured out the latest. "It's a bureaucratic vendetta. And that jerk doesn't care about Lola. Doesn't care that her leg hasn't healed yet. Doesn't care that she might end up sleeping in a crate in a cold garage."

"It's just wrong." Ardie joined me beside Lola. "Just because she's a dog, she shouldn't be treated like a slave."

The word "slave" made me think of the Underground Railroad. Could I—maybe with Ardie's help—set up a network of friends to spirit Lola away and keep her safe until all of this blew over? Would we face arrest for what might be seen as stealing police property? Was I willing to go to jail for Lola?

The answer to that was "You bet!"

But how would Lola react to a life on the run? A life in hiding far from all of us?

"What would it take to buy her freedom?" Ardie asked.

"I don't know for sure. Thousands. But they have to agree to let us buy her. And if we get involved there might be consequences for Dave. And for Lola."

"There must be some way," Ardie insisted. "Maybe a protest march. What about getting your sister to organize one?"

"Her protesting days are over. She's searching for a new career."

"Too bad. She was so good at that one."

138

"Yeah." I hated to admit it, but Iz had been a world-class rabble rouser.

"What about using social media? Or political pressure? Or something?"

The words "or something" conjured an image of Dario O'Brien grasping a few faceless honchos in the police department by their necks and shaking them the way a terrier shakes a rat. The images came with sound effects of squawking and yelping and pleading for Dario to let go.

It was a very satisfying image and I let it play for several seconds. Then I glanced over my shoulder at Mrs. B, expecting her to say she'd deal with the Lola problem. But no, she was listening to Big Chill rant on about the radio show host.

And, to my dismay, she wasn't stepping in to do something about *that* problem, either.

Until right then, I hadn't realized how much I'd come to depend on Mrs. B to handle problems that seemed too big or too knotty for me to resolve on my own. She'd formed the Cheese Puff Care and Comfort Committee. She'd gone in, guns blazing, when I'd been penalized by a bank for having too little in my account. She'd engineered what amounted to my first date with Dave. She'd negotiated a deal on my condo.

It seemed like she'd done all those things because she was my friend and because she thought of me as her daughter. But perhaps she'd seen me as so weak and needy she felt compelled to rescue me. And, perhaps, somewhere along the line, she'd come to see rescuing as enabling.

I didn't like this train of thought. And I really didn't like being someone others enabled. Sure I'd had problems when I met her, but I'll argue all day that I was honest about my situation, not needy.

Not *really* needy.

Not then.

But now?

Now I felt adrift on an endless sea. Adrift on a small raft. A very small raft. A shoddily built raft without a rudder.

And that endless sea was roiled by towering waves and populated by enormous sharks. Sharks that hadn't eaten for weeks.

Sure, Mrs. B was busy taking the lead on Verna's recovery, but this was a woman born for multitasking. This was also a woman with a soft spot for animals. And yet she didn't seem the least bit inclined to go to bat for a dog I knew she loved. I had no doubt she understood the gravity of the situation. And I had no doubt she wanted to keep Lola with us. So, why was she remaining silent? Was she feeling ill or tired? Or was I wrong about her ability to juggle tasks? Did she have too much on her plate with Verna's condition? Did she have too many irons in the fire, too many fish to fry, too—?

I gave myself a mental slap before I was sucked under by a whirlpool of swirling clichés. As you know, I have an active imagination. No, make that an overactive imagination. So I wondered how much of what I was feeling was justified.

Fearing a conversation with Mrs. B might circle around to her belief that I needed to be more proactive about my job search, I shelved the let's-talk idea. But I made a mental note to watch for other instances when Mrs. B didn't step in to deal with a problem.

"Did you hear anything I said?" Ardie asked.

I blinked. "Um, no. Sorry."

She gave Lola's head a final pat and got to her feet. "The gist of it was we should get together and brainstorm later on. But today we need to finish the alterations."

"Don't you have to drive the Chillster back to school?"

Ardie cocked her head toward the far side of the table where Big Chill and Mrs. B were deep in an animated

140

conversation about the sorry state of society. "I will when she's ready. But at the rate they're going, the gabfest won't wrap up until dinnertime."

And it didn't.

In fact, Mrs. B ordered Chinese food for all of us, including Jim and Sybil. She also tossed in a carton of shrimp fried rice for Allison who was out celebrating the end of finals and wouldn't be home until curfew.

(For the record, curfew was 9:00 PM on school nights, but since tomorrow was the one-day semester break, I didn't expect to see Allison until at least 10:30. Or later. Curfew slippage wasn't a battle I intended to fight. If Dave wasn't home when she returned, my policy was to make a note of the time on a scrap of paper from the recycling bin and hand said note to him when he appeared. Yesterday I saw he'd accumulated quite a collection of those notes on a spindle in the office. And, to my total lack of surprise, curfew slippage was still occurring. I hoped he made better progress on the investigation into Jerome Morrow's death.)

Ardie and I finished the clothing project while Mrs. B and Sybil cleaned up the kitchen. Jim, who had been drawn to Big Chill like metal filings to a magnet, invited her along to carry a bag of garbage to the containers at the far end of the parking lot. To my surprise, she accepted.

"It's good to see her with something on her mind besides Jerome, but that looked like a one-person bag to me," Ardie observed with a wink. "I could have carried it looped on my little finger."

I sniggered and reached for another faux jewel to stitch in place. "And I would have thought Jim could come up with a more creative way to cut her out of the herd."

141

"Yeah, but it worked. They say the course of true love doesn't always run smooth. But they don't mention whether it runs past a trash bin."

And perhaps, at least in this case, it did. Despite the drizzle, temperatures plunging toward the freezing mark, and the relatively short distance to the trash area, they were gone more than 20 minutes. When they returned, Big Chill's cheeks were pink and she announced Jim would drive her to Captain Meriwether to retrieve her car so Ardie wouldn't have to go out of her way.

"School is right *on* my way," Ardie muttered. "And she knows it."

We shared a wink, then turned as if we'd been choreographed and waved goodbye.

It was close to midnight when Dave slid into bed beside me, his feet cold enough to flash-freeze a quart of blueberries. I rolled into his arms and we had one of those discussions characterized more by moans and sighs than by words—at least not words forming complete sentences.

When I fell asleep I felt that if we weren't on the same page, at least we were in the same book. When I woke up, he was gone, leaving behind half a pot of cold coffee and a trail of toast crumbs.

Fortifying myself with reheated coffee, I scurried around vacuuming up bits of thread and a few grains of fried rice Allison had dropped and the dogs hadn't cleaned up. Since that was unusual behavior for them, I checked their vital signs.

Noses?

Damp and cool.

Eyes?

Clear and bright.

Teeth and gums?

No infections or swelling.

Feet?

No thorns or cuts.

Overall?

No abscesses. No lumps. No bumps.

Their physical conditions indicated no problems. But their mental conditions were, if nothing else, interesting.

Lola had camped by the door to the parking lot, her nose against the crack where the door met the jamb. And Cheese Puff, who had always been all about comfort and had viewed uncarpeted floor simply as a way to get from chair to bed to food bowl, was beside her.

I assumed Lola sensed Verna would return soon. When it came to Cheese Puff's motivation, however, I drew a blank. Perhaps, crafty little creature that he was, his plan was to win points with me and members of the Committee by following Lola's lead.

(For the record, if you think my judgment of his behavior is harsh, cast your mind back over his actions in the past. Recall, if you will, his unshakable sense of entitlement, his many refusals to obey commands, and his demoralizing strike that nearly led Mrs. B to pull out of *Still Got That Strut*. When you're finished reviewing, I think you'll agree I have every right to be just a touch suspicious, just a tad jaded, just a smidge tense in a waiting-for-the-other-shoe-to-drop way.)

Deciding to ignore both dogs for the moment, I drank a second cup of coffee while reading Stan Stewart's article. It was a long piece, packed with quotes from teachers and counselors and a spokesman for the sheriff's department. Stewart, or a photographer, had apparently staked out the radio station because the article included a photograph of Rick Rivers rushing to his car with his head down and his hands shielding his face. Rivers said nothing more than "No comment," but

143

Stewart managed to set those two words in a context that made them sound more like "I'm guilty."

A short sidebar piece featured interviews with a local journalism professor and the editor of the *Reckless River Roundup*. They shared their views on releasing sensitive information, the responsibilities of the media, and attempts to boost ratings or readership by resorting to sensationalism and inflammatory remarks.

Another story, even shorter, provided skimpy information on the investigation into the death of Jerome Morrow. It added up to what Mrs. B had gleaned last night—the autopsy report and toxicology results might shed more light on what was being treated as a suspicious death. It added that Morrow had been found in the garage on his property along the Lewis River by an officer doing a welfare check.

Resisting the urge to click on the radio and check out Rivers' reaction to the newspaper stories, I showered and dressed. Then, since Dave and I were on speaking terms again and I was willing to give up my office space, I got to work sorting through the drifts of paperwork on my desk. I was down to a heap no larger than a box of doughnuts and wondering if my brain could go a day without working food into my mental conversations, when Lola struggled to her feet and scratched at the door to the parking lot.

I'd read about canine telepathy and heard stories of dogs waiting for boats and trains. Did Lola sense Verna was on the way?

I opened the door a crack, but saw no sign of Mrs. B's car.

"Not yet," I told Lola as I closed the door.

She scratched once more and barked. Cheese Puff backed her up with a yip.

"Okay, girl, I'll assume you're picking up vibrations. Let's go outside."

144

Suspecting Bernina Burke would be lurking in the vicinity and preparing to "supervise" Verna's use of the ramp, I snapped leashes on the dogs and let them go as far as the edge of my tiny front stoop. Well, to be exact, Lola went to the edge. Cheese Puff halted at the threshold, casting a look of disgust at yet another dank day. Since we weren't headed for the car, technically I was in violation of the rules, but I took a chance Bernina would have other things on her mind.

And there she was, in all her glory, wearing a neon orange rain poncho and a pair of knee-high black rubber boots. She'd stationed herself beside the base of the ramp outside Mrs. B's unit. Her wide-legged stance and folded arms made it clear she intended to monitor every step Verna took in case she'd faked a stroke in an effort to flaunt condo regulations.

My sister stood on the opposite side of the ramp, coincidentally also wearing orange and black, and matching Bernina glower for glower. Based on past history, specifically an epic argument referred to in condo circles as The Battles of the Bulges, I doubted those glowers had anything to do with the fact they'd made identical wardrobe decisions. I also doubted, given the fact Bernina hadn't exactly emerged victorious from the previous confrontation, the condo manager was itching to fire the first volley in a rematch.

But you never knew.

# Chapter 18

Jim, sheltering beside a lightweight folding wheelchair beneath the overhang at Mrs. B's door, flipped me a wave.

"The ramp looks great," I called.

And it did. Jim had stained it gray to match the concrete walk and tacked on anti-slip strips with center lines I assumed would glow in the dark. The railings, crafted from weathered driftwood he'd found along the river, gave it a rustic appearance.

"It's easy to move," he said. "Lighter than it looks. When Verna's ready to go home, we can have it over to her place in a few minutes."

"Terrific," I praised, drawing a venomous glare from Bernina.

"Never mind her," I told the dogs. "She wouldn't like the ramp unless it was made out of potato chips and shrimp dip."

My stomach rumbled, reminding me I'd had only coffee so far today. It rumbled again, suggesting potato chips and shrimp dip would make a dandy brunch. "Later," I told it.

Whining, Lola pulled on her leash, the handle biting into my fingers. A second later Mrs. B's car crept into view, taking the speed bumps at a pace slow enough to guarantee a second-place finish in a contest with an exhausted sloth.

146

Lola lunged toward the car, but I'd braced and brought her up short. "Not yet. After Verna gets in and gets settled we'll go next door. Right now we need to stay out of the way so she doesn't take a tumble."

Lola seemed to get it. Trembling with excitement, she sat at my feet.

With a meaningful look at Bernina, Mrs. B executed a three-point turn and pulled to the curb, wheels rubbing against the yellow paint marking it as a no-parking zone. Jim rolled the wheelchair to the sidewalk. Iz marched forward, cut in front of Sybil, opened the passenger door, and leaned in to help Verna out.

Verna, face pinched and skin a gray-green, turned toward the door, and batted at my sister's arms with her left hand. She said something I couldn't hear but assumed was a garbled version of "Leave me alone. I can do it myself."

Without a trace of irritation and without saying a word, Iz leaned closer, eased Verna's feet to the pavement, and pried her from the car. As if they'd rehearsed, Jim slid the wheelchair forward. Iz turned Verna and folded her into it. In two minutes, with Sybil fluttering in their wake, they were up the ramp and inside.

"Color me impressed," I told the dogs.

Mrs. B twinkled a smile in my direction, favored Bernina with a prom-queen wave, and pulled away to park her car beneath the canopy.

Bernina tracked her progress before turning the full force of her scowl on me, making it clear I was mere seconds away from a citation, warning, and/or yet another piece of her malevolent mind to add to my collection. I stood my ground for a few moments, practicing an expression of bewildered innocence. Then I tugged at the leashes and got the dogs inside.

Lola attempted a dash to the back door, but I gave the "sit" command and she obeyed. "Five minutes," I told her as I unhooked the leash. She whined, but waited until I gave the "okay" command. Then she walked to the sliding glass door and positioned herself beside it, keeping watch on the deck.

Cheese Puff seemed in no hurry to go anywhere except to his food dish in the kitchen. He'd already devoured the contents, but now licked the rim and shoved the bowl around the room. It clunked against the base of cabinets, thumped against the refrigerator door, and clanged against the stove. That seemed to be the sound he liked best—or thought I would find most annoying—and he nosed the bowl away with a scrape of ceramic on linoleum, and shoved it again.

After the fourth clang, Lola flopped to the carpet and put her paws over her ears.

After the sixth, I picked up both Cheese Puff and the bowl, set the bowl in the sink, and carried him to the door. "Let's go, Lola."

She rose without her usual hitch and lurch. As soon as I opened the door wide enough, she shot outside. Mrs. B, obviously expecting us, stood in her doorway, a nugget-sized treat in each hand. She asked Lola to sit, praised her, scratched her ears, and offered one.

Cheese Puff thrust out his legs like a flying squirrel and clawed at the air until I set him down. Displaying not a single trace of good manners, he leaped for the nugget, but Mrs. B ordered him to sit and then dance on his hind legs. He'd refused to do that on command since they performed their routine in Las Vegas. And he refused again today.

"I'm sorry," I said. "He seems to have decided his career as a dancer is over."

"Let's see if jealousy is a motivator." She turned away from my entitled mutt and offered Lola more praise and the nugget Cheese Puff coveted.

Cheese Puff yipped in the way that said life wasn't fair and something should be done to correct that immediately.

Mrs. B ignored him.

He yipped again.

She scratched Lola's ears and told her she was the best dog in the world and there would be more treats for her inside.

Lola cut her gaze toward Cheese Puff, hesitated, then took the nugget between her teeth.

After a triple yip of annoyance, Cheese Puff stood on his hind legs and executed a series of complicated steps followed by a leap with a twist.

Mrs. B applauded and dug a nugget from the pocket of her jacket.

Cheese Puff sat at her feet to receive the treat and praise so effusive you'd think he'd come up a cure for the common cold.

I skirted their lovefest and followed Lola inside to find Sybil fluffing cushions on the sofa, my sister tinkering with the wheelchair, and Verna ensconced in a wing chair, frowning at them both. Her right hand curled in her lap, the left stroked Lola's head. The nugget lay on her lap like a get-well offering.

I bent and hugged Verna, inhaling the scents of soap and skin cream. "How are you feeling?"

"Guh." The word came up from her throat and out of the left side of her mouth accompanied by a puff of air scented with antiseptic mouthwash.

"Terrific," I burbled. "We're so glad you're out of the hospital. You'll recover much faster here with good food and your friends around."

Verna cast another frown in Sybil's direction and sucked in a breath. I plunged on. "Allison is sleeping in today because we're between semesters. I bet when she gets up she'd like to watch *Casablanca* with you."

(For the record, I planned to hedge my bet by making the viewing mandatory because of the fried rice I'd cleaned up. Allison was moving toward becoming an empathetic human adult, but her default setting on the emotional dial still broadcast phrases like "Do I have to?" and "Why can't I do it tomorrow?" and "Do I have to do everything around here?" As I've said before, admitting you're not the center of the universe is tough.)

I pointed at the stack of DVDs by the TV. "Or maybe you could watch a Cary Grant comedy. She thinks he's hot."

Iz groaned as if to say Allison was at best misguided and at worst off a rocker she might never have been on. But Verna smiled and Sybil set down a pastry box she was ferrying to the dining room table and clapped her hands. "Oooooh. *Arsenic and Old Lace* is such fun. And I love *The Philadelphia Story*."

"Cary Grant it is," Mrs. B said in a take-charge way. "But first an early lunch. And then a rest before the physical therapist arrives."

Since lunch appeared to include the contents of the pastry box, and since I had yet to get around to breakfast, I set a place for myself at the table. "We're all having tomato soup," Mrs. B told me in a soft voice. "A very thick soup. And cheese soufflé Jim whipped up. And pudding. So Verna won't feel left out during the first meal." She glanced at Iz. "Later on, of course, I'll offer a wider selection."

"Or you'll never hear the end of it."

Mrs. B cut her gaze toward Iz again. "Oh, I'm well aware of that fact, dear. Well aware."

We laughed the way you do when something is more tasteless than amusing, and she hustled to the oven to check on the soufflé that was filling the condo with an aroma of cheesy goodness.

Verna batted at my sister's hands again, but Iz made it clear help wasn't optional, tossed the nugget aside, and got her into the wheelchair once more and up to the table. Lola snatched the nugget and followed, sitting beside the chair, offering the gift once more, and resting her chin on Verna's knee.

With self-control I wasn't aware she had, Iz left her plate bare while she helped Verna get a grip on the spoon, sliced off bits of soufflé, and watched to make sure each spoonful went down as it should. The rest of us, following Mrs. B's orders, made small talk, avoiding controversial topics—a major task considering events in the news and on our minds.

Only when Verna had eaten what Iz considered to be enough did my sister attack her own lunch. And I mean attack. She went at it as if she hadn't eaten for a week and expected someone to snatch her portion away. She slurped down a bowl of soup then used the spoon to cram gobs of soufflé in her mouth. Mrs. B raised one eyebrow and I leaned close to whisper, "If she didn't like it, she wouldn't vacuum it up."

Mrs. B raised the other brow, but her reply was cut off by the doorbell.

Sybil bounced to her feet. "I'll get it."

She returned a few moments later, carrying a leather jacket. Her face was flushed, her eyes wide, and she performed that little head-twitch thing meaning "Look behind me."

I did, fastening my gaze on a tall suntanned man clad in a tight gray sweatshirt with the sleeves sliced away to reveal a set of sculpted biceps. The muscles didn't bulge, but made it clear they packed power. His thighs, in tight jeans, made a similar claim. Hot. This guy was hot with a capital H.

"G'day, ladies. Gabe Hendricks is the name. Physical therapy is my game." His voice, with a trace of an Australian accent, was as smooth as chocolate syrup. "I'm early and it appears you're lunching. Shall I return later?"

"No, no," Mrs. B responded in a breathy voice. "We're just finishing. Have you eaten? We have soup and soufflé—although I fear that has deflated."

"Just the way I like it," he answered, flashing a smile that crinkled the edges of his blue eyes. "I prefer food I can chew."

Fanning herself with her napkin, Sybil tossed the jacket on Verna's bed and trotted to the kitchen. "Would you like coffee, tea, milk, cola, lemonade, apple juice, mineral water?" She paused for breath. "Beer? Wine? Bourbon?"

Gabe laughed, the sound ringing like a bell in my chest. "Tea, please. Any kind is fine. With a dash of milk if it's no trouble."

The rise and fall of his voice felt like fingers tapping along my spine. Suffice it to say this guy pushed my sensory buttons. He could give me physical therapy any old time.

And, lest you think I'm being disloyal to Dave, I contend I may be in a relationship, but I'm not in suspended animation. I retain the right to have a fantasy life. Besides, what happens in that fantasy life could pay off for Dave later on.

"Pull up a chair," Mrs. B said with a catch in her voice. "Anywhere you like."

"Take mine." Iz, the only one of us immune to Gabe, scraped the last bit of soufflé from her plate and stood. "I'll unpack while you 'ladies' bask in the glow of a Y chromosome."

"That was Indigo Zephyr," Mrs. B told Gabe when my sister had rambled off to her lair in the office at the end of the hall. "She goes by Iz. She's here for a few days to, uh, assist Verna."

"And she looks well able to do that." Gabe raised Verna's weak hand to his lips before he sat. "And you must be Verna.

152

No worries about your little setback. We'll be dancing a tango soon."

Verna blushed and fluttered her eyelashes.

As Mrs. B introduced the rest of us, my brain played a movie. I wore a clingy, low-cut red dress and exchanged smoldering glances with Gabe as we glided across a dance floor littered with rose petals.

Sybil set a bowl of soup in front of Gabe with a thump that shattered my tango dream. I reached for my glass and gulped ice water. The resulting brain freeze dispelled the fragments of my fantasy.

Gabe went to work on the soup and soufflé, praising both the food and the way Mrs. B had set up the condo for Verna's recovery. His eyes, as blue as the Caribbean, lingered on each of us as he stressed the importance of supportive friends—and dogs—to the recovery process. He asked each of us about our lives, our interests, and our relationship to Verna. And then he asked a question that set us back on our heels. "The woman who manages this complex, the one who showed me where to park, is she a member of your circle?"

Now, if you've been following the story, you recall that Bernina Burke had been lurking in the parking lot, badgering visitors about parking rules.

"That's Bernina Burke," Mrs. B told him. "I hope she didn't harass you."

"Not a bit. In fact, once I told her why I was here and how often I'd be coming, she showed me to a parking spot under the canopy."

"Under the canopy?" Sybil asked in the same tone you might use for "Another tax increase?"

"Right. Just across the way."

Mrs. B and I exchanged glances. The spaces under the canopy were reserved for owners of two-bedroom units like mine and hers. One covered spot each. Second vehicles, or those owned by residents who dwelled in one-bedroom units, were consigned to an uncovered area beyond the canopy. "I didn't realize there was a vacant spot," she said.

"It has yellow stripes, so maybe it's not an official spot," Gabe clarified.

Darn right it wasn't an official spot. It was for emergency vehicles.

"She gave me a placard and told me I had her permission to park there every time I came." His gaze made a circuit of the table, taking in expressions that merged confusion, amazement, annoyance, and disgust. "Did I put my foot in something? I got the impression she was a friend."

Before Sybil could draw breath, and before Verna could spit out a garbled version of a word some readers might find offensive, I jumped in. "It's possible she's *someone's* friend."

"But we aren't particularly close," Mrs. B overrode me in her most diplomatic tone. "She's the condo manager, after all, and it's necessary for her to remain impartial."

*More like adversarial.*

"It's a businesslike arrangement," Mrs. B went on. "It wouldn't do for her to become too friendly and be accused of showing favoritism toward some residents. She treats us all equally."

*Equally badly.*

"I understand." Gabe forked the last bite of soufflé. "You don't happen to know if she's involved with anyone, do you? She seems like my kind of woman."

# Chapter 19

This time Mrs. B didn't speak fast enough to cover my snort of disgust, Sybil's squawk of disbelief, or the word that emerged from the corner of Verna's mouth. Due to her stroke, it rhymed with "fish" but started with a letter closer to the beginning of the alphabet.

Although her lips moved, Mrs. B didn't speak at all for a few moments. Then her words tumbled out. "What, if I may ask, are the qualities you look for in 'your kind' of a woman?"

Gabe flushed and ducked his head in the endearing way of a little boy. "Well, I'm, uh, intimidated by beautiful, confident women. Have been ever since I can remember." He fixed his gaze on me. "I could never ask you out. I could never work up the nerve."

I was as flattered as I was stunned. Never had I thought of myself as beautiful. And never, ever, ever, would I even pretend to possess much in the way of confidence. "But you could ask Bernina?"

"Yeah. First I'd have to give myself a pep talk. And I'd stock a bottle of liquid consolation to see me through if she turned me down. But then I'd stick my neck out."

He wouldn't have to stick his neck out very far. Bernina was as likely to turn him down as I was likely to skip past the cheesy snack aisle at the supermarket and go for kale instead.

"What, uh, is it about her?" Mrs. B asked. "Other than . . . what you've said."

He pondered while he sipped tea. "Well, I like a woman with a little meat on her bones."

"She's got more than a little," Sybil whispered. "She's got a couple of Virginia hams."

I snorted in delight. "And a twelve-pack of pork chops."

Mrs. B frowned at us. Sybil clapped a hand over her mouth. I studied the ceiling.

"I guess I feel the same about a relationship as I do about my work," Gabe continued. "I want to feel needed. I want to make a difference in someone's life, do them some good."

Verna patted his arm with her good hand, and Mrs. B nodded. "That might do the rest of us some good as well," she murmured.

As I cleared the table and loaded the dishwasher, I tried to imagine Bernina in a relationship and in a less-than-lethal mood. I tried to picture Bernina waving and smiling at condo residents as they came and went, Bernina filling the birdfeeders, Bernina stroking Lola's ears or scratching Cheese Puff's back.

It didn't work. The mental images I conjured were dark and filled with shadows, and I swear I heard sinister music in the background and spotted a few flying monkeys. Both dogs yipped as if they'd conjured similar images. Both scuttled to shelter beneath Verna's bed.

When Mrs. B announced she and Sybil were headed for the mall to shop for towels, I announced I was headed home and called the dogs. Lola emerged from beneath the bed, and sat beside it, making it clear she wasn't leaving Verna. I left her to it, gathered up Cheese Puff, and beat a retreat to my place.

Allison had unglued herself from between the sheets and was sprawled on the sofa watching a makeover show and eating a bowl of cereal laden with bits of sugary something the color of traffic cones. Figuring it would be wasted effort, I passed on studying the garish box in search of nutritional information.

When I noted a substantial milk slosh on the counter, I smiled to myself. Leverage.

As I did laundry, swished the dust mop back and forth along the hallway, and put together the casserole I'd made a mental promise to cook for Dave, I kept my eye on the puddle of milk. After several minutes, I also kept my eye on the sticky spoon and bowl abandoned on the coffee table when Allison went upstairs to shower and dress.

More leverage.

Cheese Puff, having filled up on soufflé and dog treats, ignored Allison's leavings, so the evidence hadn't been corrupted when she made her halting progress down the stairs, texting as she walked. I waited until she'd flopped on the sofa. Then I presented my case.

"Verna's out of the hospital. She's over at Mrs. B's. She'd love to see you."

"Okay."

I folded T-shirts warm from the dryer and counted to 100. "I got a bunch of classic movies for you all to watch this afternoon."

"Okay."

Piling the T-shirts in the laundry basket to be transported upstairs, I moved on to uniting socks with their mates.

(For the record, I had no expectation that each sock in the dryer would find a mate and that I wouldn't be left with at least one bound for the singles' drawer in the dresser. I've done experiments where I matched up dirty socks and sent only pairs into the washer and on to the dryer. Sometimes when the cycles are complete, they all match up. But often one or two go missing. I'm starting to believe scientists don't need to peer into outer space to study black holes. They could study washers and dryers instead.)

Sock mating completed with only one single remaining—a sock I swore I'd never seen before—I resumed my campaign. "It would be really nice if you went next door *soon* and made plans for a time to watch a movie."

Allison's gaze never left her phone. "Okay."

"Like now."

"Okay."

"*Right* now."

"Okay." She glanced my way. "Huh? What?"

"Go over and see Verna and set a time to watch a movie with her. Right now."

Allison sat up, her thumbs still punching phone keys. "Do I have to?"

"No. Not if you'd rather scrub the kitchen floor in exchange for me overlooking your breakfast mess."

Allison's gaze lifted from the phone screen and she took in the bowl and spoon. "It's not a very *big* mess."

The expression "it's the principle of the thing" meant about as much to Allison as advice to make her allowance last all week so she wouldn't ask for more on Wednesday and get turned down. A verbal argument, however, would get me exactly nowhere and eat up a lot of time, so I narrowed my eyes and went for a substitute teacher expression designed to convey the fact that I knew BS when I heard it and didn't expect to listen to a single syllable more.

Allison, of course, had seen the look before, so I added pressed lips to signify I stood ready to fink her out to her father. She levitated from the sofa, rinsed the bowl and spoon, stowed them in the dishwasher, wiped the counter and coffee table, and scooted out the door.

She returned in less than two minutes and began digging through the laundry basket. "Where's my pink shirt? And my new jeans? And why didn't you tell me?"

I scrambled to catch items she cast aside. "Tell you what?"

"Helloooo. Why didn't you tell me about that guy?"

"What guy?"

"The guy over there." Allison plucked the pink top from the bottom of the basket and waved it toward Mrs. B's condo. "The one with the accent."

"Verna's physical therapist?"

"OMG." She raced for the stairs. "He's so hot he's, like, on fire. He's like the surface of the sun."

"And he's, like, twice your age," I called. "And you have a boyfriend."

If she heard, Allison paid no attention, so I let her get on with changing her clothes, applying makeup, and fluffing her hair. Occasionally I giggled a little, anticipating her reaction when she learned Gabe Hendricks thought Bernina Burke was his kind of woman.

I returned from water aerobics to find she was still in the dark about Gabe's romantic leanings. While Dave bolted down casserole, Allison explained the benefits of physical therapy, especially PT of the quality administered by Gabe Hendricks. "He's so good looking and he's so strong, but he's really, really gentle. I bet that makes Verna feel safe and special."

She paused for a dramatic sigh. "And Gabe explains everything and he's really cool about Lola being so protective, and he says he sometimes works for free when people don't have enough insurance, and he smells like soap and like when we go camping in the woods and the wind blows in the pine trees, but not like that stuff you rub on when you pull a muscle. And he said he thought I'd be a natural but I have to take college classes and get good grades and probably get into a special program."

I shot Dave a thumbs-up sign. Seeing Allison interested in a career was a good thing, no matter why—or how suddenly— she'd developed an interest.

"Sounds like something you should check out," Dave said.

"Maybe the career center at school has more information," I suggested as I hung up my damp suit and towel. "And maybe you could do volunteer work and learn more about what's involved. You'd also find out whether there's anything you don't like about being a physical therapist."

"Maybe I could volunteer with Gabe," Allison gushed. "I bet I'd learn lots. I bet he's the best physical therapist anywhere."

Dave raised an eyebrow. I took that to mean he wanted to know more about Gabe—a heck of a lot more. "Tell you later," I mouthed.

"Gotta go clean up my room." Allison darted for the stairs. "Gabe says if you want to be successful, it's important to be neat and organized and know where everything is."

This was also a good thing. Before Thanksgiving, Jim had hit on the idea of claiming to be writing an article about teenagers and chores. He'd persuaded Allison to take part in a time-motion study and keep track of her tasks, the amount of time devoted to each, and how well she accomplished them. For two short weeks, buoyed by the thought of a full-page picture in a magazine, Allison loaded the dishwasher, swept the kitchen floor, and kept her room in a state that didn't remind me quite so much of a landfill. Then the winter holiday break rolled around. Schedules and routines went by the wayside, and she decided months of effort for an article that might never be published added up to too much work for too little reward. Crumbs and clutter ruled once more.

"I don't know who this Gabe guy is," Dave said once we'd heard her door slam. "But if he gets her cleaning up her mess and working harder in school and thinking about a career, I like him. As long as he keeps his hands off my daughter."

"No need to worry." I filled him in on Gabe's interest in Bernina.

"Different strokes." Dave nuked another helping of casserole. "Speaking of strokes, how's Verna doing?"

"The stroke affected her speech and her right side, but not her memory of who we all are. And it didn't affect her ability to follow a conversation and try to respond. She was alert and 'with us' at lunch."

"And your sister? How's she doing with Verna?"

"Surprisingly well." I did a quick mental review of Verna's arrival and our lunch as I drank a large glass of water. "Apparently Iz is drawing on a well of patience she's never tapped before."

"A well you didn't know existed?"

"That, too." I filled the glass again and sat across from him. For a moment I hesitated, but then, talking fast, I went for it. "I cleaned all my stuff out of the office today and Jim says he'll help get the desk out and haul it away later this week, so the space will be all yours to spread out your files. Are you making progress on the case?"

Dave shoveled in more casserole and drummed the fingers of his left hand on the table. I tried to appear as if I'd simply been making conversation and wasn't on the edge of my seat waiting for details. I was willing to bet my next paycheck I wasn't succeeding. But, to my surprise, Dave stopped drumming and started talking.

"If your idea of progress is putting more theories on the table, then I guess we're making a lot. It could be a murder made to look like an accident. A murder made to look like a suicide. A suicide made to look like an accident. A suicide that looks like murder. An accident that looks like a suicide. An accident that looks like murder."

Again, I tried to appear casual. I stood, loaded my empty glass in the dishwasher and stretched. "Well, if telling me about it will help you clear your mind, I'm here. But I picked up a job for tomorrow so I'll be headed upstairs to bed soon."

Dave resumed drumming with his left hand while scraping up the remains of his casserole with the fork in his right. The tune he created was catchy but discordant. Probably not unlike what one of his favorite bands might have come up with if members had bothered to practice. Pretending to ignore him, I opened the door to the deck and called the dogs. "Time to hit the rose garden."

Cheese Puff darted into the drizzly night, barking for me to hurry and open the gate at the far edge of the deck. Lola followed with more of a hitch in her get-along than I'd noticed earlier. When she stumbled mounting the stairs after doing her thing, I made a mental note to call her vet and ask if we should bring her in before her next scheduled appointment.

Dave had moved to the sofa and seemed immersed in the contents of a thick file folder. As you probably can guess, my fingers itched to get a grip on it, but I played it cool and went about cleaning up the kitchen and spooning a helping of casserole into a covered bowl I could tote to school. For good measure I scooped guacamole into a small container and dumped a generous handful of corn chips into a sandwich bag.

Whether I would "need" all of that depended on the quality of my pre-lunch experiences. After a morning that tested every classroom-management skill I possessed, I could devour what I'd packed in less than five minutes and then scope out what others had brought, hoping for a handout. Well, not a handout from Aston Marsden, because I might end up gnawing on six-

year-old homemade buffalo jerky. And not a handout from
Brenda Waring, because her lunches usually involved weird
combinations of ingredients and/or experimental sauces based
on a fusion of cuisines that—in my mind—never should come
within a thousand miles of each other. Most noteworthy was
the mix—or should I say clash?—of ingredients and flavors
from Norway and Samoa.

"If you're dragging your feet thinking I'll let you look at
this," Dave said, "you can keep dragging. You knew Jerome
Morrow. So did dozens of people you hang with. I think Harvey
would say you're too close to the case."

The "I think" in the last sentence was a tip-off that Dave
hadn't discussed this with Harvey Goodspeed, but was shifting
the blame to his substantial shoulders. It took me fewer than
two seconds to respond. "And I wasn't too close to the Henry
Stoddard case? The one where your buddy Detective Atwell
accused me of murder? Or the Jessica Flint case? The one
where your buddy also thought I was guilty? And then there—"

Dave closed the file. "This is different."

# Chapter 20

"Different how? How is the Jerome Morrow case different?" I refrained from stomping my feet, but only barely. "And why does that matter if it's possible I can help you solve it? Remember how I figured out Woodrow Krammer was killed with a gardening tool? Or the time I arranged things so Jackie DeWill confessed to the murder of Big Shiny? And don't tell me you're holding back because you're working with Harvey Goodspeed this time. You were working with him then, too."

Dave set the file on the coffee table. "I don't want to argue."

"Then don't." I stretched out a hand. "Give me the file."

"I can't give it to you." He stood, walked around me to the pantry, and retrieved a couple of large paper bags. "I'm going to the office to go through my desk. Don't wait up. I'll close the door so I won't disturb your sleep."

For a full minute after the office door closed, I stared at the file on the coffee table, my mind churning. Had he left it there as a test? Would he count to 100, and then swoop in and catch me peeking?

Or, scenario two, had he intended for me to look? After all, he'd used the verb "give." Did that mean he couldn't physically hand it to me, but wouldn't object if I strolled across the room and read through it while he was elsewhere?

And if I opened it, then discovered he'd intended scenario one instead of two, what was the worst that could happen?

I pondered for half a minute. The worst was he'd be angry or disappointed—probably both. Perhaps he'd give me a lecture about boundaries and controlling my curiosity. Perhaps he'd even mention that I interpreted every sign and rule and direction as having a footnote reading "except for Barbara Reed." Perhaps he'd threaten to stick to secrecy from now on and never share a single detail of a case.

If that was the worst, it wasn't too bad. And, after I apologized, admitted he was right about my lack of control, and confessed I was a sorry excuse for a fiancée, he'd forgive me.

Okay, in the interest of making it crystal clear that he wasn't a complete waffle, he might not forgive me immediately. But I was 99.726% certain he'd forgive me within 48 hours. And I was 100% certain forgiveness would be followed by the kind of bedroom activity we'd both enjoyed last night.

As I'm sure you knew I would, I decided to go for the tradeoff.

Vowing to put everything back exactly as it was, I scurried to the coffee table and opened the file.

Several times in the hours to come I almost wished I hadn't. The images captured in the photos inside the file remained burned in my brain through the night and on into the next day. As I took attendance in Contemporary World Problems and reminded seniors they had only one more semester to accumulate enough credits to graduate, bring up their GPAs, or take on extracurricular projects to impress the nice folks in college admissions offices, the scene inside Jerome Morrow's garage was superimposed over the classroom.

He lay on his back by one end of a workbench, angled between it and a pickup truck I assumed was his. I wouldn't have recognized him by his clothing. Instead of his usual gray suit and black leather shoes, he wore navy blue running shoes, jeans, a brown corduroy jacket, gray leather work gloves, and a black ball cap with "Captain Meriwether High School" embroidered on the visor in gold thread. The surface of the wooden workbench was bare except for a vise clamped to one end, and a wire brush and can of lubricating oil near the other. A large rectangular piece of what I assumed was plywood had been fixed to the wall above the bench and painted white. It was a study in organization, complete with outlines drawn in black marker to indicate where each of the smaller tools should be secured on hooks or in brackets.

The shelves beneath the bench were filled with cardboard boxes of varying sizes, each labeled to indicate the contents—nails, screws, bolts, wire, miscellaneous. Shovels, rakes, a weed trimmer, and other gardening tools hung from clips on the wall to the right. To the left of the bench was a door, solid except for a window covered with metal mesh. A lawn mower, its front wheels on a low concrete sill, butted up against the base of the door.

According to what I'd learned from scanning details of the autopsy report, carbon monoxide, most likely released by the gas-powered engine of that lawn mower, killed Jerome Morrow. Blows to the point of his chin and the back of his head possibly incapacitated him long enough for him to inhale a lethal quantity of the gas.

Was this murder? Did someone strike him, start the lawn mower, and leave him to die?

Was this suicide made to look like murder? Did he fire up the lawn mower, club himself somehow with something, and lie on the floor to await death?

Or was this an accident? Did he crank the mower and then fall and bash his head? Twice?

166

Or did he fall and then, confused and disoriented, fall again, get up, and somehow find enough focus and coordination to start the mower?

The accident sequences didn't track.

I could sell myself on one accidental blow to the head. But two?

The murder scenario seemed like a stretch. In general, motives for murder abounded—money, love or lust, property disputes, politics, revenge, drugs, or frustration, to name a few. But not one of those seemed to fit this case. No one who knew him could imagine Morrow using or selling narcotics, and no trace of drugs had been found in the cabin or in his home or truck. This hadn't been a robbery gone wrong. His wallet was still in his pocket, the truck was in place, and his expensive TV hadn't been touched. And neighbors who lived near his home in Reckless River and the cabin in the country painted him as helpful and generous with his time.

His death also wasn't due to a dispute over an inheritance. Morrow's parents had died years before, leaving next to nothing. His sole relative, an elderly second cousin, was well off. In addition, Morrow had no interest in politics, had never married, and hadn't left a visible trail of women done wrong. And as far as co-workers were concerned, sure, there were a few teachers—female and male—who carped about him. But they carped about every administrator. Had one of them become unhappy enough to commit murder? It seemed preposterous. But perhaps Morrow had a secret life. A really secret life.

As the bell rang at the end of first period, I recalled history teacher Henry Stoddard had been strangled by Susan Mitchell, chair of his department. But Susan, at the time, had been a dozen potatoes short of a bushel. Unbalanced by her dysfunctional marriage, she'd focused her energy on efforts to make the history department a shining example for other schools in the state. Stoddard, who prided himself on being a speed bump on the highway to educational rethinking and revision, had refused to change his curriculum or methods. Susan had snapped and—

The sounds of chattering voices and shuffling feet shattered my memories of the morning I found Stoddard strangled with one of his own outdated ties. I took attendance, gave this fresh batch of seniors my spiel, and set them to work filling in the names of countries and capitals on blank maps of South America. When all was quiet—or as quiet as it gets in the average high school classroom—my mind drifted again to the question of why someone would murder Jerome Morrow.

When the bell rang at the end of second period, I had nothing.

When the bell rang at the end of third period and I headed for the teachers' room where I hung out, I still had nothing. Or at least nothing except random-stranger or thrill-killer homicide theories.

And I had no reason why Morrow would have killed himself. He had no health problems and no money issues. According to neighbors, he enjoyed reading, fishing, walking in the forest, and taking photographs. He claimed to be looking forward to retirement, making a bucket list of national parks he wanted to visit.

When I reached the teachers' room, I found all my theories and doubts being covered and expounded upon. Ardie asked me if I knew anything that wasn't in the paper, but I shook my head. Technically, I knew lots of stuff that wasn't for public consumption, but I didn't let on that I'd read Dave's file and seen photos of the scene because A) I'd crossed a line, and B) what I'd seen hadn't led me to realistic answers. Telling myself Ardie would understand my lie, I ate my reheated casserole and listened as speculation ranged from serious to the seriously bizarre.

"Some people think cities are dangerous," Aston Marsden said, "but I'm here to tell you the forest isn't a playground. There are some killer critters in those mountains."

"Like coyotes and wolves and bears?" Brenda Waring asked.

"You bet. And cougars."

"So, you're saying a cougar killed Jerome?" Ardie shot a wink in my direction. "Seems if that was true we'd be hearing about a big hunt underway."

"There are other critters in the mountains," Aston answered in a low and ominous voice. "Bigger and bolder and scarier critters."

We were all silent for a few seconds, and then Doug Whitman leaned over, pinched my arm, and winked. "Like Bigfoot?"

Everyone chuckled. Everyone except Aston. "Maybe," he said.

"Have you seen one?" Brenda leaned forward and peered at him, a lock of hair falling across one eye. The hair was a sickly olive green, dull and frizzy. Brenda's efforts to salvage her do following an abortive cut and dye job back in November were not going well. "A Sasquatch? Have you actually seen one?"

"I've seen more than one." Aston smacked his palm on the table. "And not all that far from right here."

Another silence followed, and then Gertrude Suttle laughed. "Were you swilling your homebrew shortly before you spotted them?"

"Or eating the elk meat you buried in the sand to cure?" Ardie asked. "The meat we voted unanimously not to allow you to bring into this room?"

"If I recall," Doug added, "we voted it out of the school as well."

Aston bristled. "There was nothing wrong with that meat."

"Once you got past the smell," Brenda said.

"And the appearance," Doug added. "But back to Bigfoot. Why would he kill Jerome Morrow?"

"And if he did," Ardie mused, "wouldn't you think he'd kill him out in the woods? Not in a garage."

Aston shrugged.

"You don't have an answer, do you?" Brenda laughed in a snarky way that signified their relationship—if that's what you could call a few close encounters separated by deluges of disgust—was off again. "Next you'll say space aliens killed Jerome. You'll tell us the hills are crawling with little green men."

"They're not green," Aston muttered. "They're kind of silvery."

Gertrude made a timeout sign with her hands. "Change of subject. Did anyone listen to Rick Rivers this morning?"

Doug shot me a grimace of apology. "Call me a masochist, but after the paper took him to task and he made a half-hearted apology for 'crossing a line,' I had to know if he'd be able to leave it alone."

"I bet he couldn't," Ardie said.

"You win. He was in rant overdrive this morning about public education. He wants the school board to clean house, fire every administrator, and ax any teacher who's been in the classroom more than five years."

Gertrude glanced around the table. "That leaves you eating lunch all alone, Doug. Unless they hire Barbara."

"Since his plan calls for the whole board to resign after the firing is finished, I don't know who would do the hiring."

"Big Chill," I suggested.

Ardie grinned. "She'd love that. Finally she'd be on the throne instead of the power behind it."

"And she might make some good choices." Gertrude smiled at Ardie. "After all, she was the one who recruited you and assigned you to share this space with us."

As I recalled, that hadn't gone well. At least not for the first few days. Due to a warped sense of loyalty to Susan Mitchell whose chair had remained empty since her arrest, and a resistance to change that wasn't her idea, Gertrude hadn't welcomed Ardie. But, after Ardie solved the mystery behind the thefts from the Family Support Room, they'd become fast friends.

"I bet I know more about the latest Paris fashions than Rick Rivers knows about education." Aston turned to me, his beard shedding crumbs on his faded plaid flannel shirt. "Where'd he go to college?"

I thought for a few moments about the days when I worked for Rivers. He'd never displayed a framed diploma and had never engaged in a conversation with me to compare and contrast courses of study. Although he'd had nothing positive to say about higher education, he'd never zeroed in on a particular school. "I have no idea."

"I bet he didn't go to college," Brenda said.

"Or flunked out if he managed to get accepted." Aston aimed a finger at me. "You should find out."

"I could do that," I said, trying not to think about the source of the rusty red stain on the cuff of his shirt, "but I don't see the point. A degree wouldn't have been a requirement for the job."

"You mean any uneducated fool can talk on the radio?"

"If the fool can put together complete sentences and attract an audience large enough to allow salespeople to sign up advertisers, then there wouldn't be many objections."

"What can we do to stop him?" Brenda asked after a moment. "What if we picketed the radio station or something?"

"That would set him up to say we should be working on lesson plans or grading papers," Gertrude said. "And then he'd probably go on to do the math, subtracting the required number of school days from the total in the year and calling the rest of it a paid vacation."

"As if we never work on weekends," Brenda said. "Or evenings."

"Money talks," Doug stated. "If we complain or boycott or somehow put pressure on his advertisers—a lot of pressure— management would get the message."

"Well, let's find out who they are and tighten the screws." Aston aimed the finger at Doug. "Make a list."

Doug groaned. "That means I have to listen to him again."

"Unless you can think of a better way."

Doug shot me a hopeful look. I held my hands up, palms out. "Can't help. My last friendly contact over there was downsized months ago."

"It won't kill you to listen," Aston told Doug.

"It might raise my blood pressure into the danger zone," Doug said.

"You're young. Your heart can take it."

"And you're tough. Why don't you do it?"

"Truck radio's broken," Aston said.

"Listen at home. Before you leave for school."

"Listen on what?" Brenda asked in a snarky voice. "The man doesn't own a radio. Or a TV. Or an appliance manufactured since Reagan left the White House."

"And what's wrong with that?" Aston fumed. "My refrigerator keeps stuff cold. My washer washes."

"Not well," Brenda huffed. "That shirt is a disgrace."

"I'll help Doug." I crammed my words in before Aston could respond and their argument escalated to the point where Ardie and Gertrude demanded they both get out. "But I'm sick of talking about Rick Rivers. Can we change the subject?"

"Definitely," Gertrude agreed. "How do you think Tremaine will do as acting principal?"

The consensus was he'd do well and certainly be more visible. Only Aston grumped. "He'll be like any big dog that comes into a new territory and has to make his mark on every tree and bush."

"Then maybe you'd better shave," Brenda said in a sweet voice, "because you look more like shrubbery than—"

The bell drowned out the rest of her comment.

I scurried away, leaving Aston fuming and Brenda making air marks to tally her score.

# Chapter 21

At the end of the afternoon, most seniors in my classes were closer to knowing a few of the nations in South America. I, on the other hand, was no closer to a viable theory about how Jerome Morrow met his death. In fact, I'd abandoned theorizing shortly after lunch and moved on to trying to figure out what bothered me about the crime scene photos I'd sneaked a peek at last night. In the middle of fifth period it hit me—everything in the garage was in a place marked for it, or a place where it seemed to belong on a temporary basis—like the wire brush and oil can. But not the lawn mower. The killer lawn mower. It was up against the door I assumed led to the back yard, its front wheels on a low sill extending out several inches from the door.

And that was odd.

There was plenty of room for it along the side wall between a clipping-catching bag and hooks for safety glasses, earmuffs, and work gloves. Although Jerome Morrow hadn't drawn an outline of the mower, I guessed that's where he normally kept it.

If the state of his workbench was any indication, he was, if not obsessive, then at least extremely neat. So why was the lawn mower against the door?

The wire brush and oil indicated he'd been cleaning and oiling it—a task I would have done in the open space in front of the workbench where I could move around. If he'd wanted to elevate the front wheels for some reason, it seemed he would have used a couple of the bricks he'd shoved—with great precision—beneath the workbench. On the other hand, maybe the bricks made for an unstable platform. On another other hand, the sill seemed far too low. It wouldn't elevate the wheels enough for him to see the underside of the mower unless he flopped on the garage floor.

I didn't see him as the flopping type.

But there was a lot I didn't know about Jerome Morrow. And there was a whole lot I didn't know about lawn mowers. What I did know was the ones I'd used never started the first time, their tanks were always close to empty, and the gas can was usually in the same condition.

But, from the number and variety of tools, I assumed Jerome Morrow knew a heck of a lot more than I did. Maybe he could take a lawn mower apart in his sleep. Maybe he could build one from scrap metal found along the highway.

I wished I could call Dave and ask him what he thought. But that would be admitting I'd looked at the file. Of course, he knew I had. And, of course I knew he knew. But as long as I didn't admit it, he had deniability.

When I left school, the rain was doing what it does best during a Northwest winter, racketing off cars in the parking lot, sweeping in waves across the asphalt, and riding a gusting wind to spatter my glasses. Only when I got in the car and wiped them off did I check my cellphone. The text from Dave had come in almost an hour earlier. It read: "Sorry. I did all I could. Out of my control. Sorry."

"Sorry about what?" I asked the phone as I searched for a voice message, a clue of any kind. "What's out of your control?"

My mind swirling with images of what that could be and how far out of control it was, I called his cell. Naturally, I got a hollow and disinterested voice suggesting I leave a message. So I did. "What? What happened? What couldn't you do anything about? Are you trying to scare me out of my mind? Call me. Call me now. Right now!"

I started the car and ordered myself to remain calm.

(For the record, I knew darn well that wouldn't work. It never has. And yet, time after time, I continue to tell myself to take deep breaths and believe everything will work out. I tell myself to slow down, think clearly, and not jump to conclusions. Further for the record, yes, I'm aware doing the same thing over and over and expecting a different outcome is a snapshot of insanity.)

And so, 180 degrees from a state of calm, and perhaps temporarily not in possession of all my marbles, I drove home as if I was in mile 499 at Daytona and attempting to pass the leader.

Cheese Puff greeted me at the door, barking and spinning in circles, then racing to the door to the deck and back again.

Lola was nowhere to be seen.

Probably next door, I told myself.

But why wasn't Cheese Puff there as well?

Had Mrs. B brought him home because he'd interfered with Verna's physical therapy?

If so, why wasn't he sulking in his chair? Why was he so frantic?

With the Puffster under my arm, I dashed next door.

Lola didn't greet me there, either.

Verna, Sybil, and Mrs. B sat at the dining room table, a three-pound box of gourmet chocolates in front of them. The box was half empty.

Or, if you're a positive sort, the box was half full.

176

But never mind that.

I happened to recall the box was still inside its plastic wrapper when I was here yesterday. And I happened to know Mrs. B held a semi-firm belief chocolate should not be eaten before noon unless it was contained in a mug of cocoa or a breakfast croissant. That meant these women—all of whom took watching their weight far more seriously than I did—had consumed a pound and a half of chocolate candies since noon. And, since my sister was nowhere to be seen, they'd apparently done that without her help.

Further, if my suspicions were correct and this chocolate bingeing was connected to Dave's text, they'd consumed the chocolates within the past hour.

More alarming than the candy consumption, however, was the broken necklace beside the box. Pearls lay scattered on the tablecloth. A few had rolled from the table and bounced as far as the living room. One winked from beside the refrigerator. Another had made it to the pantry.

Mrs. B's necklaces were high quality. I'd never known one to break during normal wear. And I was darn sure that, in ordinary times, she would have gathered up the pearls immediately.

Hands fluttering, Sybil leaped to her feet and ran to me. "She didn't want to go. He had a badge. There was nothing we could do."

Mrs. B clarified. "An officer came for Lola. He had an order from the chief to take her to the police station for reassignment. We made him show it to us. We protested. But . . . well, he dragged her off."

This was what Dave meant by his text.

Feeling sick and dizzy, I hugged Cheese Puff until he whimpered.

"We said she wasn't ready to go back to drug duty," Sybil said between sobs. "She hasn't been cleared by her vet. Her limp was worse today."

"Wursh," Verna echoed.

"I argued, with him, of course," Mrs. B said. "We all did. Iz got so worked up she tried to punch him. Sybil grabbed her arm and stopped her."

"I did," Sybil confirmed. "I hung on like a koala. And I said if he arrested her, I'd go to jail too."

Tears stung my eyes. My sister and my friends were a little odd, but they were the best. "Where's Iz now?"

"I gave her the keys to my car," Mrs. B said. "I begged her to go for a drive and cool down."

(For the record, this demonstrated clearly that not only did Mrs. B have way more money than I did, but she was far more willing to trust and take chances. Even if I could afford to replace my car by simply writing a check, I'd never beg Iz to drive it. At least not if I was in my right mind. See, my sister's driving skills rival those of Allison—meaning those skills are, to put it mildly, severely limited. They both lack focus, are erratic, and pose a danger to other drivers. And that's when they're relatively calm.)

"Poor Lola." Tears streamed down Sybil's cheeks. "She cried all the way to his car. And he didn't help her get up on the seat."

Verna sniffled and wiped her eyes with the back of her good hand.

I carried Cheese Puff to her and placed him in her lap. He circled as if looking for a soft place to curl up, then stood on his hind legs, licked her chin, and snuggled against her neck.

"This is all my fault. Every bit of it." Without checking to see whether it was light or dark or what the filling might be,

Mrs. B snatched a piece of chocolate from the box and popped it in her mouth. "My pearls failed me. And I failed Lola."

Sybil rushed to wrap her arms around her friend. "There was nothing you could do."

"Maybe not this afternoon, but there was plenty I should have done before this." Mrs. B broke from Sybil's grasp. "When I saw your expression the day we walked by the river, and realized I was trying to project my plans for your future onto your ideas, I decided to try to break my pattern of being a meddling busybody. I decided I couldn't solve everything by pulling strings or writing checks. I didn't stop to think about how taking a blanket approach could affect my friends. And Lola."

She plucked two pieces of chocolate from the box and crammed them in her mouth. Then she jerked a pearl ring from her finger and threw it in the sink. It clanged against the side and fell into the garbage disposal.

Clearly the situation had gone from serious to grim.

Clearly it was time for me to halt this death spiral of blame and guilt.

Clearly I required chocolate.

I shed my coat, hung it over the back of a chair with my purse, and went for two dark chocolate pieces, ones with curving bumps that suggested cashews inside. "Let's all sit and be still for a minute."

To my surprise, even Cheese Puff sat. To my greater surprise, he didn't cast a single glance toward the box of chocolates.

I ate the first piece of chocolate in about three seconds. I made the other last perhaps a quarter of a minute. "This isn't good, but it isn't the end of the world."

"It will be if we don't get Lola back," Sybil said.

Verna nodded.

Mrs. B moaned.

Cheese Puff yipped his agreement.

"Okay, so we're at the point where we see the end of the world looming. But it's not here yet." I picked out another chunk of chocolate, this one with rounded bulges I hoped were hazelnuts. "Let's put our emotions aside and think about what we can do."

"What I can do is get my checkbook and go down to the police station and buy Lola back," Mrs. B vowed. "No matter what it costs."

"Let's go." Sybil clapped her hands. "Let's go now."

I shook my head and nibbled my chocolate. "Let's think before we rush off. When I brought that idea up with Dave a few days ago, he was concerned the HR person would raise a stink and the chief might feel manipulated and dig in his heels."

"Then we'll go over his head." Mrs. B scraped loose pearls into a pile. "I'll call the mayor, our legislators, the governor. If that doesn't work, I'll go higher."

I had no doubt she would. And I had no doubt she wouldn't find herself talking to someone at the bottom of a staff totem pole. Mrs. B forked out a lot of dough to politicians she supported.

"Any other time I'd say that was a great plan. But when I mentioned a similar idea to Dave, he was concerned there might be some . . . well, backlash directed at him."

"You mean they'd punish him for loving a dog?" Sybil asked.

"That's not exactly how they'd view it. But, yeah, they could demote him or transfer him to another department, change his shift so he worked nights."

"Punishment is what it boils down to." Mrs. B thumped her fists on the table. "I feel so helpless."

"Schteel," Verna whispered.

"Yes." Sybil pumped a fist in the air. "We'll steal her."

Mrs. B seemed to consider the ethics of that for three seconds, then snatched up her cellphone. "Yes. We'll steal her and hide her. I'll call Dario."

Sybil leaped to her feet. "I'll go change to something black."

Before I could smile at the mental image of Sybil as a ninja warrior or gasp at the image of Dario in commando gear, the phone in Mrs. B's hand rang.

"It's Iz," she announced as she clicked it on. "Hel— Slow down. Say that again. No, no, I'm sure you did all you could. Where are you now? Yes, she's here. Good. All right. We'll be there in a jiffy."

I stood and yanked on my coat as Mrs. B delivered the gist of the call. "Iz followed the officer downtown to the police station. Lola broke away from him. He couldn't catch her. Iz called, but Lola wouldn't come to her. She ran across the street and almost got hit by a truck. Iz lost sight of her. She's driving in circles hoping to spot her, asking anyone she comes across if they saw a loose dog."

I pulled out my phone to text Dave—in case he hadn't already heard through the grapevine. I ended the message with "GET BACK TO ME NOW."

"Let's go help search." Sybil darted for the door to the parking lot, Cheese Puff close on her heels. "I'll get my car."

Mrs. B snatched at the back of her fuzzy yellow sweater. "What about Verna?"

Verna nodded toward the door and pointed at herself with her good hand. "Um fine."

"Of course you are." With hesitant steps and a glance at the door, Sybil returned to the table and rested a hand on Verna's shoulder. "But someone needs to stay here so you don't do something silly."

"Ike wha?"

"Like eat the rest of the chocolate." Sybil put the lid on the box and sat beside her friend. "Or decide you can drive downtown and help hunt for Lola."

"Uh cuh."

"I know you could," Mrs. B assured her as she retrieved a rain jacket and a pair of rubber boots from the closet. "But you should stay here with Cheese Puff and—"

"Cheese Puff's coming," I told her. "I don't know if he knows how to track, or if he could follow Lola in this rain, but maybe if we get close he'll smell her. Or hear her. And I think Verna should come, too. Lola's stressed, but she feels a bond to Verna and that might override everything else."

Verna beamed.

"That means I can come," Sybil crowed.

"Okay. But call Jim and ask him to drive," Mrs. B said as she charged toward the door to the parking lot. "As nervous and upset as you are, you're liable to crash into something before you leave the parking lot."

I scooped up Cheese Puff and followed, digging my car keys from my purse. When we were belted in, I backed out of my covered space, set the wipers on high, and took off with no regard for the many 7-mile-an-hour speed limit signs Bernina Burke had posted recently. For once, I didn't wonder how she'd arrived at that number. In fact, I was so focused on getting downtown that, when Bernina emerged from her office and pointed a finger at me, I resisted the urge to plow through the storm water running in the gutter and douse her with a mini tidal wave.

"I'll never forgive myself if anything happens to Lola," Mrs. B moaned.

Cheese Puff whined and licked her cheek.

"I know. You're worried. You love her, too." She scratched his little orange ears. "We'll find her. I'll call the other members of the Committee and get them on the job."

"And call Allison and Josh." I tossed her my phone. "Have them patrol around the condo in case Lola comes back. And see if Dave responded to my text."

"He hasn't yet." She set the phone on the console and got busy punching numbers on hers. I got busy wondering what Dave was doing that was more important than assuring me he got my message and was searching for Lola.

Sundown was approaching at the speed of dark, and my headlights did little to carve a tunnel through the gloom. Even at their top speed, the wipers struggled to clear the windshield of a mix of rain, slushy snow, and ice pellets. I glanced over my shoulder and saw that, for once, forgetfulness had paid off. The boots I'd worn last weekend when Dave and I had joined other volunteers clearing ivy from along one of the many city trails, were where I'd left them—on the floor in the back. Beside them were Dave's boots, a couple of pairs of thick socks, and two umbrellas. Not that those umbrellas would do much good. Gusting wind would turn them inside out in no time.

Mrs. B finished her final call and wiped condensation from the passenger window. "Surely, with her leg the way it is, Lola couldn't run far. Right?"

# Chapter 22

I hesitated before I burst her bubble. "Lola's freaked out, so she might ignore the pain and push it. And the cold may numb her leg."

"So she could go a long way. She might even be back at the condo by now."

"She could be. She knows the way. We walked downtown several times before she broke her leg."

Mrs. B seized her phone, punched in a number, and gave instructions for a few members of the Committee to patrol the streets between the condo and downtown.

"There. We've covered that base." Her take-charge tone gave way to sadness and doubt. "But if what you say is true, and she pushes too hard, she could be crippled for life."

"Lots of dogs do fine on three legs," I assured her.

"I suppose. And they'd have to retire her, right?"

I didn't know the answer, so I hedged. "Probably."

"But . . . what if she feels betrayed because we didn't stop that officer from taking her? What if she doesn't come back?"

I wanted to assure Mrs. B Lola would return, but I wasn't sure I believed it. I patted her shoulder. She squeezed my hand.

If Lola didn't return home, where would she go?

My mind tossed up ideas that exploded like fireworks. And, like fireworks, they fizzled and drifted as ash. Lola had been dozens of places with Dave, mostly drug houses. She'd been to the sandwich shop. She'd been to the high school many times when Dave picked up Allison and she'd gotten plenty of attention from Allison's friends.

Mrs. B's phone rang. "Yes, Iz. Where? Slow down and say that again. Okay. Around back. Got it."

She punched the phone off. "She's behind the courthouse."

I stomped on the gas. "Has she got Lola?"

"No. But she's with someone who saw two men take her."

I punched the gas harder. Mrs. B pressed one hand against the dashboard and hugged Cheese Puff to her chest. In less than a minute we jounced across a speed bump and onto a parking lot thick with signs warning that spaces were for law enforcement or court personnel only. I paid them no mind. I felt no fear. And not simply because it was going on 5:00 and the lot was nearly empty. No, I felt like I'd donned a cloak of invincibility. I, after all, just moments ago, had disregarded Bernina Burke's speed limit signs. And lived to tell the tale.

More signage warned violators would have their vehicles towed and face stiff fines. The cloak of invincibility slipped.

"The fine is on me." Mrs. B punched at her phone. "I'll call Jim and tell him where we are. There's my car. And there's Iz. In that doorway."

I skidded to a stop behind Mrs. B's car, turned the key, and leaped out. My sister gripped the grimy shirt collar of a scrawny man with square front teeth and an overbite a beaver would brag about. He wore a puffy jacket unzipped partway. I assumed Iz had shoved it down his shoulders to immobilize his upper arms, not to make his outfit more stylish.

She raised her chin in greeting and lifted her captive so his feet left the ground and he danced in the air like a hanged man, his hands flapping. His untied shoelaces, knotted and frayed, flicked at his ankles like tiny whips.

185

"This little weasel is named Ennis," Iz said. "His friends took Lola."

"Not my friends," he yelped. "I told you. Chef and Stringer. Don't know their real names. Never met them until the cops threw me in jail. For no reason."

"Happens to me all the time," Iz snarled. "No sympathy. Why did they take her?"

"No idea."

I mounted the three granite steps to the doorway and peered into his muddy brown eyes. "*Why* did they take her?"

His gaze shifted up and away. "They didn't *take* her. She was by a bail bond place. They called her and she went with them."

"It didn't happen that way. Lola wouldn't go with a stranger." Iz lifted and shook.

He danced again, one cracked leather shoe coming loose and falling to the steps. The sock it revealed was, to my surprise, bright white.

"Okay, okay. They cornered her. And used their belts to make a leash. And tied a plastic bag around her mouth." He raised his hands as high as he could, miming tying a knot. "One of those newspaper bags. So she wouldn't bite."

"If they tied it so she can't breathe," Iz hissed, "I'll do the same to them. And to you for standing by."

"She was breathing," he yelped. "She kinda barked some."

I prodded his chest with a closed fist. "*Why* did they take her?"

"I don't know."

Iz kicked his shoe and sent it tumbling down the steps and into a puddle.

"Aww. Look what you did," he whined. "My foot will freeze."

"Too bad."

I smiled at my sister. It felt good to be on the same team. Especially since we usually weren't.

"Why did they take her?" I repeated.

Iz shook him again and the other shoe followed its mate. "Your pants are going next," she threatened. "In five minutes you'll be stark naked."

"You can't do this to me," he howled. "It's illegal."

"Ask me if I care."

"I'll have you arrested."

"Been there. Done that." Iz gestured at the rain-pounded parking lot. "First you'll have to find a cop eager to come out in this weather for an upstanding, tax-paying citizen like yourself." She shook him again, this time so hard I heard his teeth snap together.

"Revenge," he yowled. "Maybe ransom. That dog was with the cops that busted up their lab and took their crystal."

Meth cooks.

And probably meth users.

I'd been worried before, but now my anxiety increased exponentially. These guys would be about as stable as a champagne flute balanced on ball bearings atop an ice floe in a choppy sea. If their scheme fell apart, or if they decided to ditch their plans, Lola wouldn't live to make it home.

I grabbed the front of his shirt. "Where did they take her?"

"I dunno."

I gathered fabric in my fists until I heard him gasp for air. "Where did they take her?"

"I can't . . . They'll hurt me if I tell."

"And we'll hurt you if you don't." I tightened my grip.

"They'll hurt me bad."

"We'll hurt you worse," Iz threatened.

While he was weighing that, something green fluttered at the edge of my vision and Mrs. B said, "They can't hurt you if

187

they can't find you. Tell us where they took Lola and you can have this money and a one-way bus ticket to anywhere in the country."

The muddy brown eyes widened and his lips moved as he counted the bills fanned out in her hand. "A thousand dollars," he croaked.

I smiled to myself. It appeared when Mrs. B gave up on her vow not to resolve problems by throwing money at them, she jumped in with both feet. It also appeared she carried around a lot more mad money than I did. At least $987 more.

"A thousand dollars and a bus ticket," Mrs. B prompted. "Someplace warm, perhaps?"

I relaxed my grip. The muddiness in his eyes seemed to clear for a moment and I saw a gleam. "Arizona? Florida?"

"Up to you," Mrs. B reminded him. "Just tell us where they took Lola and you can be on a bus tonight."

"Or you and your wardrobe go separate ways." Iz lifted him a few inches and shook.

His head bobbled on his skinny neck and he blurted, "The park."

"Which park?" I demanded.

"By the bridge."

I groaned. The park by the bridge was my least favorite place in Reckless River. The lighting, marginal on a clear night, would be only a few degrees better than worthless given the fog and rain. But that wasn't the only thing that made me avoid the place. Years ago two little boys had been killed and buried there and few argued when people claimed their ghosts haunted the area. Although trees and bushes were kept trimmed and the huge expanse of lawn mowed, hardly anyone picnicked or played games there. Every year the city council debated improvements to make the park more attractive, and every year they kicked the can down the road.

I tightened my grip again. "*Where* in the park?"

"Down the bank. There's a shelter. By the river."

*Crap.*

Have I mentioned how much I fear falling into the Columbia again? Especially in the winter? And at night?

But this wasn't about me. This was about Lola. I damped down my fears and stared into those muddy and muddled eyes. "Which side of the bridge?"

"West." His eyes seemed to bounce back and forth. "No. East. Yeah, east."

"You better not be lying."

"I'm not."

"We'll see," Mrs. B told him in a soft but steely voice. "If you are, you'll be dealt with."

*Dealt with!*

*Yes!*

I almost punched a fist in the air.

Mrs. B was back in full take-charge, take-no-prisoners mode.

# Chapter 23

Folding the money, Mrs. B slid it into the pocket of a shirt that might have been white around the time Clinton started his second term. "A friend of ours will take you to the bus depot. When we find Lola, I'll call and he'll buy your ticket. Understand?"

Ennis nodded.

"Good." She glanced over her shoulder. "Here he is now."

Iz and I released him and he wobbled like an inflatable beach toy. And then Jim vaulted up the steps, and clamped a hand on his arm. Mrs. B gave instructions and Jim hauled Ennis to the parking lot.

"What about my shoes?" the scrawny man wailed.

Jim dragged him to the puddle where he retrieved his soggy shoes. Verna and Sybil, mouths agape, watched from inside Sybil's car, probably assuming Jim would stuff Ennis in with them.

But Mrs. B had other plans. "Give Jim your keys, Barbara. You'll drive Verna and Sybil to the park. Iz will drive me and the little prince. I have phone calls to make."

Hearing her issue orders made me feel like someone lit a candle in a dark corner of my heart. Somehow, some way, this would all work out. I tossed Jim my keys. "Dave's boots are in the back. Ennis can have them. And the dry socks, too."

It was, I thought, the least Dave could do.

I retrieved my boots and socks and hustled to Sybil's car, a cotton-candy pink hybrid model with crocheted seat covers. Verna, swaddled in a wool blanket, occupied the front passenger seat. Sybil sat in the back, beside the folded wheelchair and walker. After I unzipped my jacket and used my T-shirt to wipe the rain from my glasses, I spent a minute getting the hang of powering up. I could have cut that time by 50 seconds if I'd ignored Sybil's directions. They were detailed and descriptive, but made about as much sense to me as a crash course in quantum physics delivered in Swedish.

The wipers and defroster on Sybil's car were marginally better than mine. Or perhaps it just seemed that way because the rain was letting up and the fog lifting to rooftop level. I explained where we were headed and relayed the gist of the conversation with the weasel, and details of Mrs. B's intervention.

"Puhls," Verna said.

"That's right." Sybil leaned forward and patted her friend's shoulder. "She did it without her pearls."

"Feffer."

"Yes," Sybil translated. "Just like Dumbo the little elephant when he discovered he could fly without his magic feather."

Somehow the analogy didn't seem the least bit odd. In fact, given the group I hung with, it seemed perfectly appropriate.

In a few minutes we reached the street that ran by the park and I pulled up behind Mrs. B's luxury car. While Sybil was explaining—unnecessarily—how to power off, and I was telling her to get behind the wheel and run the engine enough to keep the car warm for Verna, a familiar vehicle screeched up behind ours.

Dave leaped out.

I did likewise, meeting him at the rear bumper and landing a punch on the shoulder of his rain-soaked jacket. "This is your fault."

I punched him again. "If anything happens to Lola, I will never speak to you again. Never!"

"I'll deserve that," he said in a rational voice. "I'm sorry, Barbara. I'm so sorry."

Naturally, his tone made me furious enough to land two more punches. Then my sister wrapped her arms around me and pulled me off.

"He tried to stop them from coming to get Lola," she said.

"Baloney."

"He did."

"Well he didn't do enough." A sob tore its way from my chest. "And he didn't call me."

"He did," Iz growled. "I took the call. You left your phone in your car and Mrs. B stuck it in her pocket."

That explained how she knew he'd tried to intervene. And how he found us here. I could almost feel myself shrink. But, like a little kid, I held my anger close. "He should have called sooner."

"Agreed," Dave said. "But I—"

"We were out looking for Lola," a male voice said. "And he didn't know what to say to you."

Iz turned me so I was face-to-face with Detective Charles Atwell. His jacket was also drenched. His expression was grim.

Conflicting emotions sent flashes of lightning across my brain. The man who once accused me of murder had been out searching for Lola. But where was he *before* she got kidnapped by a couple of ex-cons? And as for right now— "Where's everyone else? Lola's a member of the force. Shouldn't there be a whole squad here? Or a platoon? Or a battalion?"

(For the record, I have no idea whether those terms could be applied to the police department. I also have no idea how many are in a squad or a platoon or a battalion. But I think you get my point.)

"Some guys are coming along in a few minutes," Dave said.

"*Some* guys? How many is some? Three? Four?"

"Maybe six," he mumbled. "This incident, uh, well, the brass doesn't see it as a priority."

"Not a priority? Lola, your partner, isn't a priority?"

Dave held up his hands and backed off.

"She's a priority for me," Atwell said in a tight voice. "Lola's one of us."

If I'd heard that from anyone else, I would have felt all warm and fuzzy and hopeful. But since the time he'd put me at the top of a list of murder suspects and grilled me like a hot dog at a Fourth of July picnic, I hadn't been his biggest fan. And he hadn't been mine.

"Listen." He moved closer, invasion-of-personal-space closer. "You and I got into a bad pattern of disrespecting each other. I admit a lot of that's my fault, and I'm sorry."

"I bet you are."

He let that go. "What I'm saying is I think it's time we got unstuck, broke the pattern, moved on."

I was about to tell him he should move on—to Alaska or Argentina—when Iz squeezed my arms tighter to my sides and turned me toward Mrs. B. "Calm down, dear," she said. "Anger isn't helping."

"I know that," I raged.

"Then let it go," Iz hissed.

She didn't say "And grow up while you're at it." She didn't have to. I heard it clearly in her tone.

Coming from my sister, who seldom exhibited adult behavior, the advice made me laugh.

Well, it wasn't really a laugh. The situation was too dire for that. It was more of a strangled, snorting chuckle. Just enough for a reality check.

I relaxed. Iz released me, and I wiped my glasses on my T-shirt. The heavy rain had blown past, leaving a persistent murky mist that created ghostly auras around the few streetlamps. Somehow, those fuzzy orbs of light made the park seem even bleaker and more desolate.

"There," Mrs. B said. "Now we can all focus on getting Lola home. Dave, what's the plan?"

"Step one would be for us to get down the bank, find the squat, and assess the situation," Atwell said. "See how many are there and what their mood is. See if we can open a channel of communication. Find out what their demands are."

"Obviously you'll tell them I'm prepared to pay a substantial ransom," Mrs. B said.

Atwell grimaced. "Bad move."

"But I have plenty of—"

"Money's not the issue." Dave took her hands in his and bent to look into her sapphire eyes. "If you pay these jerks, word will get around. Fast. Every lowlife with a habit to feed will be out stealing dogs."

After a long moment, Mrs. B nodded.

"Good. I'll make it clear that's not on the table." Dave pulled out his phone and turned to Atwell. "Reception's good here. I'll call you when—"

"No." I grabbed the soggy sleeve of his jacket. "You can't go."

"I have to. Lola's my partner."

"Exactly. Those guys grabbed her because she led you to their meth operation. But you made the arrest. If they hate her, they *really* hate you."

"She has a point," Atwell said without even a faint touch of disgruntled irritation. "I'll go."

"You'll slide into the river trying to get down the bank in those shoes." Dave pointed at Atwell's black leather brogues and turned to me. "Are my boots still in your car?"

This was no time to mention they were at the bus depot and he'd never see them again. "Uh, no."

"I'll be fine," Atwell said.

Before anyone could suggest he was delusional, a wreck of a vehicle skidded to a stop behind Dave's. That wreck was familiar. Dario O'Brien had secured it last summer to give Allison driving lessons. Dario himself was behind the wheel.

And Dario, I realized when he stumbled our way, was drunk as a skunk.

(For the record, I'm pretty sure that's a figure of speech with a rhyme to it. I've never seen an inebriated skunk—not in a bar, not at a party, and not in the wild. And right now, with Lola in jeopardy, I don't have time to speculate about how the saying came to be or whether skunks like their liquor neat or on the rocks, shaken or stirred.)

"Dario," Mrs. B said.

"Muriel." He lurched to her with a zigzag motion, bringing with him a strong scent of gin and lime. "You aren't home."

She held him at arms' length. "Obviously not."

"I wanted to surprise you but you aren't home. I called Jim. He said to come here." Frowning, he studied the mist-shrouded park. Perhaps it was the moisture in the air or the alcohol in his system, but his voice seemed rustier than usual. "Why are you here?"

"Dario. Focus." Mrs. B raised both hands and smacked his cheeks three times. "Why are *you* here?"

"They cancelled the show."

"And you handled the decision like an adult and got drunk."

"But not drunk enough." He fished an airline bottle from the pocket of his gray trench coat and struggled to unscrew the top.

Mrs. B pried it from his hands and tossed it to Iz. "You were thinking of quitting the show anyway."

"Yeah. But not until I was ready." He rocked onto his heels and took a few backward steps. Steadying himself with a hand on the roof of Sybil's car, he bent to peer in at her and Verna. "Good evening, ladies. They cancelled the show. Now I can't quit."

Mrs. B made a "come here" gesture toward Dave. He stepped up, gripped Dario under the arms, and righted him. Mrs. B smacked his cheeks again, harder and faster. "Dario, we don't have time for a pity party. Sober up and get a grip. Lola's been kidnapped."

"Lola? That's funny." Dario boomed out a laugh. "Cheese Puff's the one who gets kidnapped."

"Not this time." Using words of few syllables, Mrs. B gave him a short version of the story.

When she finished, Dario shook himself free of Dave's grip. "What are we waiting for?" he asked Atwell. "Let's us guys go get her."

"We will," Atwell told him. "As soon as we get backup. We don't know how many are down there, or what they have in the way of weapons."

"Ah. This calls for reconnaissance." Dario tore off his tie, ripped a few buttons from his shirt, and stepped to the gutter. Stooping, he grabbed a double handful of mud and leaves and smeared the gunk on his face and coat.

"What are you doing?" Mrs. B asked.

196

Dario smiled, scuffed his shiny black leather shoes against the curb, and smeared gutter gunk on them and on his slacks. "You need a man of the people—those people."

"Meth cooks and drug addicts?" Dave asked.

Dario responded by cocking his head and lifting one eyebrow—something I thought was quite a feat for a drunk. Something I couldn't manage cold sober. Then he swept Mrs. B into his arms and kissed her. "Muriel, I love you more than life itself."

"I know that," she sputtered. "You don't have to prove it."

"Exactly why I'm going, Kitten." He kissed her again, then reached in his trench coat pockets and removed half a dozen airline bottles and two half pints of a nasty yellow something. He studied them, frowned, and shrugged. "Not enough. But you go to war with the arsenal you have."

With a clink and clatter, he dumped the bottles into his pockets again and headed off across the park, waving his phone in the air. "I'll be in touch."

"We can't let him go," Mrs. B cried.

"He's a hard man to stop," Dave observed.

I dug a tissue from the pocket of my jeans and wiped mud from Mrs. B's chin and cheeks. "He'll be okay." I steered her around to the passenger side of her car. Cheese Puff stood on the seat, front feet pressed against the glass, nose sniffing air seeping through a gap at the top of the window. "Why don't you get in your car and get warm? Snuggle with Cheese Puff."

"Good idea." Iz opened the door.

But as Mrs. B reached for Cheese Puff, he shot from the car and took off in pursuit of Dario.

"Stop," I ordered.

"Come," Mrs. B called.

"Sit," Dave shouted.

Cheese Puff, his usual less-than-obedient self, kept going. In a few seconds he closed on Dario.

"Catch him," we yelled in unison.

Dario turned. As Cheese Puff passed, he made a diving tackle.

Cheese Puff skittered to one side, danced a circle around Dario in the muddy grass, and took off again.

"Hope Dario didn't break his 'arsenal' in that fall," Dave muttered.

Atwell snorted. "Or something that would hurt worse."

Dario got to his feet, patted his pockets, and shuffled a few steps. Then he ran, pumping his arms. He moved far faster than I imagined a man his age and size could, especially an inebriated man wearing dress shoes and running on slick and bumpy ground. In no time, he was swallowed by the foggy dusk.

# Chapter 24

"The poor little prince," Mrs. B wailed. "Those men will kill my sweet Cheese Puff."

"Ten bucks says he'll be fine," Atwell said.

"Twenty bucks," my sister chimed in. "You treat him like an antique glass ornament, but he's as tough as an old salami sandwich."

I hated to admit my sister was right, but she was. "He's fast, he's strong, and he's smart." I ushered Mrs. B to the seat Cheese Puff had vacated.

"And sneaky." Iz slid behind the wheel, started the engine, and fiddled with vents and knobs. "Don't forget sneaky."

Again, she was on the money. Cheese Puff *was* sneaky. And lately he'd been getting sneakier, hopping on the dining room table more often, crawling into the refrigerator when Allison left it open while she hunted for a snack, climbing the pantry shelves and knocking down sacks of sugar and flour, overturning the hamper in the bathroom and making a nest in our dirty clothes. The few times he'd been caught in the act he'd displayed not the least bit of anything even remotely resembling guilt.

"Plus, he has more lives than a cat," Dave added.

"But we don't know how many he used up before Barbara found him," Mrs. B sniffed.

True.

Like Cheese Puff's exact age, his past was shrouded in mystery, although somewhere along the line he'd been neutered —a fact Mrs. B lamented often while speculating about how adorable his puppies would have been. As if what the world really needed was more adorable small dogs with huge attitudes.

"Dario will call as soon as he can." I tucked her coat around her legs so it wouldn't get caught, then retrieved my phone from the dash, closed the door and spoke to her through the gap at the top of the window. "Make sure your phone is on."

"It's on." She held it up, cradled in both hands like an offering.

A display at the bottom indicated the time. A minute past 5:00. It seemed like at least half a day had elapsed since I got Dave's text and came racing home and then to the courthouse and here.

Iz leaned across the console and said something I couldn't hear. Mrs. B responded in a soft voice. Iz pulled out her phone, tapped in a number, and spoke in a rumbling murmur. Mrs. B transferred her phone to the console, dug in her purse, and passed what looked like credit cards to Iz.

I bent closer to the window to ask what they were up to, but Dave wrapped his arms around me and drew me against his chest. I pulled away, then let go of my anger and leaned into the soggy warmth of his embrace.

Atwell took shelter in Dave's car, but we stood together in the chilly mist, gazing across the park. Night was tightening its grip and inky shadows stalked from beneath the evergreens like hungry wolves. Feeble lighting high on the bridge created a faint sheen on the wet grass. Cars moved across the span with flickers of white and red light, and their tires made a muffled swishing sound. I wondered how much Dario would be able to

200

see in the light from his phone. The riverbank was studded with rocks and roots, tangled with blackberry canes, and littered with slick mats of fallen leaves. I hoped he didn't tumble and end up in the river. Hampered by his heavy coat and the volume of liquor he'd consumed, he'd be dragged under in no time.

After a few minutes, Dave kissed my forehead. "Cheese Puff will be fine."

"I'm not as worried about him as I am about Lola. She's hurt. She's traumatized."

"She's a trouper."

"She's been betrayed. And even if we get her away from those thugs, we might not get to take her home."

"We'll get her home," he said, his voice grim.

"How? You couldn't stop them when they took her for reassignment. How will you get her back after this?"

Before he could answer, headlights probed the gloom and a car pulled up behind Dario's. Another familiar car. With another familiar driver—reporter Stan Stewart.

"Great," Dave muttered. "You had to call this clown. Now the chief will never get off my case. I'll have to hunt for jobs in Tennessee or Texas or—"

"I didn't call him," I hissed.

Dave snorted in disbelief.

"I didn't." But only because, in the bedlam since Lola went missing, it hadn't occurred to me. Sympathetic coverage of Lola's plight might guarantee a better future for her—and for us. So I was darn glad Stewart had turned up.

"Well I'm not saying a word," Dave said. "If my name lands in the paper attached to a quote, I might as well turn in my resignation."

"I blew off a transportation hearing and my editor blew a gasket," Stewart said as he slouched our way. A camera hung from a thick strap around his neck and he pulled a notebook and pen from the distended pocket of his usual jacket. "I hope this story is as good as your friend said it is."

"Friend?"

Stewart flipped pages in his notebook. "Muriel Ballantine. The Las Vegas dancer rich lady who got arrested in the Big Shiny case last year. She called on your phone 15 minutes ago."

Dave cast a withering glance at Mrs. B's car.

I refrained from sticking my tongue out, but vowed that later he'd pay for not believing me.

A car door slammed and Detective Atwell joined us.

"Let me see if I got this right." Stewart flipped another page. "A drug-sniffing dog was about to be reassigned to a new partner when she ran off and was taken hostage by men she'd led police to during a drug bust, men named Chef and, uh, Stringer. They have her in a camp by the river. They may have taken her in retaliation for their arrests. They may demand ransom."

"That's the gist of it," I said. "So far."

Stewart studied the terrain before turning to Atwell. "So what's the rescue plan? Is there a special police team on the way? Snipers? Helicopter? River patrol?"

"No comment."

Stewart turned to Dave.

"No comment."

"Come on, guys." Stewart checked his watch. "Don't make me call dispatch and have them page the information officer. She doesn't like me much *during* business hours and now it's after 5:00. It could be hours before I hear from her. It could be tomorrow."

Atwell shrugged.

Dave followed suit.

Stewart turned to me once more.

I opened my mouth.

Dave made with a don't-get-me-in-more-trouble expression.

Atwell went with a watch-what-you-say glower.

I took a breath, but before I could say anything, a dog barked in the distance. Not just any distance, but the distance situated on the other side of the park.

"Lola!" I shouted. "Cheese Puff."

Mrs. B powered down her window. "Do you see them?"

"No. But I thought I heard Lola bark."

Sybil and Verna powered down their windows.

Dave whistled, high and shrill.

A dog barked again. Closer? Maybe. The fog, growing thicker by the minute, made tracking sounds difficult.

"Lola! Cheese Puff!"

Dave whistled again and jogged toward the river. Stan Stewart stopped slouching and leaned in that direction.

Mrs. B got out of her car, crossed the sidewalk to the edge of the grass, and added her voice to mine. So did Sybil. Even Verna cried out. "Ohah. Ohah."

Her weak voice and garbled delivery brought tears to my eyes. Through the shimmer, I spotted moving shadows on the far side of the park. The shadows were low to the ground and coming our way. I pointed. "There."

Mrs. B yelped with delight. "Come on, Lola. Come on, Cheese Puff."

And they came, Lola wobbling along with her bad leg bent up close against her belly, Cheese Puff with his teeth fastened in the end of the leather belt looped around her neck. He held his little head high and pranced like a tiny show horse going for a blue ribbon.

"That her?" Stan Stewart asked.

"Yes. The Golden Retriever."

"What's the other one?"

"Our little hero," Mrs. B informed him in a voice that said he should know better than to ask. "Cheese Puff."

"Great shot." Stewart hustled toward them, camera clicking and flashing.

"That's my brave little boy," Mrs. B called. "And my good girl."

Keeping her gaze on them, she backed across the sidewalk and opened the rear door of her car. "Come get warm and dry. Come on, my darlings."

As the dogs reached the sidewalk, Cheese Puff bounced to his hind legs and danced to the car, Stewart snapping photos all the while.

"Isn't he precious?" Mrs. B enthused. "He's a star."

Sybil and Verna oohed and aahed.

"He's a ham," Dave said.

"USDA certified," I agreed.

Cheese Puff leaped into Mrs. B's car, dropped the belt, and yipped as if to tell Lola she could make it. When she hesitated, Dave moved in. Lola snarled at him and shied away.

"I'm trying to help you, Lola."

Lola snarled again.

"Back off." I plucked at the sleeve of Dave's jacket. "She doesn't trust you."

Dave's shoulders slumped. "I get it, Lola. I'm sorry."

Lola grunted, gathered herself, pushed off on her good rear leg, and thrust her upper body onto the floor of the car. Cheese Puff yipped, turned in a circle, and licked her muzzle. She grunted again, scrabbled at the carpet, and dragged her hindquarters aboard.

Mrs. B closed the rear door, snatched her purse from the front passenger seat, turned a thumb up to my sister, and slammed that door. Iz gunned the engine and, with a squeal of tires, made a U-turn and took off, barely avoiding a collision with a pair of police cars.

Dave turned to me with the look of a man who has discovered the pea isn't under the shell he picked, a man who just lost his last dollar. "Why do I think she's not taking the dogs to the condo?"

# Chapter 25

Mrs. B glanced at the officers spilling from the cars and rushing to speak with Detective Atwell. Then she flashed Dave a smug cat-that-ate-the-canary smile.

I recalled the huddled conversation with my sister and the transfer of credit cards. The word "sanctuary" leaped to my mind, and I shot her a wink.

Dave raised his hands in surrender. "Fortunately, because it seems I don't have a choice in the matter, I'm wild about deniability."

"Good." Mrs. B patted his shoulder. "Now go get Dario before he hurts those nasty men."

But Dave didn't have to.

Dario, muddier and more mussed than when he departed, emerged from the gloom.

Stewart nudged me. "Who's that?"

"Dario O'Brien."

"Ah." He made a note. "The assistant producer of the showgirl reality program."

"Former assistant producer. The show's been cancelled."

He made another note.

"He volunteered to do some reconnaissance."

Stewart glanced toward Dave who had joined Atwell and the reinforcements. "Is he working with the cops?"

I laughed. "No. And, off the record, he's not a guy most cops would go to for help. Or vice versa. Dario's kind of a law unto himself."

Stewart made yet another note.

"If I were you," I said, turning my back so Dave, if he'd honed that particular skill during years of surveillance, couldn't read my lips, "I'd talk to Mrs. Ballantine."

"Got it." Stewart headed her way.

She brushed past him and threw herself into Dario's outstretched arms.

"I was so worried."

"About what, Kitten?" He lifted her as if she weighed less than Cheese Puff and nuzzled her neck. "Worried I'd bust their ugly heads and Dave would have to arrest me for assault?"

"Well . . . yes. Did you hurt them?"

"Only if you define 'hurt' as doing nothing to stop them from swilling the world's cheapest tequila."

"Ah. And while they were drinking, you freed Lola."

Dario kissed her and set her on her feet. "I'd like to take credit so you'd reward me until I begged you to stop, but getting Lola loose was all Cheese Puff. When I climbed down there—well, to be honest, I did more falling than climbing—I spotted him burrowed in a pile of leaves next to the tree where they had her belted. He gave me an I've-got-it look, and I decided all he needed was someone to block their view."

Dario squared his shoulders and set his feet in a wide stance. "If there's one thing this big body is good for, it's providing cover."

"I can name some other things it's good for," Mrs. B purred.

Atwell cleared his throat, interrupting the ensuing clinch. "How many are down there?"

"Four," Dario answered. "And the way they were emptying the bottles I brought, they should be knee-walking drunk in no time."

"The wind has a vicious bite to it." Mrs. B raised the hood of her raincoat. "And it's starting to rain again. Perhaps, they won't resist. Perhaps, when they realize their leverage is gone, they'll decide they'd rather be in jail than out here."

"Wish I had that choice," Dave muttered. "The chief's going to rain down a load of misery on me."

"I think not." Mrs. B patted his arm and cast a meaningful glance at Stan Stewart who was hovering at Dario's elbow, scribbling in his notebook. "As I'm sure Mr. Stewart will make clear to his readers, it's not your fault Lola was taken hostage. In fact, you were about to risk life and limb to rescue your canine partner when a civic-minded man just happened by and assisted a daring little dog with the rescue."

I pressed my fist against my lips to smother a laugh. The best political spin doctors had nothing on Mrs. B.

She twinkled a smile at the reporter. "If you'd like to talk with Lola's attorney, I'd be happy to arrange to have him call you."

"Lola has an attorney?" Atwell barked out a laugh. "Ten bucks says it's Angus Drummond."

"No wonder you've had such amazing success as a detective," she said without even a minute trace of sarcasm.

Atwell beamed and puffed out his chest.

I put more force behind my fist, grinding my lips against my teeth.

Stewart made a note and handed Mrs. B his card. "He can reach me at the number on the back. The sooner the better."

"Angus is familiar with newspaper deadlines. He won't leave you hanging." She slipped the card into the pocket of her raincoat. "Now, Dario and I intend to go home and put on some dry clothing and order in dinner for ourselves and our friends." She tapped Stewart's notebook and told him her address. "Perhaps you'd like to join us after you cover the arrests? I expect you'll have more questions. And you'll need a little sustenance while you write."

Stewart managed what passed for a smile. "Sure."

"Wonderful. We'll set a place for you. I have some snapshots of Cheese Puff performing in Las Vegas I'll share with you." She nodded at me. "And Barbara has Lola's veterinary records. You'll want those."

"Great." Stewart bobbed his head. "Definitely."

Dario jerked a grimy thumb toward the chevron of slicker-clad officers headed across the park. "Better hustle, son, or you'll miss the trash collection."

Stewart tucked his pen and notebook away and took off at a trot.

"I'd better go along." Dave touched my arm. "Are we good for now?"

"Of course you are," Mrs. B answered. "This was a bump in the road, a tempest in a teapot. We'll have everything straightened out in no time, I promise."

I wasn't so sure this had been only a highway bump or a teapot tempest. I also wasn't sure I liked the use of the word "we" in Mrs. B's last statement. While I was delighted she was back to her old self, it sounded like she was taking charge of too many things. But this wasn't the time to toss that on the table for discussion.

She clapped her hands. "Now kiss and make up and move on."

I hung back.

Dave did likewise.

It seemed we were on the same wavelength.

Kissing would be easy. Making up, not so much. And as for moving on, well, Dave and I accumulated quite a heap of emotional baggage in the past few days. We'd need time to unpack each piece, time to examine, compare, and determine what we could let go of and what we couldn't—at least not right away.

Dario opened his coat, wiped his hands on his shirt, clamped them on our shoulders, and shoved us together. "Get on with it. I need a hot shower and a big bowl of spaghetti and meatballs."

I felt like a kid caught fighting on a school playground and forced to make peace with my opponent—or at least go through the motions. When Dave's lips met mine in an unyielding way, I knew he felt the same.

"There now," Mrs. B said. "Barbara, if you'll go with Sybil and Verna, Dario and I will follow. We'll help Verna get inside. Dave, I'll set a dish aside for you, and one for Detective Atwell. I suspect he receives few dinner invitations."

I stifled a giggle.

Dave sighed, gave me a we'll-talk-later look, and took off across the park.

Mrs. B, dialing up Jim to tell him to put Ennis on a bus, climbed in the driving-lessons wreck with Dario. When Sybil announced she was no longer upset and intended to drive home, I recognized the futility of arguing, belted myself in the back seat, closed my eyes, and pretended I was on an amusement-park ride.

"Ohah?" Verna asked. "Urt?"

"Yes," I said, trying to ignore the zigzag motion of the car and marveling that Verna seemed unaffected. "She's hurt, but she'll get good care." The best Mrs. B's money could buy.

"Where did Iz take her?" Sybil asked.

"I don't know." And I didn't want to. Like Dave, I was wild about deniability.

After pondering the question for a few moments, I concluded my sister and the dogs were somewhere in Portland. Iz had a network of friends and acquaintances from her days as a motivational—or rabble-rousing—speaker on the women's empowerment circuit. I bet some of them would jump at the chance to help shelter a dog in Lola's situation, especially a female dog, and more especially if they didn't have to shelter Iz as well. When you looked up "most demanding guest on the planet," there was a picture of my sister. As for Cheese Puff, I had no doubt he'd turn on the charm and do whatever needed to be done to ingratiate himself to those who harbored him.

"Ohah," Verna said in mournful voice.

Telling myself I might be able to prevent a crash if I saw one coming, I opened my eyes and patted Verna's shoulder. "I'm sure Lola misses you, too. But I don't think she'll be away for long."

Not with Mrs. B bringing money and influence to bear. And not with Angus Drummond on the job. The high-powered attorney came out of retirement whenever she crooked a diamond-ring-laden finger. And, of course, the morning would deliver an edition of the *Reckless River Roundup* and Stan Stewart's article to doorsteps around the city. I suspected a groundswell of public opinion would help sweep aside official objections and red tape.

But, given the way Lola had snarled at Dave, would she want to come home once the path was clear?

What started out as dinner quickly became an impromptu party. Everyone ate too much, drank too much, and—with the exception of a few of us who had suffered impairments or were carrying grudges—talked too much. Allison complained she never got included in the really good stuff and added with a pouty face that Verna's physical therapy appointments with Gabe fell during school hours when she couldn't be there. Jim supplied snippets of his rambling conversation with Ennis as they'd waited for word Lola was safe. Dario regaled Stan Stewart with aw-shucks details of his venture to the squat by the river. Stewart recounted details of the arrest, clicking away at the keyboard of his laptop as he spoke.

Mrs. B did most of her talking on the phone and in a low voice. As she fielded and made calls, the expression on her face changed from delighted to concerned to fearful to hopeful to encouraged. Each change slapped me with a fresh wave of curiosity and anxiety. After half an hour, I felt seasick enough to pass on a second dessert.

To add to the queasy feeling, Detective Atwell steered me down the hallway to the small office where my sister had set up camp. I won't go into descriptive details, but let me assure you it was a messy camp. A really messy camp. The kind of camp that would have had a scout leader ripping off badges.

"I meant what I told you this afternoon," Atwell said in a gruff voice as he closed the door. "I think it's time we bury the hatchet."

Naturally, my brain brought up images of parts of Atwell's anatomy where I'd most like to bury a hatchet. Or a knife. Or an ice pick. Or even one of those tiny flat wooden spoons that used to come with ice cream cups—and maybe still do. Since I'd moved on to using a soup spoon to eat ice cream out of the container, I hadn't given those Lilliputian spoons much thought.

"Focus," I told myself. Steeling my nerves, I looked into the depths of Atwell's snake-like eyes just long enough to see that he appeared sincere.

"All right," I agreed. "Consider the hatchet buried."

But not too deep.

Because I reserved the right to dig the hatchet up at any time.

"Dave, um, is a good friend and he, uh, means a lot to, um, both of us."

The little hesitations in that sentence made me think of Atwell as almost human. Almost.

"He and I are a good team." Atwell actually shuffled his feet. "You and Dave make a good team, too. It's, uh, sometimes helpful to get other views from, uh, those who have no knowledge of the basics of law enforcement and investigative procedures."

See how he is? Just when I thought we were picking up speed on the freeway to Friendlyville, he took the off-ramp to Backhanded Compliment City. That, as you know, is only a bridge away from Insult Island.

I didn't attempt to hide my huffiness. "It seems to me my 'lack of knowledge' and my 'views' helped both of you on the Woodrow Krammer case. And led to an arrest in the murder of Big Shiny."

He winced. He hesitated. Finally, in a grudging tone, he said, "I won't argue."

I noticed he said "won't" instead of "can't." Seemed like he didn't intend to bury his hatchet too deep, either. But I didn't call him out. No point in opening a hatchet-burying-depth discussion. If we did that, we'd be in this room far longer than was healthy for either of us.

(For the record, I estimate the maximum amount of time Atwell and I could spend in an enclosed space was somewhere south of 17 minutes. For cramped enclosed space littered with my sister's sweats, knock off 10 of those minutes. I have no scientific basis for arriving at those numbers, so you'll have to trust me.)

213

"The case he's working on with Harvey Goodspeed . . . it's important that he solves it. Fast. Especially now that Lola . . ."

Atwell didn't finish. He didn't have to. I got the picture.

"So, are you saying I should ask him to share details of the Jerome Morrow case? And, if he does share, are you saying I should feel free to offer my views?"

"No. No. At least, uh, I'm not saying anything like that first part. Not in an, um, official kind of way."

"So this discussion is off the record?"

He rubbed his chin with a thumb and forefinger. "Isn't that a term journalists use?"

"Well, yeah. So?"

"So you're not a journalist."

*Sheesh.*

"I took journalism courses in college."

Later, however, I'd gone to work for Rick Rivers. That disastrous career choice wiped out everything I'd been taught about being fair and balanced. Only by holding my nose—and reminding myself I had a mortgage—had I hung on to the ability to tell right from wrong.

But I didn't mention any of that to Atwell. What I said was, "There's a journalist in the next room. Shall I get him?"

"No. I've had enough of that guy and his questions to last me a year. What part of 'no comment' doesn't he get?"

"He gets all of it. It's his style to keep pushing and asking questions."

"With a style like that, he should take up telemarketing. It might pay enough for him to get a new jacket."

I stifled a laugh. Atwell, whose wardrobe choices did nothing to disguise the shelf of gut above his belt, was hardly an authority on fashionology. "All right then, back to what you were saying. Unofficially—and so far off the record we're not even in a position to see the record if, indeed, there *is* a record

214

—if Dave, at some future date, shared a few details of the case, then I might feel free to share my thoughts in return. If, that is, I developed any ideas that weren't obviously harebrained due to my lack of the least bit of knowledge of investigative procedure."

Confusion tap dancing in his eyes, Atwell drew lines in the air as if trying to unsnarl the sentences and determine what I'd said.

I glanced out the tiny window facing the parking lot. Rain was pounding down again and I heard a rumble of thunder, but I wasn't worried lightning would strike me for lying. If you noticed, I hadn't actually lied to Atwell. Dave hadn't *actively* shared details of the case. In fact, unless he'd dusted for prints, for all he knew I hadn't opened the file. I might have—for once —bottled up my curiosity and left the case folder untouched. And, since we hadn't discussed the case after the evening he left the folder on the coffee table, I had no idea whether he'd formed any new theories about Jerome Morrow's death.

Atwell stopped drawing air marks and shrugged. "Yeah. What you said."

"All right then, I'll agree. But, given that my relationship with Dave has been significantly fractured due to our divergent views concerning Lola, the communication pump will need to be primed." Taking a cue from his frown, I elaborated. "In other words, if you feel my input would be valuable, you should initiate a conversation with Dave wherein you indicate it might be to his benefit to take advantage of the resourceful woman with whom he shares a domicile."

Atwell made finger marks again and I smiled to myself. Nothing like multi-syllabic words and a little legalese—correct or not—to assert conversational dominance.

With a grunt that signified either agreement or indigestion, he opened the door and returned to the living room. I wouldn't go so far as to say he stomped along the hallway, but neither did he amble, stroll, sashay, or cavort.

I followed, emerging from the office just as my sister entered through the door from the parking lot. Ignoring her dripping trench coat, I grasped her arm. "How's Lola?"

# Chapter 26

"It looks good." To my surprise Iz gave me a hug. Granted, it was a brief, one-armed hug. Nevertheless, it was a hug. "Let's go in and I'll tell everyone as much as I can."

I helped her peel off her coat, took the fedora she'd clamped over her short brown hair, and tossed them over a chair in her temporary lair. When I reached the living room, Mrs. B and Sybil were in full flutter mode, filling a plate and getting Iz settled at the table beside Verna who beamed and repeated, "Ish. Ish. Ish."

To my surprise, Iz beamed back.

Well, to be scathingly honest, she pretty much just twitched a smile in Verna's direction before laying waste to a slice of lasagna about the size of the average home dictionary. I noticed she didn't ask if it was meatless—it wasn't—or inquire whether the ingredients were locally sourced. Either she was so hungry she didn't have time for her usual culinary interrogation, or she'd come to a fork in the path of personality quirks and chosen the trail toward less carping. Because, the truth, as you well know, is that when you look up "omnivorous," there's a picture of my sister eating her way through the full range of food items in my refrigerator and cupboards.

By the time she swallowed the last bite, everyone was gathered in the vicinity of her chair. And everyone was silent except Verna. "Ohah?" she asked every few seconds. "Ohah?"

Iz pushed her plate aside and patted Verna's shoulder. "I won't tell you where she is or who did the operation, but the surgery went well, and she should be fine. If the hardware holds. If the bone sets like it should. And if there's no further injury or infection."

That last word made me feel queasy all over again. I gripped the back of Verna's chair and glanced at Mrs. B.

She appeared pale and had a tight hold on Dario's hand, but her voice was firm. No, it was beyond firm. It was like tempered steel. "Lola is with one of the best vets in the Northwest. And, of course, no expense will be spared for her treatment."

She raised her chin, revealing all six strands of the pearl choker she'd donned before dinner. "And no interference with her recovery will be tolerated from petty bureaucrats or anyone else."

"Ohah urt," Verna said.

"Yes, dear," Mrs. B told her. "Lola is hurt. But in a strange way that works in her favor. And ours."

"Meaning the department won't want her back," Dave said. "And Angus Drummond can make a deal."

"Precisely. But I've asked him to hold off on negotiations until tomorrow morning when those concerned have had time to absorb the details of Mr. Stewart's article."

"Wide-ranging article," Stewart corrected. He shoved the platter of garlic bread across the table toward Iz. "Tell me more about the surgery."

Iz bit into a heel of bread, scattering bits of crust as she spouted details. Lots of details. Three slices of garlic bread worth of details.

"You watched?" I asked when she stopped talking and turned her attention to the enormous wedge of chocolate cake Sybil set before her.

"Every minute," she confirmed.

That seemed odd. When I was young and prone to cuts and scrapes, she had two approaches to dealing with my injuries. The first involved assessing the damage with a fleeting glance and telling me to stop sniffling and handle it myself. The second involved dumping half a bottle of hydrogen peroxide on the affected area and slapping on salve and a bandage—all faster than a pit crew changing a tire at the Indy 500. And, although Iz had been involved in protests resulting in bloodshed, she'd never been among those patching up the injured.

It also seemed odd my sister had watched because, no matter how smart and sensitive she might be, Lola was a dog. And Iz ranked dogs low on the scale of creatures she thought were worth the air they breathed. Frequently she'd claimed to be allergic to dogs, although I'm pretty sure she did that so she wouldn't be expected to hold or pet a pooch. I've never noticed any evidence of allergies in the way of rashes, sneezing, or difficulty breathing.

"Of course I watched the surgery." Iz patted Verna's hand. "Lola is important to you . . . to all of us. Besides, I had to hold Cheese Puff up so he could see what was going on. Otherwise he wouldn't stop howling."

I choked on a laugh. Iz had often said she wanted nothing to do with Cheese Puff because he was male, entitled, and "just a dog." I suspected another reason was he had the ability to play the cute card—a card missing from her deck.

For his part, Cheese Puff had made it clear through body language—including the occasional passing of gas—that Iz didn't belong in his universe. But, desperate times did indeed call for desperate measures. And it wasn't politics alone that made for strange bedfellows.

"Eez Uff?" Verna asked. "Surgy?"

"Yeah, he watched the surgery. And now he's sleeping next to her."

Sybil clapped her hands. "The little darling."

"I'll buy some special treats for our hero when he gets home." Mrs. B turned to Dario. "We'll grill him a steak."

Dario rolled his eyes as if to say he'd rather grill Cheese Puff, but I suspected he'd be ready with a barbecue fork when the time came. He might not adore Cheese Puff, but he adored a woman who did.

After all the excitement, I decided to make myself unavailable for subbing on Friday and didn't set the alarm clock. By the time I got downstairs, wearing the yellow bathrobe I wished would manage to lose itself, Dave was about to leave. "Dropping Allison at school," he mumbled through a last bite of toast. "Then to the county offices."

He tapped the paper spread on the dining room table. "No outright lies in the story, but plenty of truth stretching. Your friend Stan Stewart has a future as a fiction writer."

Meanwhile, Rick Rivers, also known for stretching the truth—not to mention bending, tearing, obscuring, and perverting it—had a different kind of a future in store. He didn't know it yet. And neither did I, until the phone rang a few minutes later.

"That horrible man," Mrs. B cried. "Saying Lola is 'only a stupid dog' and should be put down if she can't do the job she was brought in to do. Saying her medical care is a waste of money. Saying—"

"I'll be right over."

In less than a minute I was pouring myself a cup of coffee, nodding to Mrs. B in her silvery kimono, nodding to Dario resplendent in purple pajamas and a gold satin bathrobe, nodding to Verna propped up in her hospital bed beneath a puffy green comforter, nodding to my sister, clad in camouflage sweats and lounging in a recliner beside Verna's bed. All were listening to the rest of what Rick Rivers had to spew. The gist of that spewing? First, the men who took Lola were criminals, but so were the people who had whisked away what amounted to city and taxpayers' property once she'd been freed. Second, Lola wasn't a "real police dog" because she didn't attack and bring down bad guys. And third, cops who couldn't keep hold of a dog explained why crime was skyrocketing in Reckless River.

"Is it?" Dario asked after Mrs. B snapped off the radio. "Is crime going up?"

"No," I said. "As a matter of fact crime is down—except for the white-collar variety. There was an article in the paper last month. If he was the type who bothered to check facts, Rick could have found the report and statistics with few taps of his computer keys."

"Speaking of checking, Muriel," Dario said, "and checking accounts . . ."

Mrs. B cocked her head. "Yes?"

"Isn't it time you bought that fool's soapbox out from under him and sent him packing?"

"I second that idea." My hand wavered between a plate of mini cinnamon rolls and a bowl of biscuits. I went with a cinnamon roll, vowing to eat only one. "Since you've abandoned the experiment in non-meddling, there's no reason not to. You've been looking for a new project."

She favored me with a faint smile followed by a not-so-faint sigh. "Except I don't know anything about running a radio station."

"I'm unemployed right now," Dario said. "Take me some time to get up to speed, but if the rest of the staff stayed on, it shouldn't be too hard." He aimed a meaty forefinger at me. "Do you think they'd hang around?"

"Possibly. The radio job market is shrinking. Finding a spot is tougher than it used to be."

"We could offer financial incentives for those who stayed," Mrs. B suggested. "And better health insurance at a lower cost."

"That would get my attention." I eyed the plate of cinnamon rolls again. They were so small. Less than two inches in diameter. How many calories could one have? Especially if I picked one that wasn't dripping butter?

"Sounds like it's a go," Iz said.

"Oh," Verna echoed.

"I suppose it is." Mrs. B's voice held a mix of resignation, relief, and realism. "It's probably a larger project than I wanted, but as soon as Angus concludes his negotiations with the police department, I'll have him look into how we go about it." She paused, sipping her coffee and studying the silent radio. "I imagine it won't be as simple as buying a car."

"Not if the government's involved the way I bet it is," Dario said.

"Angus will probably want to bring in an attorney who specializes in this kind of thing," I told her. "And it could take time to get the paperwork together and submitted and approved."

"Paperwork," Dario snorted. "Bureaucrats. That jerk Rivers could be on the air a year before we get the key to the door to boot him out of."

Mrs. B frowned and chewed at her lip. "And if he knows the ax is falling, there's no telling what kind of poisonous opinions he'll broadcast."

We all pondered that horror in silence. Then, thanks to a mental energy burst provided by the second cinnamon roll, I had an idea. "What if your offer to buy included some kind of financial incentive for 'cleaning house' before the seller signed an agreement."

Dario grunted. "Under the table and off the books?"

I shrugged. "I'd never advise Mrs. B to do anything illegal, but I'm sure Angus could find some 'creative' ways to strike a deal."

Iz turned a thumb up. It might not seem like much of a sign of approval to you. But, given the source, I considered it right up there with a blue ribbon or gold medal.

"I'm sure there's a way to be creative without being unscrupulous." Mrs. B snatched a pad and paper from the counter and made a note. "I'll have Angus explore the possibilities."

"You might see if Dario could come on board early. Maybe as second in command or as a consultant until the deal closes," I said. "And you'll also need to be ready with a replacement for Rick Rivers. Someone to fill in until you take full control and find a permanent host."

"Angus moves quickly. We might not have much time." Mrs. B drew squiggles around the edge of the paper. "Who could we get to replace that repugnant piece of slime?"

The words "piece of slime" caused a name to pop into my head. Before my better judgment could stop them, my lips blurted it out. "How about Jake?"

"Jake?" Mrs. B mused.

"Jake?" Dario considered.

"Ake?" Verna asked.

"Jake?" Iz howled.

"Just a thought," I said. "He doesn't have radio experience, but he loves to be the center of attention. And if there's one thing Jake can do, it's talk."

"He *is* full of ideas," Dario added.

"Mostly stupid or illegal ones," Iz amended.

Mrs. B poured herself another cup of coffee. "He couldn't be worse than Rick Rivers."

"He wouldn't be better," Iz insisted.

Defending my ex was new territory. Scary and stressful territory. Caving to demands for sustenance from my fat cells, I buttered half a biscuit and drizzled on honey. "He's available. He needs money to pay the fines he got for not having a license or insurance for that wreck of a bus. He could start as soon as Rivers is out of the building. Plus, Jake is used to losing jobs and reinventing himself, so if you fired him later, he'd take it in stride."

"What if we hired a producer?" Dario asked. "Someone to steer him and rein him in?"

"That's a great idea." Mrs. B turned to me with a hopeful gleam in her eyes. "Maybe you—"

"No." I dropped my biscuit and made the sign of the cross. "No way. Nohow."

"Not even for a few months?" she wheedled.

"Not even for a few minutes." I bent to scoop up the biscuit. Naturally it had landed honey-side down, leaving a sticky smear on the linoleum. Where were the dogs when you needed them?

Iz turned both thumbs up to my refusal.

Wow. That was like getting a gold medal *and* a silver cup *and* a crown of laurel leaves.

"Not even if I offered—?"

"Not even." I dropped the biscuit in the trash under the sink. "Like I said, radio jobs are declining. There are probably plenty of young and hungry producers who would jump at the chance." Of course, they might jump more slowly and not as high since that chance was located in Reckless River and involved working with my ex-husband.

"All right." Seizing a napkin, Mrs. B wiped at the smear. "I understand how you feel. Would you help Dario find those people?"

"And check their resumes? And help interview them?" he asked. "Or at least tell me what to look for?"

"Sure. I'd be happy to. I bet Stan Stewart would have some ideas about talk topics. Heck, you might even be able to hammer out a deal with the paper so he could do live news reports on weekday mornings."

"Great idea," Dario said. "Could be good for our operation and theirs."

"You're talking like you're already running the place."

"Might as well get in the habit. When Muriel makes up her mind, things have a way of moving at neck-snapping speed."

True. I hid a smile, reached for the half of the biscuit I hadn't trashed, and slathered on butter. "Speaking of moving, have you heard anything about Lola this morning?"

"She's doing well," Mrs. B said with a smile. "They got her up and she went outside and managed to do what needed to be done. And the little prince was never more than a few inches from her side."

"Cheese Uff," Verna said.

"Good job," Iz told her. "You got the cheese. This afternoon you work on the puff. Now let's get you up and showered and ready for your boyfriend Gabriel."

Verna giggled and patted her hair with her good hand.

"I should get dressed too." I stuffed the biscuit in my mouth and headed for the door. "Keep me posted on what Angus comes up with."

# Chapter 27

What Angus was up to apparently unfolded at snail-like speed; hours went by with no word on the free-Lola negotiations. I puttered, filed my nails, reorganized my closet, and then drove to Captain Meriwether High School to check in on Big Chill. To my relief, every hair was in place and her fresh silvery stick-on nails were flawless. But there was no softness in the eyes behind a pair of rhinestone-studded glasses. "Are you here because Dave cracked the case?"

"I wish." I sat in the less-than-comfortable chair in front of her desk. "As far as I know they haven't reached a conclusion about the cause of death. But the situation with Lola set our relationship back a few notches. We're speaking, but our communication is as deep as the water I splashed through on my way across the parking lot."

The Chillster glanced out the window behind her desk and scanned the rain-washed parking lot. "The weather report says we'll have sun tomorrow."

"I'll believe it when I see it."

A sunny day in January would be a nice change, but clear skies generally meant colder temperatures and a biting Coho Wind. That was the winter tradeoff in the Pacific Northwest. When a high pressure system set up east of us, wind funneled through the Columbia Gorge. At least, that's what I've observed.

226

I'm not an expert on the weather. Or, as you've probably noticed, on much of anything else.

"Jim tells me Muriel hired Angus Drummond. He's as high-powered as they get in this neck of the woods, but I thought he retired."

I noted Jim's name at the start of her first sentence, and also noticed she'd seemed to linger over it, but I didn't ask the questions that popped into my mind. There'd be time later. "Angus Drummond is retired as far as his other clients are concerned, but he misses butting heads with the system and her cases give him the opportunity. Besides, I think he's a little bit in love with her."

"Easy to see why. She's a firecracker."

"Takes one to know one." I shifted my buns in search of a more comfortable position. "How are things here?"

"We're holding on. Tremaine's doing a great job. He's everywhere."

*As opposed to Jerome Morrow who usually seemed to be nowhere.*

I told myself I wasn't speaking ill of the dead. For one thing, I was thinking, not speaking. And for another thing, it was the truth.

"Tremaine's got everyone working on personal reflections for the memorial service. Whenever we're allowed to have a service. For closure." She crossed her fingers. "I hope they rule it an accident. It's too horrible to think someone murdered Jerome. But if that's true, it could be months before they catch the killer. And then there would be a trial."

And the last thing folks at Captain Meriwether High School needed was to be associated with another murder, and have another trial hanging fire.

"And it's even more horrible to think he might have killed himself. Not that I believe he did, not for a minute, but . . ."

I didn't prod her to finish that sentence. She had known Jerome Morrow better than any of us, but I doubted their relationship included soul-searching talks—often fueled by long hours, late nights, or a drink too many—where people revealed their deepest feelings about love and life and death. If Jerome Morrow had taken his own life, she'd never stop wondering why, never stop searching the past for clues, never stop feeling she should have seen it coming and said or done something to change his mind. At her age, with her stressful job and spiking blood pressure, that would do her no good.

She narrowed her eyes. "Are you sure you don't know anything about the investigation?"

I crossed my heart. "Positive."

She twitched her nose and tapped her nails on her desk in a way that suggested I wasn't being entirely honest. I crossed my heart again. She narrowed her eyes, but then gave it up. "At least that pathetic excuse for a radio personality has stopped saying hateful things about Jerome. I'm sorry he's harping on that poor dog and the police, but it's a relief not to hear him blaming Jerome for everything wrong with education and society in general. If he starts in again I won't make the effort to talk Aston Marsden out of setting a bear trap on the seat of his car."

Now there was an image—Rick Rivers with his hind end between the jaws of a bear trap. I savored it for a few seconds before I stood, nudged the door closed, and leaned across her desk. "Between you and me, the Rick Rivers problem should be resolved shortly."

Big Chill's eyes sparkled. "How shortly?"

I didn't pause to consider the lack of grammatical merit to that question. "Shortly after Angus Drummond winds up negotiations to arrange for Lola to 'retire' from the police force."

"He'll file a lawsuit against that loud-mouthed lunatic?" She frowned. "That could drag on for years."

"But a sale could be wrapped up a whole lot quicker."

"Muriel's going to buy the radio station!" Big Chill applauded. "I could hug her neck."

"What about mine?" a deep voice asked.

I turned to see Jim had opened the door a few inches and was peering through the gap. From the corner of my eye I caught a blush washing up Big Chill's neck and dyeing her cheeks. Her fingers fluttered. And then she got a grip. "You'll have to wait for a hug until I know you better," she said in a prim voice.

Jim smiled, his Father Christmas beard rippling as his facial muscles moved. "Then let's go to lunch and get started on that."

"I can't. I never go to lunch." She surveyed the phone, the computer, and the stacks of paperwork on her desk. "Things . . . things happen when I go to lunch."

"Things happen when you don't." I grasped her elbow and raised her from her chair. "Go to lunch. I'll hold down the fort."

"But what if the superintendent calls for Tremaine?"

"Then I'll find Tremaine. I'll round up a few student government kids and have them track him down. If that fails, I'll use the PA system."

Big Chill glanced from me to Jim and then back to me.

"Go to lunch. You deserve an hour off." I seized a pen. "I'll take detailed messages of every phone call. I'll keep a log of everything that happens."

She took a step toward the door and hesitated again.

"Seriously." I gave her a push. "How hard can it be to cover for you?"

Famous last words.

Along with the phone calls—of which there many and mostly of the parental concern/complaint variety—there were the up-close-and-personal interruptions. I'd forgotten Big Chill was the person everyone came to with their questions and problems. Sometimes they came because they honestly couldn't find answers and solutions elsewhere. But mostly they descended on her because it was easier to dump the problem in her lap, stand back, and let a take-charge person take charge.

Example 1. Aston Marsden.

He prowled in, silent as a cat thanks to a pair of fur-lined moccasins. "Where's Wilhelmina? What are you doing here?"

"I'm covering for her. She went to lunch."

"What?" He rocked on his heels, shaking his head and tugging at his mangy beard with both hands. "She never goes to lunch."

"She did today."

He studied the desk calendar as if he expected the numbered square for today would contain a notation indicating a holiday or observance he wasn't aware of. Then he tapped the unmarked white space beneath the number with a grubby finger. "Hmpfh. She might have let me know."

I considered a number of comments about the chain of command and where I felt Aston should reside within it. I settled for a blank stare.

"I need staples."

"They're in one of the lower cabinets in the business office."

"I know. That's way over on the other side of the building."

"Pwah. It's a hundred yards. Maybe less. A mere stroll for a mountain man like you."

"I'm in a hurry."

"Then *run* to the business office."

"Wilhelmina always lets me take some of hers."

His grousing eroded my patience like a flash flood in the desert. I raised my voice as I clipped off words. "Wilhelmina's not here. She'll be gone for an hour. Maybe more. Go to the business office."

Displaying a profound inability to listen and absorb, he rounded the desk and yanked out a lower drawer, bashing my shin.

I howled, half with pain and half with annoyance.

He leaped back, rubbing his ears. "Stop that yowling. What's wrong with you?"

"Me?" I rubbed my shin. "What's wrong with *you*? Were you raised by wolves?"

"There's nothing wrong with me." He aimed both forefingers at my head as if they were six-guns and jerked them several times. Then he left, yelling over his shoulder, "And there's nothing wrong with wolves."

"I'm wild about wolves," I called, being all about getting in the last word. "Wolves don't use staplers."

Example 2. Brenda Waring.

I had my jeans rolled up to my knee so I could examine the scrape on my shin when she hove into view, belching and thumping her sternum with her fist.

"Where's Wilhelmina?"

I shoved my jeans over the scrape. "She went to lunch."

"She never goes to lunch."

"She did today."

"Hmpfh. I have indigestion."

She followed up her statement with a three-second belch that sent the odor of garlic and onions drifting my way like a toxic release from a chemical weapon.

If she was hoping for sympathy, she'd come to the wrong place and arrived at the wrong time. "Eat your own cooking?"

"As a matter of fact, yes. But that's not the reason my stomach is upset."

*I bet!*

Brenda's concoctions—billed as cutting-edge or creative cuisine—had given me indigestion plenty of times. And that was just from smelling them.

She belched again. "This uncertainty has me on edge. All I can think about is poor Jerome and what will happen to the rest of us now that he's gone."

An interesting point. Jerome Morrow hadn't exactly run a tight ship, and he hadn't been the type to rock it. A new principal, on the other hand, might not be as tolerant of some of the teaching methods and character quirks that seem to abound at Captain Meriwether. Even Tremaine Scott, who'd had a year to study the staff and realize some of their methods actually worked, might propose changes.

"You're lucky you're just a sub and you're not affected by politics and policies. I wish I had a boyfriend who supported me so I could afford to work only when I wanted."

Boy did she have that wrong—to varying degrees, but still wrong. My patience, stretched as thin as cut-rate aluminum foil, tore. I made no attempt to control my testiness. "What brings you to the nerve center of CMHS?"

"I told you." She thumped her sternum again, releasing another belch. "I have indigestion. I need antacid tablets."

"Try the nurse's office."

"She's out. The office is locked up."

"Get the key from the attendance office."

"That will take too long. I'm in a hurry. Wilhelmina always has a bunch."

Like Aston, she came around behind the desk.

Having learned my lesson, I drew up my knees and turned away from the drawers on the left side of the desk. Unfortunately, she seized the drawer in the center and yanked.

I howled once more and rubbed my knee.

"Stop," Brenda ordered. "You sound like a coyote."

She yanked the drawer again and rammed it into my hand.

I howled again and pushed the drawer in, catching her fingers.

Her howl harmonizing with mine, Brenda freed her hand and waved it in the air.

Doug Whitman stuck his head in the door. "What's wrong with you two?"

"Don't get me started." I struggled from the chair and stood on my good leg. "And don't tell me you're here because you're in a hurry and you need paper clips or pencils or—"

"Sticky notes," he called as he made a U-turn. "On my way to the business office right now."

Brenda cradled her injured hand and cast a glance at the desk. "I don't suppose I could just look in the—"

"No."

"But Wilhelmina always—"

I hopped at her, flapping my arms like an enraged chicken. "Wilhelmina is at lunch. And I see why she never leaves the building in the middle of the day. You all can't seem to manage the simplest tasks on your own."

"But she—"

"She puts up with it. She's stuck. And you're stuck." I pushed Brenda out the door. "When she comes back from lunch I intend to tell her things have got to change."

But, of course, I didn't.

Big Chill, like Mrs. B, was a force of nature. And who was I to attempt to alter a force of nature? Especially when I needed that force of nature to put in a good word for me should a position open up at Captain Meriwether. And no, I wasn't worried about Aston and Brenda putting in bad words. They had their oddities and faults and failings, but they didn't hold grudges. At least not for long.

# Chapter 28

"Angus is making great strides," Mrs. B told me when I dropped in to check the status of everything and everyone. "Of course, nothing is certain until the papers are signed, but it appears Lola will retire and the police department will purchase another drug dog."

"Using money from an anonymous donor?"

"Exactly," she said as she pried the lid from the box of chocolates we'd nearly wiped out yesterday. "A donation from a resident concerned about crime."

I pawed through the box, searching for a dark chocolate treat not likely to have jelly inside. I settled for one with a Brazil nut. Not in my top five nut choices, but it would have to do. "How large a donation?"

"Far below their opening offer. And there will be no charges against Iz." She twinkled a smile. "Angus drives a hard bargain."

Dario grunted, shifted in his armchair, and lowered the book he'd been reading. I spotted the word "radio" on the cover and assumed he was doing research. His expression said he could have driven a harder bargain than Angus. It also said the attorney better not get ideas about being more than Mrs. B's legal representative. "Maybe when he finishes driving bargains he should try driving with Allison."

Mrs. B giggled and danced over to plant a kiss on his forehead. "Angus is a fine man with a great legal mind. He's never flinched in a courtroom, but when it comes to the real world, I doubt he has your nerve."

I swear, Dario made a noise like a cat purring—a very large cat. A cat the size of, say, a well-fed adult male Bengal tiger.

"Now." She turned to me and clapped her hands. "While you're here, dear, you can help me change the sheets on Verna's bed."

"Okay." I glanced around, for the first time noticing Verna and my sister weren't in residence. "Where's Verna?"

"Your sister took her for a drive." Mrs. B lowered her voice. "Iz wouldn't say, but I have a feeling she took her to see Lola and Cheese Puff."

"Verna got worked up after physical therapy," Dario said. "Couldn't remember the rescue. Thought Lola was still in the squat."

I pulled sheets from the bed. "That's not good."

"No, it's not." Mrs. B removed the pillowcases. "But I'm told it happens to stroke patients. So we'll cross our fingers and hope this is a one-time glitch."

"And hope riding with Iz doesn't get her more upset."

Dario snorted.

"Iz promised to be extra careful." Mrs. B came to my sister's defense. "Besides, she's never had any *serious* collisions."

"That we know about," I muttered.

"Well, what's done is done." Mrs. B marched to the kitchen and loaded the washer. "And I've been extremely impressed with the way she's cared for and encouraged Verna."

Her tart tone made it clear the subject was closed, so I filed the comment that a white-knuckle drive with Iz might act like an electric shock to the brain and stimulate memory. To make sure I didn't speak, I ate another chocolate, this one filled with marshmallow. Not even as high as 20 on my list of favorites. Perhaps, if I left the lid off, Mrs. B would notice a fresh box was needed.

She started the washer, returned to the bed, and shook out a fitted sheet. "So far Verna doesn't seem to have lost any memories from the less-recent past."

"Knows she used to be a court clerk," Dario added. "Knows who we are. Knows she's not in her own place."

"Does she remember falling down the stairs?" I smoothed the top sheet and made an attempt at a military-style corner—an attempt pathetic enough to have me drummed out of any corps.

"Apparently not." Mrs. B wedged a fat pillow into a fresh case. "And to my way of thinking, it would be a blessing if that piece of memory was lost forever."

"I agree. But when she's able to go home, it may come back."

"I'm afraid of that." Mrs. B shook the pillow. "But we can't allow her to go home until we do something about all those precarious piles. It's dangerous."

"Dave told the rescue team we'd make it safe for her." I shook out the comforter and smoothed it.

"So we haul it to the dump," Dario said.

Mrs. B sighed. "That's probably the sanest course, but I don't want to be responsible for throwing away things she collected and saved for years."

"*I'll* do it." He flexed his muscles and puffed out his chest. "Rent a truck and clear it in a day."

"And you'll explain to Verna what you did and why?" I asked.

"Yeah. Sure." Dario's tone was tough, but his chest deflated.

"I'd pay to be there for that," Mrs. B said with a trill of laughter. "She'll slice your ears off."

"And maybe other parts of your anatomy as well," I added.

Dario crossed his legs. "Somebody's got to do something."

"Yes," Mrs. B said with a longer and louder sigh. "Perhaps if we all got together . . ."

"Getting together is a good idea." I took the pillow from her and put it in place. "Get the whole Committee involved. Get Lana Dylan from the sandwich shop. Stage an intervention. Make sure everyone delivers the same message about hoarding and your desire to help."

"Good idea," Dario said in a voice heavy with relief.

"All right. I'll reach out to some experts to see how we should go about it. We have time before Verna will be ready to go home." Mrs. B dusted her hands, closing the subject. "Now, on to other things, dear. I've changed my mind about getting your friend Paulette to advise me on renovating your old condo."

"You're not going to rent it?"

"Not in a conventional way."

"Meaning I won't have a lease," Dario said. "So she won't have to give notice before she throws me out on my ear."

"The ear you won't have if you haul off Verna's hoardings," I reminded him. "So you're leaving Las Vegas?"

"It's time. I love the glitz and glitter, but it gets old. And this radio gig sounds interesting." He shot me a wink and flexed his muscles again. "Plus, someone's gotta be around for when Muriel needs a little heavy lifting. Or any of the other little services I'm happy to perform at all hours of the day or night."

He followed up with a leer that caused Mrs. B to blush a vivid shade of scarlet.

Time to steer this conversation elsewhere before they got too friendly. "So, Dario, you'll be in charge of the renovations and upgrades?"

"No point. For all I cook, the microwave's plenty. Paint looks okay, and where it isn't I'll hang a picture or maybe a dartboard. Then I'll shove my stuff in."

Hanging pictures over paint gouges. Shoving stuff in. Paulette would be horrified.

"All I need is a getaway." He glanced at the bed we'd just made. "For when things get too crowded here."

*As they had a way of doing on a semi-regular basis.*

"A man needs space."

"A room of his own," I seconded.

And with that I returned home to help Jim move my desk out of the office soon to become Dave's cave.


Allison was out with Josh when Dave came home well past 6:00, lugging his messenger bag as if it weighed 50 pounds. I assumed the file on the Jerome Morrow homicide was thicker, but still didn't contain a definite cause of death. Remembering my talk with Detective Atwell last night, I pasted on a smile and helped Dave out of his rain jacket.

"Already ate," he said by way of greeting. "Need beer."

His clipped delivery and lack of pronouns told me I couldn't expect dazzling conversation, emotional sharing, or details of the case. But perhaps I could nudge him into the mood. Or, if that failed, perhaps I could wear him down.

So I cleaned crumbs from the silverware drawer that always seemed to stick open except when it stuck closed, and rearranged the order of the cereal boxes in the pantry. And I chattered.

Or perhaps I prattled.

Most likely, I did a bit of both.

239

First I updated him on Lola's condition and the negotiations for her retirement. He smiled in a bleak way. Not so bleak I assumed he'd gotten a ton of blowback, but with enough frost to indicate what he'd heard from the cop shop hadn't been what you'd call warm or encouraging.

I moved on to a more detailed description of my visit to the high school. He said nothing when I told him how distraught Big Chill was about two of the possible outcomes of the investigation into Jerome Morrow's death. He raised an eyebrow when I mentioned she'd gone to lunch with Jim. He rolled his eyes when I described—complete with a display of the bruises on my shin, knee, and hand—Aston and Brenda descending on the office.

Taking those as signs he was listening, I moved on to my sister and Verna. Both of Dave's eyebrows lifted when I praised Iz for patient encouragement and for going the extra mile by driving Verna to see the dogs and hopefully refresh her memory.

"I know," I admitted. "I never thought I'd say so many nice things about Iz. But I never thought she'd develop empathy. Although, I suppose she had it all along, or else she wouldn't have taken care of me when I was a kid."

I abandoned my mostly-for-show cleaning and straightening, and plopped on Cheese Puff's favorite chair. "Anyway, we're hoping this is just a glitch because Verna's memory of the past seems solid. Except for the night she had the stroke. She doesn't remember feeling strange or falling down the stairs. If Lola hadn't alerted us, she might have been there all night. And if she'd bashed her head, she might be in a coffin now."

Dave did the side-to-side-lip-press thing he does when he's following along and considering. He was, in essence, nibbling at the bait.

Now for the hook.

I opened my mouth.

"Jerome Morrow didn't have a stroke," Dave said.

*Dang.*

He spotted the hook before I got it in the water.

But he spoke. And in a complete sentence.

That was good, right?

I considered ways to keep the conversational ball rolling. Asking "Are you sure?" was out. He knew I knew the autopsy would have revealed a stroke or heart attack. Asking what else they'd ruled out seemed too pushy. So I went with a simple "Oh."

For a long moment silence hung between us like one of those shower curtains that isn't transparent but isn't opaque, either. Translucent. That's the word. If silence could be translucent, this was it.

And then the curtain fell and Dave spoke again. "He didn't have a heart attack, either."

Perhaps his words came because he was tired or frustrated or attempting to make amends for the whole Lola thing. Or perhaps he talked because, as Atwell indicated, he was ready to admit I often had ideas that were creative, interesting, or unique. And sometimes right on the money.

I nodded.

"He wasn't poisoned."

Poison hadn't even entered my mind. I abandoned the nod in favor of a soft "Hmmm."

"Or stung by a bee. Or stabbed with a hat pin."

Also things I hadn't considered.

I felt a sense of loss, the way I had as a little kid when my mother told me she'd thrown out a frayed and moth-eaten blanket because I was getting too old to drag it around with me.

241

Dave was good at this investigation stuff. Dave didn't need my help developing theories.

The sense of loss deepened. What if it wasn't only theorizing Dave didn't need me for? What if he'd decided life with me—and my friends and Iz—was too complicated, too exhausting? What if having a room of his own, a man cave, wasn't enough to allow him to feel like an individual? What if he was having second thoughts about the engagement ring he'd presented me with in November?

(For the record, if there's one thing I excel at, it's the ability to whip up a gigantic batch of insecurity from only a few ingredients. An off-hand comment or sidelong look could work like yeast to make the dough of doubt rise until my ego was smothered by it. Heck, some days my self-esteem was in such sorry shape I didn't need ingredients other than those on hand. All I had to do was step on the scale, glance at my bank balance, or recall my marriage to Jake.)

Without the excuse of dogs to take out, or lunch to put together for school, I feigned a yawn, stood, and headed for the stairs. My intention was to crawl into bed, assume a fetal position and fold a pillow around my head, thus muffling the sounds of life going on without me. Unfortunately, the pillow hadn't been made that could block out the anxious little voice in my head. It would be in sky-is-falling mode within five minutes. Five minutes after that, my stomach would be in the kind of knot a hangman would envy, my toes and fingers would be cold enough to chill a martini, and the twitch in my left eye would kick off at double speed.

"It's, uh, early," I stammered. "We had a long day yesterday. I think I'll—"

"Do you want to look at the file?"

# Chapter 29

Dave didn't utter the word "again" before the punctuation mark, but his tone made it clear the question wasn't complete without it.

The rising dough of doubt fell.

Dave wanted my help! He wasn't about to pack up and leave! At least not in the next few minutes.

I tamped my elation down with a couple of deep breaths and a long glance at the kitchen clock that prompted Dave to say, "Unless you're too tired."

"Uh, no. I'll take a look. If you're sure it's okay."

He gave me a wry smile. "In the past year I've revised my thinking about what's okay and what's not. In fact, I now consider the word to be subjective and flexible."

With a shake of his head, he drew the file from his messenger bag. "Since I met you and your cohorts, I've discovered Okayland is a bigger place than I once believed. A bigger place with a whole lot of diverse and interesting terrain—much of it not on any map I've ever come across."

Talk about backhanded compliments.

If, indeed, that *was* a compliment.

I ignored the issue, planted myself in Cheese Puff's chair, and reached for the file. In a few seconds I was sorting through the photographs taken inside the garage, searching for shots of the thing that had been bothering me since I peeked at the file the other day—the out-of-place lawn mower. "How did the mower get there?"

Dave frowned and I held up the picture to clarify. "It's against the door. With its front wheels on the sill."

"I don't know. When I looked in the window and spotted Morrow, the mower was like that. I had to shove to get the door open. Later on, I put the mower back for the photos." He pointed at the picture. "Harvey thinks Morrow had just finished cleaning it. See the brush and oil at the end of the bench?"

"Yes." I'd noticed them before and come to the same conclusion.

"Harvey thinks he planned to use them again after he mowed. But the killer cancelled his plans."

"Killer" was not a word Big Chill wanted to hear. "So Harvey's leaning toward murder?"

"Not leaning hard, but he's leaning."

Dave finished the beer and squeezed the empty can making a series of crinkling metallic sounds. Maliciously, I wondered if the noise reminded him of one of his favorite bands.

"And what are you leaning toward?"

"I'm more swaying than leaning." He slowed the metallic beat. "The blow on the chin and the one to the back of his head suggest homicide . . ."

"Suggest?"

"There's no evidence anyone else was in the garage. Not a hair. Not a print. Nothing."

We both knew that unless a killer was extremely careful—or extremely lucky—there would be something, some little trace. "No defensive wounds?"

"He had minor cuts and scrapes on his hands. And a couple of bruises. Neighbors said they saw him cutting brush and digging holes for fence posts a few days before I found him."

And he'd been wearing gloves when he died. Gloves that could have protected his hands.

That left us with death by accident. Or suicide.

I stared at the photo of the lawn mower again. And at the oil. And at the wire brush. Was I bugged because things were out of place? Or was there another reason?

As I've said, I don't know much about lawn mowers. Before my brother died, we had a beautiful lawn, lush and dark green during the months in Nebraska when grass wasn't blighted by cold. My father fertilized it every spring, dug out weeds that dared venture among the blades of grass, watered it during the heat of summer, and clipped it to a uniform height.

After Bryce's death, when my parents checked out emotionally, the mower seized up from lack of use and the grass turned spotty and yellow-brown. It got mowed only when the boy down the block needed a few bucks and came by with his machine. He was a scrawny kid and the mower was hard to start. Sometimes he couldn't pull the cord hard enough to bring it to life and Iz would have to do it, straining and sweating.

Sweating.

Because it was summer.

And this month was January.

"Where does Harvey Goodspeed live?"

"I don't know."

"In a house? An apartment? A condo?"

"Why? What does where Harvey lives have to do with anything?"

His tone indicated my questions were right out of the pack marked "Waste of Time" or perhaps the one labeled "Dumb as They Come."

That, as you can imagine, made me want to prove my queries were legitimate.

And, okay, it made me want to do that with a dash of attitude. A large dash.

"It has more to do with what might be a gap in Harvey's knowledge. And maybe in yours."

"Gap?" He scowled. "What gap?"

"Maybe not so much a gap," I soft-pedaled my response. "Let's call it an observational lapse brought on by the stress of events."

His scowl muscles relaxed a bit.

I plunged on. "Condos and apartment buildings often have mowing services on contract. If the managers aren't like Bernina Burke, and they don't run off the crews, guys come around and mow on a regular basis, even through the winter."

Dave rubbed the stubble on his chin. "So?"

"So lawns are wet and muddy in January. Plus, it's cold and sunlight is at a premium, so grass doesn't get too long. If you own a home and can't afford a service, you might not make the effort to mow unless you absolutely have to. And if you do mow, you probably wear boots and rain gear."

"Hmm."

"We haven't had a break in the rain for weeks—at least not much of a break." I tapped a photo that showed more of the scene in the garage. "So if Jerome Morrow was going out to mow, why did he have on running shoes and a corduroy jacket? They would have been soaked through in five minutes."

Dave narrowed his eyes. I could almost see the wounds in his pride, see him considering whether he could insist he'd thought of that already, and see him wondering if I'd buy his claim.

And I hadn't even used my smug, take-that voice.

"I think Harvey's right about Morrow cleaning and oiling the mower. But I think his intention after that was to start the mower, see how it was running and rolling, decide if it needed more attention, and then shut it down and do that. Or put it back where it belonged if nothing else needed to be done."

Dave blew air between his lips as if to say I was splitting hairs. I rushed on. "What I can't see is why he'd have the wheels up on the sill. It's too low to let him look underneath to check the blades. And, if we're not letting go of the mowing theory, it would be a pain to take the mower outside through that door, especially if there's an outer sill to get past."

"Huh." He sat up straight, snatched the rest of the pictures and flipped through them. "And why take the mower out that door when he had plenty of room to roll it past his truck? If he raised the overhead door, he wouldn't have to jockey it over the sill."

A good point. And a point that, unfortunately, took us back to where I didn't want to go—the suicide theory. Or the murder theory. Maybe the killer—the killer who hadn't left a trace—struck Jerome Morrow, then used the mower to block the door and make it harder for him to escape if he came to.

"Does the overhead door have an automatic opener?"

"No, it's old school. You have to unlock it from the outside and turn a handle to retract a bolt." Dave mimed that action. "Then lift from the bottom."

"And if you're inside?"

"Retract the bolt and lift." He flexed his shoulders. "Thing's heavy."

A killer could probably handle that on his way out, but lifting the door would be more difficult for a man suffering from carbon monoxide poisoning, a man with a head injury. I flipped through the file in search of the autopsy report. "What's the conclusion about the bruises on the back of his head and on his chin? What kind of a weapon does Harvey think the intruder used?"

"Actually, the one on the back of his skull was most likely the result of a fall."

"And the other? The one on the chin?"

"That one we're not so sure about."

"And by 'we' you mean you *and* Harvey?"

"Mostly Harvey. He says the intruder punched Morrow." He mimed an uppercut to his own chin. "Stunned him and knocked him down."

"And you think . . .?"

"I'm no expert in bruising—although I know more than I did a week ago—but it doesn't look right to me." Dave closed his fist hard, making the points of his knuckles stand out.

I did the same, twisting my fist back and forth and pressing it against my chin in various places and ways, then holding my arm out and giving it a series of soft uppercuts. "What if the intruder was wearing thick gloves? Or wrapped something around his hand? Or her hand?"

Even as I asked, I knew we were back to the lack of physical evidence. "Stupid question," I admitted. "No fibers, right? Or other stuff?"

"Only dirt and grease from the gloves Morrow was wearing. In several places on his face." Dave mimed scratching an itch below his right ear and then rubbing another below his left eye and one along his jaw. "Which could have gotten there in a perfectly normal way."

"Maybe the killer put on Morrow's gloves," I suggested in a tone that implied I hoped not.

"Been there. Checked that," Dave said.

I motioned for him to hand over the photos and went through them once more. "If this was a suicide, why try to make it look like something else? So the insurance would pay?"

"He didn't have insurance. At least not that we've found yet."

"And he didn't have close family he wanted to protect from the truth. Unless you consider Big Chill as family. And still, don't you think the way he went about it was . . . unnecessarily complex and difficult to execute and, uh, pretty much contrary to reflex?"

"Contrary to reflex?" Dave squinted at me. "What does that mean?"

"Maybe that's not a good way to say it but, see, I can buy the part where he starts the mower and puts it up against the door to make it tough to escape if he changes his mind. And he could hit himself on the chin easily enough—although I don't know if he could do it hard enough to leave much of a bruise unless he used a wrench or something. And then he'd have to put the tool back where it belonged. And after that, he had to fall straight back and bash his head. I couldn't do it. I'd automatically twist my body and fling out an arm to break my fall. I might splinter my elbow or break my collarbone in the process."

Dave stood, shot me a look that said I was full of it, and flopped on the sofa without turning or trying to break his fall.

"Seriously? That doesn't count as a reenactment. The sofa's soft. I dare you to go outside and fall on the parking lot."

He crossed his arms and gave me a look that said he'd do that right after I did. "It's not impossible, though, is it?"

"No," I admitted grudgingly. "But if the fall didn't knock him out, he'd have to lie there for—well, for as long as it took for the carbon monoxide level to rise to the point where he'd lose consciousness. Lie there fighting the survival instinct, the will to live. That takes a lot of inner strength. And a total commitment to ending it all."

And I couldn't see Jerome Morrow—a man who'd spent the past few years avoiding conflict by hiding, and handling tough decisions through impersonal memos—doing that. Besides, unless he'd been lying to his neighbors and Big Chill, he'd been looking forward to retirement and the years ahead.

"Okay." Dave acknowledged my point with a slight nod. "So let's say he got the mower running and waited until he felt the effects of the carbon monoxide before he took the fall."

I mulled that for a moment. "Then he'd risk being too weak or dizzy or confused to follow through with the blow on his chin and the fall. And, really, why do that? If he was intent on killing himself, there were dozens of other ways he could have gone about it. And plenty of ways to make it look like an accident."

I stood and paced to the dining room and back—not a long walk. "He could have driven his truck into the river, or crashed into a tree or a bridge. He could have gone for a hike and taken a dive off a cliff. He could—"

"You really hate the suicide theory don't you?"

"I don't *hate* it."

"You hate it."

"Okay. I think it stinks." And not just because of the effect on Big Chill of calling Morrow's death a suicide. I wheeled to face him. "And *you* think Harvey Goodspeed's murder theory stinks."

"It has some holes," he admitted.

"It has holes you can drive a bus through." I ticked the largest off as I paced. "No motive. No physical evidence."

"None we've found yet. Harvey has a gut feeling something will turn up."

"Well, Harvey has the gut to have a feeling with."

Dave didn't acknowledge what I thought was one of my finest snarky remarks. Instead he sat up and crossed his arms. "Harvey has years of experience investigating homicides."

"Yeah, well when you're a hammer, everything looks like a nail. And if you're a homicide detective, maybe everything looks like murder."

He stood and, as they say, got up in my grille. "Why are you so determined to rule out murder or suicide?" His voice was so tight the words seemed to have been screwed into place with brute force.

I didn't step away. Instead I jabbed a finger at his chest. "Why are *you* so determined not to call it an accident?"

"Because I can't visualize how an accident happened. I'll buy that he could have fallen and hit his head and knocked himself out. But the rest—the mower by the door, the bruise on his chin—doesn't fit."

"You're not even trying to make it fit. Maybe he got the bruise on his chin earlier."

"And the mower by the door?"

"Okay, maybe the door latch was broken and he kept the mower braced against it until he could fix it."

"If you reach any harder you'll dislocate your shoulder."

"And if you don't reach at all your muscles will lock in place. Especially your brain muscles."

(For the record, I have no idea if there are muscles in the brain. Some day, when I have absolutely nothing else to do, I might seize a few minutes for research. But right now, as you can see, I'm busy having an argument. I'm also busy wondering how a discussion became a dispute that seemed headed for donnybrook magnitude.)

"I'd be willing to reach if I saw anything to reach for," Dave said.

"Well, maybe you should open your eyes and you might see something."

"And maybe you should calm down."

251

"And maybe you should review all the reasons why I haven't been calm recently. That might give you a clue why I have no intention of hopping the train to tranquility!"

He stomped to the coffee table and gathered up the photos. "Forget it. Just forget you saw any of this. Forget we talked about it."

"Forgetting! Wow! What a great investigative technique. Did you learn that from Hardly Nospeed?"

Dave went on reassembling the file and said not a word.

That, of course, made me even more furious.

Fury, of course, made me hungry.

Ice cream.

I needed ice cream.

And I needed it fast.

No time for a bowl. This was an eat-out-of-the-carton situation.

I flung the freezer door wide and seized the only carton on hand—mint with chocolate chips. Definitely not my favorite. The mint would make me burp like a set of bagpipes in the hands of a rank amateur. But it was cold, creamy, and tasty. And, bonus, it was also loaded with fat and calories and not even close to being on the foods-that-are-good-for-me list.

Now for a spoon.

I grasped the handle of the silverware drawer and tugged.

It slid out an inch.

And stuck.

I tugged again, harder.

The drawer didn't budge.

I squeezed two fingers of my other hand inside the handle and gave it the grunting kind of effort made in a gym. Or so I'm told. Except for the gym at Captain Meriwether High School, I haven't been inside one in years. And the effort I'd seen most kids putting out at school wasn't enough to generate power for

252

more than a few low-wattage light bulbs. But then, back in the day, I'd done all I could to avoid breaking a sweat in gym class. Now, however, I was motivated. Seriously motivated.

The drawer gave me another half an inch. Not enough to get two fingers inside and wiggle out a spoon.

I eyed the dishwasher. It was loaded with dirty spoons. It would take only a few seconds to wash one.

No.

This was war. The drawer was the enemy. And I would triumph.

"Want help?" Dave asked in a low voice.

"No!" Accepting help was admitting defeat.

No drawer would defeat me.

I returned to the one-handed grip, widened my stance, bent my knees, leaned back, and gave it everything I had.

The drawer shot out.

My grip slipped.

My hand recoiled.

The thumb edge of it slammed into my chin.

I staggered and fell.

The back of my head cracked against the stove.

Fireworks exploded inside my skull.

# Chapter 30

Cascading pinpricks of bright color faded to black.

Black gave way to red and orange and yellow flames of pain.

I heard myself groan.

I heard Dave ask if I was okay.

*Stupid question.*

*Of course I wasn't.*

But I couldn't seem to form words to say I didn't know. Couldn't do more than groan.

And I couldn't seem to see anything except those flames.

"I'm calling for help," he said. "Don't move."

*As if that was possible.*

Wait!

*Was* moving impossible?

Was I paralyzed?

A blast of cold fear knocked down the flames of pain in my head.

All went black once more.

Could I move?

I wanted to know.

I didn't want to know.

But I *had* to know.

I willed my fingers to flex.

254

After what seemed like an hour, they did.

I crossed them and sent a command to my toes.

After a long moment they obliged. They wiggled. Then they got my ankles involved.

I uncrossed my fingers and rotated my wrists.

"Paramedics are on the way." Hands folded around mine. Dave's hands.

"Open your eyes, dear," a second voice ordered. "Open your eyes and look at me."

*My eyes were closed?*

I freed my hands from Dave's and felt my eyelids.

Definitely closed.

That explained the blackness—or at least some of it.

I lifted my eyelids.

Dark gave way to light.

A bright light.

One of those tiny intense flashlights in the grip of Mrs. Ballantine.

I slammed my lids back down.

"Her pupils aren't dilated," she announced. "And they're both the same size. What else should I look for?"

"Ask her if her head hurts," Dario suggested.

*Really?*

"Of course my head hurts." I opened my eyes again, this time without effort. "I bashed it on the stove."

"Irritability's a symptom." Dario tapped his phone. "And delayed responses to questions."

"You're going to be fine, dear." Mrs. B patted my cheek. "The experts are here now."

And they were, subjecting me to more bright lights and questions, getting me on my feet, watching me walk, checking my balance, checking my vital signs, and checking my memory.

I didn't exactly ace all the tests, but I didn't fail them, either. Still, Mrs. B insisted I go to the hospital.

Since my health insurance plan covers less than a skimpy thong bikini, I declined.

Mrs. B said she'd pay.

I declined again and walked in slow circles around the dining room table, holding an ice pack to the back of my head.

The paramedics shrugged and headed out.

Mrs. B conferred with them at the door.

Dario consulted the Internet again and then asked me questions he said would test my brain. Naturally, his questions smacked of Las Vegas. "What are snake eyes? Which card has the man with the ax? How many ways can you make 21?"

I was busily tossing out number combinations when Mrs. B returned. "It's all decided. You'll come next door so we can keep you under observation," she announced in a no-arguments-accepted voice

"You've got the immediate world over there already," I protested. "Dave can keep—"

"He took off when the paramedics did," Dario said.

*The coward.* I bet he felt responsible for my fall and couldn't face me.

Mrs. B pulled a jacket from the closet and laid it across my shoulders for the short walk next door. "He said it couldn't wait until morning. He said you'd understand."

*Hah! Never!*

"He said the sheriff was pressuring Harvey Goodspeed to call the case one thing or another and they had to go up there and check out your theory." Dario opened the door to the deck and offered his arm.

Head swimming, I clutched a dining room chair. "Go where to check out what theory?"

"Well, he was talking so fast I couldn't make much sense of it." Mrs. B took my hand and tugged me toward the door. "Something about a lawn mower."

*Really?*

"And the starter rope." Dario closed the door behind us.

"The *grip* on the starter rope," Mrs. B corrected. "Or maybe *his* grip on the rope. Like I said, he was talking fast."

But it made sense to me. Having witnessed my kitchen catastrophe, Dave realized Jerome Morrow's death could have been an accident.

And later that evening he proved he was far from a coward. "You were right," he told me, not caring that everyone in Mrs. B's condo—especially my sister—was all ears.

"I was?" I played dumb, easy to do with a throbbing headache. "About Jerome Morrow's death?"

"Yes." He planted a long kiss on my lips. "We may never know for sure, but I'm casting my vote for accidental death. See, I think—like you said—after he cleaned the mower, he decided to start it up to see how it was running."

Moving to the center of what little clear space remained in Mrs. B's condo, Dave mimed pulling the starter cord on a mower. "His gloves were old and worn slick. I think his grip slipped and his arm recoiled and he hit himself in the chin and fell back and bashed his head on the floor. Just like you did when the kitchen drawer stuck."

"Won't stick anymore. I fixed it." Jim hung his head. "Sorry I didn't get to it before you—"

I waved off his apology. "If you had, Dave never would have given up his suicide theory."

Dave scowled.

Mrs. B interrupted any protest he might launch. "And the mower climbed the sill and hit the door? Is that possible?"

"Yes," Dave said. "According to people who know a lot more about mowers than I do—and that's pretty much everyone in the known universe."

"Depends on the height of the sill and the power of the mower," Jim added.

"Right," Dave agreed. "And the angle of approach."

"You'll never know for sure," Dario said, "since the only witness is dead."

Something about his tone and choice of the words "witness" and "dead" gave me a chill. Once again I wondered about Dario's past. Then I put that aside. "Do you think you can sell this to Harvey Goodspeed?" I asked. "Will he buy a mower as killer theory?"

"More?" Verna asked. "Kher?"

"Right." Iz lowered Verna's bed to sleeping position. "I'll explain it in the morning and you'll work on two-syllable words. Now it's time to get your beauty rest. You want to look your best for Gabe."

Verna giggled, plucked the sheet up to her chin, and closed her eyes.

"I'll sell the theory hard." Dave lowered his voice. "With an emphasis on how buying it will make Harvey's life easier."

"How?" Mrs. B asked.

"If he sticks to his murder theory," I explained, "he has to hunt for a killer who didn't leave a trace."

"And if he goes with suicide," Dave added with a nod in my direction, "he's stuck explaining why a man as organized as Jerome Morrow chose a convoluted, failure-prone method."

"He also has to stand up to a storm of protest if he goes with a suicide call," Jim said. "Wilhelmina will see to that. He'll wish he retired before this case came up."

I nodded, imagining Big Chill with a picket sign marching outside the sheriff's office. I guessed she had enough personal

258

time accumulated to protest until she wore out every pair of shoes in her closet. "Speaking of retiring, have you given more thought to moving into Harvey's job?"

"I've given it plenty of thought." Dave tapped his head and took my hands. "But that's all. I haven't said a word to Harvey. And I won't until things are settled with Lola, and you and I have a long talk."

"Who says he can't learn?" Iz asked.

Dave's grip on my hands tightened, but he said nothing except, "Let's go home so you can get some rest."

Early the next morning, after making sure I had no ailments greater than a goose egg and a slight headache, Dave walked me over to Mrs. B's and took off for a meeting of the minds with Harvey. At my suggestion—whispered because Verna was fast asleep and I guessed my sister and Dario were also in dreamland—he planned to stop for a dozen doughnuts. At Mrs. B's suggestion, he planned to add crullers, cinnamon rolls, and maple bars. "Not to bribe Mr. Goodspeed," she'd insisted as she walked Dave to the door. "Or spike his brain with sugar. But I'm sure he'll think better on a full stomach."

I refrained from wondering aloud if Harvey's stomach was ever empty. I also refrained from asking what qualified as "better" thinking. After all, it appeared he'd be Dave's boss for the next few months. Although I had yet to discuss the situation, it was clear Dave's only route back to the Reckless River cop shop was across a number of burned bridges and would involve the eating of crow and perhaps other substances. The smart thing was to get gone. And working for the sheriff's department beat snagging shoplifters at the mall.

Mrs. B pulled a pan of cornmeal muffins from the oven and popped one onto a plate for me. While I sliced and slathered it with butter and honey, she said in a voice devoid of apology. "I

259

took the liberty of suggesting Angus might roll Dave's future into his negotiations for Lola."

I wasn't surprised. She was almost always a step ahead of me. "How are the Lola negotiations going? And what do you hear from the vet?"

"Angus should have the papers signed this afternoon. Lola will be a civilian tomorrow, and she'll be adopted by the end of next week."

She popped out a muffin for herself and sat across from me at the table. "That's where it gets tricky."

The sweet and buttery bite of muffin in my mouth took on the flavor and consistency of dried oatmeal mixed with potato flakes and sawdust. "Tricky? What does that mean?"

Mrs. B put a finger to her lips. "Ssshhh. Don't get upset, dear. It means there was a great deal of resistance to allowing Dave to adopt her. The feeling is they'd be rewarding him for not following the rules and for defying authority."

It took half a cup of coffee to do it, but I swallowed the muffin. "What about me?"

Her hands fluttered like butterflies might after sipping an energy drink. "They feel that would be the same as allowing Dave to adopt her."

"Then what—?"

"They ruled me out as well. It seems I'm a thorn in their sides." Before I could say anything, she went on. "Your sister is even closer to the top of their black list than I am and, besides, I can't imagine Iz taking care of a dog. Josh is too young. Dario isn't a resident yet."

I groaned. "So Lola could end up anywhere. With anyone. She could be tied up all day. Sleeping in a crate. Eating crap dog food."

She reached across the table and patted my hand. "Don't worry. We hit on the perfect candidate, someone they can't turn down unless they want Angus to play the discrimination card."

She turned her head slightly and glanced toward the hospital bed. "Someone Lola loves and protects. Someone who could benefit from a canine companion."

I flashed on an image of Verna's condo, towering piles of clothing and furniture, teetering stacks of boxes and newspapers. "I don't think—"

"She'd be close by," Mrs. B said quickly. "Just a few doors away."

"But—"

"We'll see her every day."

"But Verna's place is a—"

"Of course it is. But we'll deal with that."

"With or without her permission?"

Mrs. B glanced toward Verna's bed and put her finger to her lips again. "Without, if we must. We'll explain we feared if Bernina learned of her hoarding she'd call the health department and social services, so we moved the, uh, excess to storage."

"Under cover of darkness?"

Mrs. B blinked.

"Because when Bernina sees us carting all that stuff out, she'll go nuclear. She'll call every agency she can think of."

Mrs. B chewed her lower lip.

I chewed a thumbnail.

"I'll think of something." Mrs. B fingered her double string of pearls.

This was a problem requiring a whole lot of pearl power. But I was sure she knew that, so I refrained from advising her to make a run for the jewelry box and a few more strands.

Iz trundled from her lair a few minutes later and got Verna out of bed and to the bathroom. She had more control of her arm and leg today and her words were easier to understand. So we all got it when she demanded the walker, waved Iz off, and got to the table on her own. We also got that she wanted to go to her place for scarves and jewelry so she'd shine for her next physical therapy sessions with Gabe.

I shot Mrs. B a questioning glance. She fingered her pearls and pointed to the thick drops pattering on the deck. "It's raining again, Verna. You'll be soaked by the time you get there."

"And there's no ramp at your place," I pointed out.

"I'll help her," Iz volunteered.

"Up the stairs to the bedroom?" Mrs. B asked. "They're so steep and narrow."

"Why not let us bring some things over here?" I suggested.

"Great idea," Mrs. B yelped.

"Myself," Verna insisted, mastering both syllables.

"But there's no need for you to stress yourself. We're happy to help. And we know your style," Mrs. B wheedled. "And the exercise will be good for us."

"Do it myself," Verna said.

My mind tossed out a slew of phony reasons why she couldn't go to her condo—broken pipe, snake in the plumbing, squirrel in the heat vents, intruder lockdown alert for the entire complex, high wind warning, magazine salesman camped on the doorstep, religious group in search of converts, eclipse of the sun.

Mrs. B locked her gaze on mine. I shook my head. All of my ideas added up to nothing that would work.

"All right," she told Verna. "I'll go wake up Dario. We might need his help for the stairs. When you're dressed we'll all go over there."

We dragged out the process as long as we could. Dario dawdled over breakfast. Mrs. B checked the weather radar and insisted we wait for a period of light rainfall due in shortly after noon. I got Iz aside and explained the situation, and she added to the delays by phoning to check on Lola and Cheese Puff. Mrs. B scooted upstairs where Verna couldn't hear and phoned Sybil. She came by to make sure Verna had booked Mrs. B's TV for the Sunday mystery and brought along several magazines. In typical Sybil style, she launched a lengthy and one-sided discussion of the state of the fashion industry that ate up half an hour.

When we could delay it no longer, Iz pushed the wheelchair down the ramp and along the sidewalk to Verna's condo, all the while reminding Verna anything she selected had to be easy to get on and off. Mrs. B, her expression grim, unlocked the door, I unfolded the walker and set it just across the threshold, and Dario and Iz helped Verna up the steps and inside.

# Chapter 31

And there in the narrow entryway, bunched like bananas, clustered like grapes, mashed like potatoes, we waited for whatever was to come. Other than tossing spoiled food and pushing back piles to make room for the paramedics, the place was as we'd found it less than a week ago.

Verna's gaze swept the cluttered hallway. She peered into the living area beyond. The left side of her mouth drooped to match the right. Her eyes narrowed. "Crap," she said.

I cringed. Mrs. B flattened herself against the wall beside me.

Verna's eyes flashed. Her face turned the color of beet soufflé.

(For the record, I've never seen a beet soufflé, and I hope never to encounter one. I view beets the way Superman views kryptonite or Dracula views a cross.)

"Crap." Crablike, Verna propelled herself sideways along the limited space in the hall.

At the base of the stairs she glanced up. "Junk."

At the edge of the living area she paused. "Trash."

By inches, she jerked the walker around and glared at us. "Who?"

We exchanged puzzled looks. Was it possible she didn't remember collecting all this and packing it in? And, if so, was that memory lost forever?

"Who?" Verna asked, her voice rising to as much of a shout as she could muster.

No one answered.

Verna slammed the walker against a stack of boxes and spit each syllable of her question: "Ber-ni-na?"

Mrs. B and I exchanged startled glances. It took her only a second to seize the initiative. "Who else? Who else would cram a bunch of garbage in your place without asking permission?"

"And who else would do it while you're in no condition to argue?" I chimed in.

Dario kicked a box. "Probably bought out a storage locker at one of those auctions."

Iz followed suit. "A really disgusting storage locker. If she paid more than $50 she got taken to the cleaners."

"Now, don't you worry about this mess." Mrs. B scurried along the hallway to Verna's side and gave her a hug. "I'll see that Bernina Burke is dealt with."

"I'll help," Dario growled in a voice that made me swallow hard.

"Count me in." Iz delivered a one-two punch to a cardboard box.

"But first things first," Mrs. B said. "We'll rent a truck, round up Allison and Josh and Luke and some of their friends, and get everything that isn't yours carted away."

Tears welled from Verna's eyes and ran down her cheeks and into the crevices of her left-sided smile.

"What are friends for?" Mrs. B blotted Verna's face with a tissue plucked from the pocket of her rain jacket. "Now, don't give Bernina another thought. When I'm through with her, she won't have the nerve to ask what happened to her junk. She'll avoid the subject like the plague."

"She'll avoid it so hard that if you mention it," I said, "she'll pretend she has no idea what you're talking about."

"Right," Mrs. B agreed. "So you put this mess out of your mind and go on upstairs and pick out some pretty things."

"I'll give you a piggyback ride." Iz folded the walker and got into position.

Verna shook her head. "Too heavy."

"You're tall, but you're skinny as a rake. I bet you don't weigh more than a sack of groceries."

Verna giggled, but shook her head again.

"Tell you what," Iz said, "you let me carry you up and I'll let you come down on your own—sliding on your butt if that's the way you want it."

"Sounds like a deal to me." Dario put his big hands around Verna's waist and hoisted her aboard. "Hang on." He lifted her weak arm and leg into place. "Enjoy the ride."

Iz grunted once, then leaned far forward and charged the stairs.

Okay, she charged like an aging bull on a scorching day at high altitude, but charge she did.

"I'll have to give Iz a bonus," Mrs. B said when they'd disappeared around the bend in the staircase. "She's doing a wonderful job with Verna. I think she's found her niche."

"I wouldn't have bet on it, but you're right. Maybe instead of a bonus you could pay for a training program of some kind." I lowered my voice a shade. "After you convince her she doesn't already know everything."

"Good point, dear." Mrs. B twinkled a smile. "Your sister does occasionally exhibit more self-confidence than ability."

A nice way of saying Iz could be all about bluster and BS.

Mrs. B clapped her hands and gave out assignments. In a few moments, Dario took off to rent a truck and secure a supply of cardboard boxes, I got to work rounding up a posse of teenagers and alerting Dave and Jim, and she contracted for a large storage unit. "Verna may not recognize all this as hers right now, but there may come a day when her memory returns."

"A day when we'll have a lot of explaining to do."

"Yes. But we won't cross that bridge until we come to it."

I envisioned a swinging bridge made from fraying rope and broken boards sagging across a deep chasm studded with sharp rocks and cacti with needles long enough to knit a sweater. "And you'll be in the lead when we step out onto said bridge?"

She winced, but then nodded and clapped her hands again. "Let's get to work."

"Wait a minute. What about Bernina?"

Mrs. B froze. Then her fingers clicked her pearls like a rosary. After a long moment she pulled her phone from the pocket of her raincoat and punched in a number. "Hello, Gabe," she purred. "If I asked her, would you like to take Bernina out to a movie this afternoon? And then dinner? My treat, of course."

We started the minute Gabe and Bernina drove off. With only a brief break to help Verna back to Mrs. B's with half a dozen bright scarves and two hats, and another break for pizza, we had the job done by 9:00 PM. We'd bundled stacks of paper and tied them with twine, packed up kitchen items that were chipped or cracked or seemingly useless, sorted through existing boxes for valuables, and numbered each box. Those numbers went on a master list with a brief note of the contents. The same list contained notes about furniture, carpets, and linens moved to storage. All the good clothing remained

267

behind, sorted by type and color and packed into boxes that were, in turn, packed into the closet in the second bedroom.

Some of the furniture we discovered beneath piles and heaps and stacks also remained behind. "These pieces are old, but they're quality," Mrs. B said as she examined a mission chair. "So is the carpet. I'll arrange to have everything cleaned and we'll pick up a few bright throw pillows." She raised her hands. "But that's all. No more excessive shopping for me."

"Except for things for Lola," I added, my voice cracking. "Bowls for food and water. Treats."

"You'll see her every day." Mrs. B kissed my cheek. "You'll get used to her being a few doors down."

Would I?

I supposed I might.

After all, people get used to all kinds of things, even painful or inconvenient things. But that didn't mean they liked them.

Mrs. B danced around what seemed to be an acre of open space where heaps of hoardings had stretched to the ceiling just hours ago. "It feels so light and airy. *I* feel so light and airy. I'm not stuck anymore."

And with that she began making plans for beefing up my resume and coaching me for job interviews. Twirling and tapping faster, she called out thoughts about a summer wedding on the deck, or perhaps an early fall aisle walk on a cruise.

By the time she got to possible names for the baby Dave and I would have, my head was spinning. I slumped in the dusty mission chair, reminding myself she meant well and looking back fondly on the days when she had lost momentum.

Carolyn J. Rose

Also by Carolyn J. Rose:

The Catskill Mountains Mysteries
*Hemlock Lake*
*Through a Yellow Wood*
*The Devil's Tombstone*

The Subbing isn't for Sissies series
*No Substitute for Murder*
*No Substitute for Money*
*No Substitute for Maturity*
*No Substitute for Myth*
*No Substitute for Mistakes*
*No Substitute for Motives*
*No Substitute for Misinformation*

And others
*Nightfall Bay*
*An Uncertain Refuge*
*Sea of Regret*
*A Place of Forgetting*

With Michael A. Nettleton
*Death at Devil's Harbor*
*Deception at Devil's Harbor*
*The Hard Karma Shuffle*
*The Crushed Velvet Miasma*
*Drum Warrior*
*Sucker Punches*

Carolyn J. grew up in New York's Catskill Mountains, graduated from the University of Arizona, logged two years in Arkansas with Volunteers in Service to America, and spent 25 years as a television news researcher, writer, producer, and assignment editor in Arkansas, New Mexico, Oregon, and Washington. She's now a substitute teacher in Vancouver, Washington, and her interests are reading, swimming, walking, gardening, and NOT cooking.